Adam's Fall
(Touch of Tantra)

By Liv Morris

Copyright © 2014 Liv Morris

Createspace Edition: February 2014

Cover artwork by: Okay Creations

Editing by: Write Divas

Proofing: Marla Esposito

ISBN-13: 978-1496060815
ISBN-10: 1496060814
1.   Adam's Fall—Fiction   2. Fiction—Romance   3. Romance—Erotica

TO LAUREN

TABLE OF CONTENTS

Chapter 1

The monotonous sound of the cable news program echoes in my private hospital room. The television acts as my connection to the outside world. The last thing I want to experience right now is silence, so I crank the volume up a couple of notches. Left idle, my thoughts will drift back to the ugly, tragic scene from a couple of hours ago where Simon's body lay cold, his lifeless eyes staring ahead, judging me. I shake my head, and try to clear the image from my mind as the talking heads drone on and on. I perk up when I hear the name of my asshole father, Xavier Thorpe.

"Xavier Thorpe, and his conglomerate Thorpe Industries, are coming under fire from city officials in Indianapolis. Thorpe Industries closed the Republic Manufacturing plant on Friday with plans to ship production to an overseas facility. The decision left two thousand workers unemployed."

"What a fucking prick," I mutter under my breath.

"Gary Fredrick, the mayor of Indianapolis had this to say, 'Wall Street may love Thorpe, but he is despised here on Main Street. He's nothing more than an industrial sociopath. Wiping out industries and people's dreams in places like Indiana without even a forethought.'"

An industrial sociopath! That's a brilliant and perfect definition of Thorpe and his greedy business dealings. He ruins lives to line his own pockets.

The news anchor moves on to the next story and I see my photo flash across the screen. *Great.* They're already reporting on Simon's shooting.

The photo shows me dressed in my Armani tux. The image reflects a man who is at the top of his game, conquering his world. The man of bravado I was such a short time ago. Now I'm sitting by myself in a hospital room, surrounded by my own demons.

"No one from Kings Capital has given an official comment concerning the alleged love triangle between the now-deceased Simon Edwards, his ex-fiancée Marta Llewellyn, and the CEO of Kings Capital, Adam Kingsley.

However, authorities confirm that Edwards, a founding partner and top executive of Kings Capital, was fired last Wednesday. It is also confirmed from hotel security footage that Edwards was the alleged shooter earlier today in the incident in front of The Pierre that injured Adam Kingsley.

One Wall Street analyst, Stuart Cross of IEF Securities, believes Mr. Kingsley's high profile image and this morning's shooting will hammer Kings Capital stock. Cross foresees Kings Capital facing big questions from clients and key shareholders. He says, quote, "This event may even affect Adam Kingsley's ability to continue as head of Kings Capital."

My world spins as every word spewing from the reporter's mouth lands accusingly on my shoulders. To the outside world my guilt is automatic, whether it is true or not. The so-called prediction by this analyst hits me like a punch in the gut. This clusterfuck surrounding Simon could infect every part of the company and my leadership.

"Who the hell are these 'inside sources'?" I hiss through my clenched teeth. Red-hot anger courses through every cell in my body. Anger at myself, anger at Simon, and anger that no one will ever know the truth. There was no love affair between Marta and me. It was a forgettable fuck that I wasn't aware had morphed into a twisted obsession on her part.

As seething fury causes my body to shake, and I breathe in deeply, calming myself down, an image of Simon flashes in front of me. He's lying on the sidewalk where he was shot. He's not dead, though. His are eyes full of life while his mouth twists into a mocking smile of hate. Closing my eyes, I bury my head in my hands, stunned by what has to be my stressed-induced imagination. Upon opening my eyes and clearing my head, the unworldly vision of Simon disappears, but my rage remains.

"Fucking lies. Goddammit!" I shout at the mocking faces glowing from the television as the soothsayers continue divining my doom. In my blind rage, I grab the closest object I come in contact with. My keys. With the television as my bull's-eye, I hurl them forward and flinch as the stitches in my side protest my violent movement.

The keys miss their mark and crash into the stark white wall, falling with a clack when they hit the floor. I'm not sure if my rage is directed at the gossipmongers or if I'm trying to squelch Simon's appearance in my mind. I decide it's likely both.

Hayes, a physical incarnation of Goliath and my personal bodyguard, pushes my door open, his hand inside his navy jacket. The banging commotion and my yelling likely drew attention from behind the closed door.

"What the hell is going on?"

I scoff at his overreaction since he knows I'm the only one in the room. The ghost of Simon is unseen by him, but I swear I hear Simon's voice mocking and wondering how an oaf like Goliath killed him. Again I shake my head, knowing my ears are playing tricks on me.

A nurse peeks into the room around Goliath as if she's waiting for the red, angry dust to settle. "Are you okay, sir?"

"Yes, yes. I'm okay," I grunt impatiently as I rub my head. Goliath strides to my side, more relaxed now that there isn't an immediate threat. The nurse has already disappeared from sight. Who I'd like to see appear at the door is Kathryn, but I haven't a clue where she is since we were separated downstairs.

"Listen, I really need to get the hell out of here. Would you try to locate my doctor?" I peer up at Goliath. He saved my life, so I owe him some respect. There's no reason to crucify him for being concerned about my safety, so I curb the angry tone in my response.

"You bet. I'll get the nurse right on it." Goliath resembles the dutiful soldier eager to help out his ass of a commander.

The hospital moved me to a private room before stitching up where the bullet grazed me. I was given VIP status the instant they found out my name. Now I need to escape this place and figure out how to handle all the negative press. Kings Capital will not be tarnished by what happened today.

When the door shuts behind Goliath, my phone vibrates and rattles across the side table. Messages and texts, no doubt. I glance over the incoming list and find the one person I want to speak with most missing in the rundown.

Kathryn.

I have no idea where she is now. I've been texting and calling her relentlessly because Peters sent her away without my consent. He claims his intention was to keep Kathryn from being caught up in the middle of everything. I told him he could go to hell; she needs to be here with me.

Fuck, she was almost killed by Simon because of me. I ached to have my arms around her, run my hands through her hair, and smell her familiar scent.

I call Kathryn again. I wait impatiently for her to answer, and after a couple of rings, she finally greets me.

"Hi, Adam." The sweet and simple sound of her sexy voice weaves through me like a witch's spell, calming my anger. I exhale some of the tension before I speak.

"Beautiful, where are you?" I hear the faint murmur of people talking close by her.

"I'm sitting in the hospital cafeteria. I've been on the phone with my mother. I wanted to tell her about today before she saw it on the news. She freaked, of course, and is worried about you. I told her you were okay—at least I think you are." There's a hesitation in her voice.

"I'm going to be fine. Just a few stitches. I'm as mad as hell Peters kept you from coming up here with me."

When the orderly was wheeling me upstairs, Peters had a crazy notion to tell Kathryn to wait downstairs until things cooled down. I told him he overstepped his authority, and Kathryn should've been the first person in my room after the doctor left.

I want her with me. I need her with me. I considered firing his ass when I found out what he'd done. But after seeing the news report and the media shitstorm brewing around me, Peters may not have been completely wrong to send Kathryn away. Getting Kings Capital out of this mess is likely to be one of the hardest fights in my professional life.

"I wondered if you knew what he said to me. I figured you might be upset, but there was no arguing with him in the ER." Her voice reflects some anger. "Can I come up now? Is the coast clear?"

"Hell yes, you can come up here. I've straightened everything out with Peters and... I need to see you." I don't want to sound like a sappy, lovesick teenager, but it was the fucking truth.

"I need to see you, too." Relief shoots through me. Letting my true feelings show is new territory for me since vulnerability isn't one of my strong suits.

The door to my room opens and a man in a white coat walks in.

"Kathryn, my get-out-of-jail-free card just walked in through the door. I'm in room 1401. Please come up."

"I'll be right there." I'm relieved when I sense the urgency in her voice, too.

With my doctor approaching, I place the phone on the table next to me, fully aware that I've ignored everyone else who's tried to reach me and have likely pissed them off.

Dr. Payne—interesting name for a man of medicine— stands next to my bed and holds a clipboard in one hand while he flips through the attached paperwork.

"Sorry I had to run off." He's been gone almost an hour since he left me, saying he'd be right back. "I was needed in the ER. We're a little short staffed today."

"I understand, Dr. Payne," I reply as he lays the clipboard on the bed. "But I'm ready to get out of this joint."

"There's no reason to keep you here any longer. Your injuries are minor. However, we have to do things properly. A nurse will be here in a few minutes with your discharge papers."

"Great." My dry sarcasm earns me a slight smile from the doctor.

"A little warning of what to expect from your injuries. You will have some bruising and tenderness around the stitches. You were very lucky today. Things could've been a lot worse."

"I know." Those two simple words contain a thankful acknowledgement. I think about the angle of Simon's gun.

If it had been pointed a few inches over, I would be Simon's roommate in the morgue.

"Give it a couple days and this injury will be a distant memory, I assure you."

"I don't think anything about today will be a distant memory anytime soon."

"True. The media is camped out on the sidewalk and flooding the PR department with calls." Dr. Payne shakes his head in disgust. "I do hope things work out for you, Mr. Kingsley."

"Thanks. Me, too." The doctor's smile is warm, and I can tell he's genuine in his reassurance.

"Now, before we get the nurse started on your discharge paperwork, I'd like to discuss the matter of the tests you had us run. I have to say it was a highly unusual request under the circumstances. Most gunshot victims don't request to be tested for STDs, but we should have the results by Friday."

I'm unsure what the tests will reveal. I've been careful and never fucked anyone without a condom, but nothing's foolproof.

"I'll email you personally on Friday with the results. Your nurse will bring in the papers to sign." Dr. Payne offers his hand. "Take care of yourself, Mr. Kingsley. And no more shootouts."

I force out a short laugh and shake his hand firmly, saying, "I'll try to stay out of trouble."

The door blows open and Kathryn breezes into the room. With each step she takes, my chest feels lighter as the weight of my worries about my guilt and business begin to lift. Her presence brings me hope that my torn and fucked up life can be righted. Goliath follows her inside, towering behind her.

"Looks like you have company." Dr. Payne smiles as he glances between Kathryn and me. "Sign your papers and you're good to go."

Kathryn glides over to the bed and stands by the doctor. Giving me a nod, Goliath retreats back toward the doorway. His stance reminds me of a soldier on duty. He's taking this saving my life thing pretty damn seriously, but I do owe him the very air I'm breathing. I can never thank him enough for saving me so I can be with the lovely woman smiling in front of me. For those two things alone, I'll be forever grateful to him.

"Hi, beautiful," I say, focusing my attention back on Kathryn. She's a sight to behold this morning. Her hair cascades around her shoulders in thick waves. All I want at this moment is to hold her tight and run my fingers through the soft strands.

"Hey," she says with the most dazzling smile I've seen, and it warms my soul to know a woman like her cares for a dickhead like me.

"Doctor Payne, this is Kathryn Delcour, my woman." She side-eyes me, surprised and maybe a little ticked off by my possessive comment. What can I say? The term just rolled off my tongue, so I shrug my shoulders, having no defense.

"Good morning, doctor." Kathryn greets Dr. Payne with a handshake. The effect she has on the good doctor is evident as his body subtly moves closer to hers. She's a basic man magnet.

"Good morning, Ms. Delcour. Our patient should be discharged in a few minutes. I think he's had enough fun around here for one morning. Well, I'll leave you to it, Mr. Kingsley."

"Thanks, doctor. Oh, when will I get the stitches out?"

"They're dissolvable so there's no need. Get some rest and take a few days off from the Street if you can. You've been through a hell of lot and are lucky to be alive."

"I wish time off was possible, doctor, but thanks."

The doctor gathers his papers and leaves the room. Now I need to get Goliath on the other side of the door, too.

"Hayes." Kathryn moves to the side when I speak, so I now have full view of Goliath. "Wait in the hall, please," I say to him. "I'll be leaving soon."

"Yes, sir." He nods and retreats.

Once I hear the click of the large wooden door shutting, I take Kathryn's hand in mine and bring it to my lips. I kiss her knuckles with a brush of my lips, never taking my eyes from hers.

"Adam," Kathryn whispers. Her one word has so much meaning behind it. She sits down next to me on the bed. "You know, this morning could've been so much worse. How are you feeling? Okay?"

Her eyes begin to glisten, and I'm awed that this strong woman is moved to tears. For me. No longer able to stand the distance between us, I envelop her in my arms, burying my face in her hair, and getting a rush from her sweet scent.

"I'm doing fine. Better now that you're here. I made it through with nothing more than a little scratch." I point to my wounded side. "All's well that ends well."

My words aren't totally true because I still can't seem to shake the memory of Simon's dead eyes, and know I'm headed for a shitstorm on Wall Street after hearing the news earlier.

"Yes. It is." Kathryn brushes the hair away from my forehead. I lean into her gentle touch as she runs her fingers over my scalp.

"You know how good that feels? It's been a hell of a morning." She only answers with a smile and I close my eyes, relishing the attention she gives so freely.

"I'm so sorry for everything that happened to you today. You deserve so much better than me."

Before she can respond, I kiss her like there's no tomorrow. I want to possess every inch of her as I roam my hands over her silky dress. Simon could have ended her life or mine, instead we're alive and together and for some unknown reason, she still wants me.

"I'm here with you now, Adam," she murmurs in between my desperate kisses. "We can get through what happened today."

"I hope you're right, beautiful. After what you've been through, your strength amazes me." My words boil over with worry. Anger and fear of the future mix together, and I hold on to her as if she's my lifeline, knowing she can see me through the troubles ahead. But am I selfish enough to drag her through the public storms stirring around me? It's a question I'm not prepared to answer.

Chapter 2

As my nurse, Marla, explains the doctor's discharge instructions to me, Eddie strides through the door. Hopefully he's brought clean clothes for me to wear home. I called my housekeeper, Rosa, for her help. She was a frantic mess after she answered the phone, speaking so fast I could barely understand a goddamned word she said.

Forced to nearly shout over her chatter, I assured her I was alive and coming home today. She praised Jesus, Joseph, and Mary and finally calmed down. I can only imagine what poor Eddie endured when he met her at my apartment to retrieve my clothes.

"Hey, Eddie," I say as he approaches the bed.

"Morning, sir." Eddie raises his hand, and he's holding my black Bosca duffle bag.

"My clothes?" I question although I know the answer.

"Yes, sir." Eddie places the bag next to my bedside table and turns to Kathryn. "Good morning, Mrs. Delcour."

"Good morning, Eddie." Kathryn stretches up on her tiptoes and gives Eddie a kiss on the cheek. My happily married driver now has a blushing grin on his face. "That's a thank-you for all you've done today."

While the paramedics were prepping me for the ride to the hospital, Eddie tried to comfort Kathryn. She wasn't hysterical, but she was clearly traumatized. He drove her straight to the hospital, following close behind the ambulance, and according to Kathryn, he ran red lights when she told him to step on the gas.

He bows to her, and I think she's embarrassed this poor man beyond words. But finally Eddie begins to speak, "My pleasure, ma'am. Sir, I'll wait outside for you with Hayes."

"Pardon me, Mr. Kingsley," the nurse interjects since her instructions were interrupted. "I'd like to advise you on your aftercare."

"My apologies, please go on." I want to get out of here, so I give her my full attention.

"Thanks. You'll need to keep the stitches as dry as possible." She hands me a stack of bandages.

"Yes, ma'am." I nod and smile back at her. She becomes disarmed, turning several shades of red while looking back and forth between me and the papers in her hand.

"Well, I think I've gone over everything." She pulls a pen out of her pocket, and hands it to me.

When I reach for the pen, I flinch. Moving too quickly sets off a sharp pain through my ribcage. I try to hide my reaction, but I'm pretty sure I failed.

"Adam, are you all right?" Kathryn moves closer in concern, and I need to set her mind at ease.

"I'll be fine." I try to wave away her worries. "I need to remember to move more slowly. That's all."

"I'll bring you some pain meds before you leave." My nurse sets her papers on the raised table in front of me, pointing to a signature line. "If you'll sign right here."

"Thanks," I say with a wink after signing the papers. My nurse blushes and looks away.

Kathryn rolls her eyes at the exchange. I can't help it, but I feel a little twinge of satisfaction knowing that maybe Kathryn's a tad jealous. Or maybe I'm reading her wrong and she's only annoyed at me.

"You're good to go now, Mr. Kingsley." Marla tears apart the papers and gives me a signed copy.

"Appreciate it, Marla."

"You're more than welcome." She returns my wink before walking away.

Marla heads to the door, and a mocking Kathryn takes her place. Oh boy, here it goes. So much for sympathy.

"Really?" Kathryn lifts her brow, and I know she saw everything, including the wink good-bye.

"What?" I reply, playing dumb.

"Oh, never mind." Kathryn laughs while shaking her head. "It's your snake-charming ways."

"Get over here." I move my legs over the edge of the bed and stand up carefully, still wearing the piece of shit hospital gown over my pants. I cover her hand with mine, needing to connect with her.

"It's okay. You had the same effect on me, too," she says while threading our fingers together.

"Lucky for me, I did. Because I don't even want to think about where I'd be if I hadn't." I place my left arm around her, cautious to keep my right side still. "I can't wait to be alone with you later."

"Me, too," she whispers while leaning into my chest. She stiffens as she tries to be watchful with my injury.

"Hey, I'm tough. Like the man of steel," I boast, then pull her harder into my side—the good one.

"Steel?" She gazes at me with smiling eyes. "Yes, I can confirm that."

"If we keep this up, I think everyone else will confirm it, too."

Now that I have my discharge papers, I've had enough of this flimsy hospital gown and I'm ready to change into the clothes Eddie brought me. Kathryn helps me get dressed and promises to help me *undress* later... and I can't fucking wait.

Eddie and Goliath are outside my room, waiting to take me home. I haven't checked my phone once since Kathryn arrived. She can be a bit distracting, to say the least. I scan through the missed calls and texts, realizing the report I heard earlier has detonated a PR bomb at Kings Capital. Meg Daniels, my communications director, practically begged me to call her back. Yes, the shit has hit the fan.

"I think we're ready to leave, finally." Ignoring the demands for my immediate attention, I move away from the bed, fully dressed in black designer track pants and a matching jacket with a pocket the perfect size for stuffing my phone out of sight.

"I'm so grateful you're okay." She clasps my hand. "I don't think I could stand losing someone important to me again."

"Me, too, beautiful. I felt the same way when I saw you with Simon and all because of me."

"Everything happened so fast. By the time I figured out what was going on, he was waving the gun around, and then you rescued me. I can't tell you what went through my head when I heard the first gunshot," she says, her voice shaking with emotion. "And then I saw you go down."

"Ah, babe. You were so brave today," I say, comforting her and hoping to soothe her worries. "I have to believe I made it through with barely a scratch for a reason."

"Me, too." She nods and caresses my arm softly letting me know how much she cares.

Hand in hand we walk to the door, ready to leave. When I open it, I'm surprised by what I see standing in front of me. Peters and Tom, my business partner at Kings Capital and longtime friend, are blocking our exit from the room. Ah, *shit*.

"I kept them out while you were changing, sir." Goliath addresses me before the other men speak, as though he's trying to win more brownie points, but I'm thankful he barred the door.

"Good move. No need to give everyone a show." I laugh as I face my new guests in the hallway. But I feel the effects immediately when a pain hits my side from the small chuckle rippling through the muscles in my abdomen.

"Fuck," I mutter under my breath and grab my side.

"Easy, Adam." Kathryn's by my side, gently rubbing my arm.

"I'm all right," I say, straightening up to my full height. "The pain's more a twinge than a constant ache."

"That bad, buddy?" Tom asks with a concerned look on his face.

"Only when I see your ugly face." I tease him back and grip my side more. "And right now I'm really hurting."

"Good one." Tom chuckles because it's usually me on the end of *his* jokes. It does feel good to pick on him for a change.

Tom turns to Kathryn and introduces himself, holding out his paw. "Tom Duffy."

I can't miss the hint of mischief in his eyes.

"Kathryn Delcour. Nice to meet you." Kathryn shakes his hand, a broad smile on her face. It's impossible not to like him. He's just one of those guys everyone wants to call a friend.

"And Peters we *all* know." I acknowledge him with a tip of my chin and see that he's dressed like it's a workday. All business. "I take it you didn't like the text I sent you earlier?"

"You're correct, sir." He stands a little straighter as he speaks his mind. "Perhaps we can discuss things inside your room."

Peters looks around him as if what we have to talk about is top secret.

"We're in a hospital, for Christ's sake. I don't think I'm in any danger here. But okay, if for no other reason than we need to clear the hall."

I turn to Kathryn before I let the new entourage of guests back into the room I was hoping to leave behind.

"Beautiful, would you mind giving us a few minutes? I have a feeling this powwow with Peters and Tom could take a while, and I hate to bore you." She looks confused, likely wondering why I'm dismissing her. The truth is I don't want her knowing about the crap in the press concerning the shooting.

"Sure, I can take a hint when I'm not wanted." She gives me a wink followed by a quick kiss on the cheek. "How about I get you a coffee. Cream, right?"

"Yes, thanks." I pull her close to me so I can whisper in her ear. "And believe me, babe, I've never wanted anyone like I want you."

Releasing her, I turn back to the men in front of me. "All right, gentlemen. This better be good. You're keeping me away from this pretty lady."

"Goddammit, Adam. You've got it bad." Tom tries to hit me on the arm, but I give him a death glare. He pulls back, realizing I'll be in pain if he does. "Sorry, buddy. I got carried away."

"I'll leave you boys to your business." She shakes her head at the testosterone-filled crowd before turning to leave.

As she walks away, the eyes of every single man standing next to me follow her sweet little sashay. All I can think is *yes, by God, that sweet little ass is mine,* and the other eyes fixed on her are starting to piss me off.

"Okay. Enough gawking, *boys.* You have ten minutes, tops, because I want to get the hell out of this place. I swear it's like fucking Grand Central Station around here."

I turn to face Eddie and Goliath. "You two wait outside. And pull up a couple of chairs for fuck's sake."

I push back through the door and both Peters and Tom follow behind me. I'm actually happy to see Tom. I think it will take us both some time to fully process what's gone on since Wednesday night.

I sit back down on the bed as Tom and Peters pull up chairs. "So, Peters, I'm assuming you've heard the latest news. The media has linked me to Simon's fiancée and claim a love triangle is the motive behind his actions."

"Yes, sir. The media circus you're facing needs to be handled carefully." Peters sits back in his chair. It looks like he's about to give me news I don't want to hear. "I've been downstairs trying to keep reporters out of the hospital. They're sniffing for blood, and I want to keep Hayes guarding you at all times until things settle down."

"Fuck." I bury my hands in my hair. I owe Hayes my life since he killed Simon to save me. A split second later and Simon would've blown my head off. "Okay. I'll let him stay around for a little while longer."

"Good." Peters' lips form a sly grin now that he's won the point with me. "I just got off a call with the detectives who were initially on Simon's case. They want to speak with you this afternoon."

"*Great.*" I don't disguise my frustration. I wanted to decompress and spend the rest of the day alone with Kathryn. So much shit has gone on since we've met, and now it looks like a quiet afternoon isn't in the cards, either. "What exactly do they want?"

"Just basic questions surrounding the shooting so they can close the case. I believe they want to speak with Mrs. Delcour, too.

"She's been through enough since she met me." I want to keep Kathryn from getting tangled in the web of my troubles as much as possible.

"It's too late for that. The local news covering the shooting is calling her an innocent bystander. They haven't connected the dots that she was outside of The Pierre *with* you."

"Dammit," I say under my breath. This is more unwelcomed news.

"They've tagged her as the *Widowed Heiress*," Peters continues. "Since her late husband was wealthier than her own parents. And they were Vanderbilts, too."

"I had no idea her late husband was that wealthy."

"It was all in the background report you asked me to do on her," Peters says in his defense. I was sidetracked by her photos on the front of his report. With everything else going on, I haven't given the report another glance because I had Kathryn, the real thing, with me instead.

"You had a background report done on her?" Tom, who's been silent, finally inserts himself in our conversation. It's clear he doesn't approve of Peters prying into Kathryn's private life one damn bit. "That's really low, buddy."

"I wanted to know more about her after we first met." I put my hands up, trying to concede some ground to Tom. "I swear I don't normally do this type of thing. Back me up here, Peters."

Sneaky Peters smiles. "He's right. This is the first time he's asked me to run a background check on a woman for personal reasons."

"Remember who we're talking about here." I stop and have to laugh. "I've never been interested in anyone for over an hour... two, tops. That says something, right?"

They both look at each other and shrug, but Tom has a knowing grin spread across that big mug of his. One I'd like to smack right off because I know there will be more jabs at my expense later. All along the lines of the fact that the mighty playboy, Adam Kingsley, has finally fallen.

"Back to Kathryn and the media. I want to keep her out of this whole debacle as much as possible. Peters, keep tabs on this situation and alert me the second you see anything that even remotely connects her to me."

"Unless you keep your relationship underground, it's only a matter of time before they find out," Peters says, and I know his words are likely the truth.

"After a couple of news cycles, this will be forgotten if we play it right. I want the press on my ass, not hers. Anything else, Peters?"

"Nope." He stands. "I'll meet you back at your apartment. I'm going to scout for the media. The Pierre is usually good about keeping cameras away, and there's always the service entrance if need be. I'll instruct Eddie with the logistics once I know more."

"Fine." I remember one more important thing before he heads out. "Make sure you call my lawyer. I want him in attendance during the detective's questioning. Got it?"

"Yes, sir. See you, Mr. Duffy." Peters shakes Tom's hand before exiting the room. I feel the tension in the room leave as he does. Peters is invaluable to me, but he's intense as hell. I also win very few arguments with him. He's like the bossy uncle I never had.

"Forget about the press shit for a minute. I want to talk about Kathryn," Tom says, starting in before the door's fully shut. He's moved his chair right in front of me. With his football player build, I'm going nowhere until he's finished. "She's quite the woman to tame you this quickly. Patrick and I always bet it would be this way. One solid whack from the right woman and you'd fall like a dead tree. Boom! So what are you two? Boyfriend and girlfriend?"

"Yes, I'm pretty much willing to be her *anything* right now." It's the truth, because I would wear any label for this woman. I regain my composure and say, "I have no idea where this thing between us will go, but she hasn't run screaming from me yet. Even after almost getting shot by Simon and hiding me from him last week."

"Well you know how to show a girl a good time." Tom wiggles his bushy brows. "Maybe she's an adrenaline junkie. Or just after your junk."

"Funny." I smile, remembering how she went after said junk. "If you and Patrick are going to give me a hard time about possibly settling down, it'll be no different than all the times you called me a male slut."

"Hey, you're right, man." Tom gets a deadpanned look on his face. All kidding aside. "I'm happy for you, but mostly I'm fucking happy you're still with us."

"Me, too. When I think about everything, it seems like a dream. Then I move a little and feel the pain in my side and I know it's real."

"I still can't believe our Simon is gone. It's obvious mentally he left us a long time ago, but holy shit, we've been together since college. Things weren't supposed to happen this way. Even Patrick is pretty shook up."

"I can imagine." Patrick, the stoic one of the group, is our other business partner. Patrick, Tom, Simon, and I started Kings Capital together. Four high tech wizards from MIT. All for one and one for all. Now with Simon gone, we are down to three.

"Patrick's coming back from Boston today. He called and told me to get my ass to the hospital since you haven't answered a single communication from any of us. Meg's already formulated solid talking points for us if we're questioned by the media." Tom raises his finger, prepared to count off the suggestions from Meg.

"First, stress that Simon was removed from his position at Kings Capital on Wednesday. Completely disassociate him from Kings when he started acting crazy. Second, we are to say we offer our condolences to his family for the tragedy that occurred. Third, we are to conclude that we wish we had known he was suffering so we could have gotten him help."

"I have to say Meg's brilliant, and everything you just said is completely true." I pause and take a deep breath. "If we'd only known."

"No kidding." Tom tilts his head, and I can feel a question coming on. "What do you think it was? And I'm confused about the whole love triangle thing blowing up in the news involving you."

"I know the main reason he snapped. It's ugly." I glance at the floor and prepare to bulldoze through the truth. Tom goes still in his chair, which for him is quite the feat.

After clearing my throat, I say, "I slept with his fiancée—way before he met her. Don't remember it, either. She was just some random hookup in the Hamptons. But she became obsessed with me. Used Simon the entire time to try and get to me."

"No way." Tom shakes his head, anger brewing in his eyes. "One of your casual fucks, I take it."

"Yes," I say and bow my head, ashamed. Which is something new for me, and I don't fucking care for it at all. "When she broke off the engagement with him, she told him everything, and he snapped. He really loved her."

"Goddammit, Adam." Tom stands up and turns his back to me. The symbolism of his stance is significant and one I likely deserve. "I shouldn't be upset with you, I suppose, but using women like you've done for years... it came back to haunt you, didn't it?"

"I know." I agree with him. Simon's face, with the same mocking smile, and the word *karma* flash through my mind.

Tom turns to me, his face scrunched in anger. "You better learn from this goddamned mistake. Actions have consequences. They set wheels in motion. You're a genius, so figure your shit out."

"I think I have." My voice is nothing more than a whisper, enforcing my guilt.

"I sure as hell hope so. I don't know Kathryn well but—"

As he speaks, the door opens and Kathryn comes walking in as if on cue, holding two cups of coffee.

She must feel the heaviness in the room between Tom and I because the worry lines deepen between her brows.

"I interrupted something, didn't I?" Her question is as intuitive as she is.

"We were just finishing up. No problem." Tom tries to ease the palpable tension but eyes me in a way that tells me this conversation isn't over, not by a long shot.

Shit. I have a hell of lot to prove to him, Kathryn, and even myself. If I become a truly better man there will be only one reason for my change. Kathryn.

Chapter 3

We're finally pulling away from the hospital after making a covert escape. Goliath had me exit through an underground staff-parking garage. We'd hoped going out that way would keep the media from getting shots of me.

Tom left quickly after Kathryn came back with coffee. He hardly said a word of good-bye to me. The once jovial Tom couldn't get past my indiscretions and the effects they had on not just me but Simon.

Kathryn sits by my side in the back of the SUV. She's been quiet ever since Tom left. Her pensive mood is driving me nuts since I have no clue what's going on in her mind. Our only connection is our hands as we hold them together.

"Kathryn? What are you thinking?" I'm half-afraid to hear what she will say. Maybe she's having second thoughts about us. I've put this woman through a hell of a lot since we met. I have no frame of reference for being with someone like her, either. I am pathetic and out of my league. It's a feeling I don't care for but I can't seem to shake it. I wipe a little sweat over my brow and silently curse to myself because sweat has always been a sign of weakness to me.

"I don't know." She lowers her head and bites her lip. I fear she's holding back words I don't want to hear. "I was hoping we *weren't* going back to your place."

"Is that what's bothering you?" This I can work with. I think. I give her hand a reassuring squeeze.

"Yes, I'm not quite prepared to go back to The Pierre and see where it all happened." She looks at me, eyes pleading, asking me to keep her from having to relive today's memories.

Memories of Simon holding a gun to her head, me being shot, and Hayes killing Simon right in front of us. It all makes sense now. After Tom left, I told her we were going back to The Pierre, and she went silent after that. I should have known this would bother her.

"Ah, beautiful." I place my arm around her shoulders, choosing to ignore the pain below my ribs and focus on her because this usually strong woman *needs* me. "Let me ask Eddie what entrance of the building we're taking."

"Hey, Eddie," I say over the low music. The partition is already down in the SUV. We didn't feel it was necessary for privacy today. "Where are you dropping us off at The Pierre?"

"Peters wants us at the building's entrance on Fifth. It's a quicker walk to the elevators, and he said the paps are waiting on the sidewalk by the Sixty-First Street entrance, closer to Barney's."

"Great," I answer, both relieved and in agreement with the plan. I nudge Kathryn with my arm. "No worries, babe. We won't be near where everything happened."

"Good. I'm not ready to face that place yet." The relief in her is evident as she snuggles into my side. Again I suppress the pain. She needs me, and damn if I don't need her even more.

I hold her tightly until we hit Sixty-Third Street. I know we are getting close and need to prepare for a quick exit from the vehicle as the SUV makes the turn onto Fifth Avenue.

"We're almost there," I tell her. Kathryn pulls away from my side and looks up at me. "I'll lead, so stay close to me. There will be no waiting for Eddie or Hayes. Once the wheels stop, we'll step out onto the sidewalk and hurry toward the door."

She nods, agreeing with me. I look out my window and see Eddie pulling up to the entrance and stop the SUV. The sidewalk's signature black and white checkered tiles greet me as I exit with Kathryn by my side.

We jog toward the double doors. I'm holding my side like I'm fucking Napoleon. The pain radiates through me with each footstep on the pavement.

"Adam, are you okay?" Kathryn asks once we're inside. By now I'm doubled over and panting like a damn pussy. She's rubbing her hands over my back.

"I'll. Be. Okay." I spout out my words one by one between breaths. "Just. Need. To. Catch. My. Breath."

Stuffing the pain away, I grab her hand and start for the elevators. I'll relax once I'm upstairs in my apartment. I hear a commotion behind us and glance over my shoulder long enough to see Goliath with his arms stretched wide. Apparently, the paps have realized I just arrived and tried to follow us inside. Fortunately I listened to Peters and kept Goliath around to keep the paps out of the hotel. Hopefully they didn't get a view of Kathryn with me and her connection to me is still a secret. I don't want her drawn into this clusterfuck.

"That was close," I say, finally able to breathe normally as we near the elevators.

"Does this happen to you a lot or is it just because of the shooting?"

"It's the shooting and Simon's death. Other than a few photos at events and the occasional press conference, the media pretty much leaves me alone."

"Good. I can't imagine living like this. I'd go crazy. I'm too independent."

"That you are, beautiful." I nod to the elevator attendant as we approach him.

I'm thankful he monitors who enters these elevators. Only registered guests and residents are allowed up from here. They must show their keys, and I've even seen the guard check their validity by asking for their IDs. It's great security The Pierre offers.

We stand outside the residents' elevator. Guests of the hotel aren't allowed to enter this one. I punch in my code and we wait for the elevator to arrive. Out of the corner of my eye, I see a group heading our way. Something isn't right about them, though. Before I can react, lights flash and my name echoes around the marbled hallway.

"Jesus," I utter under my breath and move quickly to stand between them and Kathryn. A protective gesture I hope was in time and keeps them from photographing her.

"Shit, Adam." She collapses into me as I practically scoop her up and move into the waiting elevator. My side roars in pain as the questions from what must be reporters begin.

"Mr. Kingsley, who is that with you?" yells one reporter.

"Why did Simon Edwards attempt to kill you this morning?" shouts another.

The elevator closes as the last question lingers in the air.

"Rumors are that you had a relationship with his fiancée. Is this true?"

I shake my head in disgust because Kathryn knows about the press leak now. The reporters shouldn't have found out about Simon's fiancée, and I can only imagine it was the police who tipped off the press. Those detectives were idiot bastards who hated me. It was apparent in their questioning. They thought I was a cheating, rich asshole, to put it mildly.

"Fuck, fuck, fuck," I yell while leaning back and hitting my head against the shiny chrome wall in frustration.

Kathryn places her hands on my hips, so I tilt my head down to see her gazing up at me. Her eyes are soft and show me a depth of understanding and compassion I don't deserve but need like the air I breathe.

"Adam," she murmurs to me in a comforting way. I place my hands on her waist to bring her closer to me as the elevator carries us up to my floor. "I'm glad you told me the truth about Simon. You could've hidden the reason behind this entire mess from me, but you didn't. So don't let them get to you. Simon's actions weren't how a normal person would react. He was a sick, sick man."

"I did set the stage, though. Deep down I want to believe you're right. But the simple fact is my actions have put us in this whole mess. It's the kind of gossip that the media thrives on. Salacious and outrageous and I don't want your name drawn into this. That's my only worry. It will take a little time, but after a while, the media coverage will die down and move on. Another scandal or disaster will wipe this story off the front page." I hope my predictions come to pass. I know Wall Street has the memory of an elephant. Traders and analysts never forget.

"Do you think they got a clear view of me?" I hate that she has to even ask me this question.

"I don't know. I'll have Peters check the news feeds for me. He said he'd meet me back here. Until now, you haven't been connected to me. I think the term was 'innocent bystander' from the news reports so far."

"I'm glad I reached my mother before she saw the news about me... and you."

"I should've had you go home instead of coming here with me or at the very least had you come into the building without me. I wasn't thinking. Truth is I don't want to be apart from you right now." My selfish desires for her have put her in the spotlight.

"And there's no place I'd rather be." She removes her hands from my hips and cups my chin.

Her fingers glide over my jaw with the lightest of touch and I relax into them. This woman unravels all the knots in me and lays me bare. I tighten my hold around her waist, not wanting to let go as the doors to the elevator open and we exit onto my floor.

"Peters," I yell as I enter my apartment with Kathryn behind me. I'm livid and he's going to get an earful. He walks around the corner that leads to the kitchen. He must have been back in the butler's bedroom.

"Yes, sir." Peters keeps his distance in the large living room. I can feel tension vibrating off me in angry waves.

"The fucking reporters were downstairs shouting questions at me." I have my fists wrapped into tight balls at this point. I need answers.

"I was assured the hotel staff was guarding the lobby and only registered guests were being admitted. My apologies, sir."

"Obviously, they let some of those fuckers slip through. Kathryn and I dodged into the elevator as the reporters screamed questions at me. One being, did I sleep with Simon's fiancée? I think I know how they found out, too. Those damn detectives. And there will be hell to pay if they leaked it. I'll have their badges."

"Nothing is sacred, Mr. Kingsley. I'm not saying you shouldn't be upset, but in this day and age, there's no controlling leaks. Even the president has trouble with his own staffers." Peters' words grate at me and offer no relief.

"When they come for the interview at three, I want you here and putting their feet to the fire. You're good at that. If they did leak it, we need to know. I'm not answering one question until we address this with them. Got it?" I run my fingers through my hair in frustration because the control I need in this situation remains out of my grasp.

"Got it." I can tell he wants to leave the room and escape my wrath as he backs away from me, but I'm not quite finished yet.

"Another thing. Check the news feeds. I want to know if the reporters recognized Kathryn."

"Will do." Smartly he flees to the back of the apartment.

Now it's just me, Kathryn, and my dark mood in the room. I wonder what Kathryn thinks of my ugly tirade. I glance over and see a worried look stretched across her beautiful face. A look that I put there.

Frustrated with myself and needing to calm down, I walk over to the wall of windows overlooking Central Park. The green on the trees is beginning to show the signs of spring. New beginnings. I lean my head against the glass and hope somehow fate or God will give me the same chance because I sure as hell have fucked my life up.

"Adam." Kathryn moves to my side and rubs her hands down my back. I close my eyes and take a deep breath before facing her. Control is what I need right now, not my abominable temper.

"Sorry, beautiful." She's here beside me, understanding, accepting. "Clearly, I'm not the man you deserve. Have I scared you away yet?"

"You're kidding, right?" She answers back with a smile, and every fear fades away. "Believe it or not, you're the first man in two years I've wanted to be with. I don't think my feelings are *that* fleeting. Actually, I rather like you. Besides, I'm known for taking cocky rich boys and turning them into men."

I bring her in my arms, and she giggles at my sudden move, likely not expecting it with my injury. But I couldn't care less about the pain. I brush aside the hair that's fallen in her face and press my lips against hers. Hard. The kiss is backed by a feeling so intense I can't begin to name its source. It's beyond my heart, more like the marrow deep in my bones.

"Thank you," I whisper as I bury my face in her hair. The smell of her perfume intoxicates me. "I've learned my lesson and need you to teach me how to be a better man. Before we've hardly begun, I fear I'm going to drag you through my muddy reputation. Staining me might be deserved, but marking you is a sin."

She pulls away a few inches and tilts her head. There's a quizzical look in her eyes. "You really think you're unworthy because you've made some mistakes in your life, don't you?"

"After the last few days, yes. I think it started when I wasn't there for my mother when she took her life. It did something to me."

"It's tormented you." She does that wonderful thing with her fingers in my hair that I love.

"Yes," I say and pull her closer, loving how her softness molds into me. We fit perfectly.

As we silently hold one another, I hear footsteps against the wood floor. I look up from our embrace, expecting to see Peters, but it's Rosa, instead.

"Rosa." Partially releasing Kathryn, I turn us toward my housekeeper. "I didn't know you were here, but I'm glad to see you."

"Oh, Mr. Kingsley." She practically runs to where we're standing. Once she's closer, I can make out the tears brimming in her eyes. "I was so frightened. When I watched the news this morning, I worried that you might be dead, too."

"Like I told you earlier when we talked, I'm going to be okay. I promise. I was extremely lucky. It could have been much worse." I smile down at the petite woman whose concern for me, her often-distant employer, surprises me. Rosa eyes between Kathryn and me. It's time for an introduction.

"I'd like for you meet someone very special to me." I can't disguise the pride I feel having Kathryn at my side.

"She's the lady on the TV." Rosa's volume rises with excitement and her eyes become wide as she recognizes Kathryn. "But they say you weren't with Mr. Kingsley."

"As you can see, she is very much with me." I lean down and kiss Kathryn on the top of her head. "Although we're keeping it hush-hush for a while."

"Oh, this is very good." Rosa's sad expression changes to one of sheer delight as a broad smile graces her face. "Hello, Miss..."

She pauses, needing help with Kathryn's name. I step in with the introductions. "Rosa, this is Kathryn Delcour. *Dr.* Kathryn Delcour, in fact."

"Please, you can call me Kathryn," she says while giving me a sweet tease with her eyes. "It's a pleasure to meet you, Rosa."

Rosa has taken Kathryn's hands and raises them in the air, surprising Kathryn as she inspects her from head to toe. Kathryn glances up and gives me a "what's up with her" look. I shrug my shoulders because I haven't a clue.

"You're very beautiful," Rosa finally says.

"Thank you," Kathryn responds, and I detect a little relief in her tone.

"And you're Mr. Kingsley's girlfriend, right?" Rosa's signature grin lights up her face.

Kathryn begins to laugh, and I become tense wondering what her response will be. "Yes, I guess you could call me his girlfriend."

"This is very good." Rosa takes Kathryn's arm and leads her toward the kitchen. "So many nights he's here in this big old apartment all alone."

"Is that right?" Kathryn glances over her shoulder at me with a wicked smile on her face. She appears to be enjoying Rosa's rundown of my habits, and it makes me feel like a fucking child.

"Yes, he never has company." Rosa shakes her head as if my lifestyle is a crying shame, and truthfully she's dead-on in that view. "You're the first girlfriend I've met."

"So I've heard," Kathryn says with undeniable sarcasm.

"It's about time he looked to the future. What good is life unless we have someone to share it with, right?"

"Rosa, those are very true words. Don't you agree, Adam?"

"Yes, beautiful, I do." I twist a strand of her long hair between my fingers as I walk behind her.

"I have food for you both in the kitchen. I fixed my meatloaf, your favorite, Mr. Kingsley."

I swear my stomach growled at the mere mention of Rosa's cooking. Her meatloaf reigns as my favorite comfort food and reminds me of my childhood. My mother's was a touch better, but I think the added love for me she put into her recipe made the difference.

"Bring it on!" I can smell the aroma of what awaits us the closer we get to the kitchen. "You're going love her meatloaf, beautiful."

"Rosa, can I help you with anything?" Kathryn moves closer to Rosa, who's pulling the meatloaf out of the oven, I plant myself at the kitchen table since that's where some of the food is already laid out.

"No, dear." Rosa waves her off after setting the piping-hot dish on the table in front of me. "I've got it all under control. I've been off for a few days and need to earn my wages."

"Where were you when we came in, Rosa?" I'm surprised she didn't hear me yelling at Peters. It's likely my neighbors heard me two stories below.

"I was in the laundry room." She pulls a pair of ear buds out of her pocket and shows them to us. It's quiet around here since I'm gone all day, so she's constantly listening to something. "I was just finishing this new audio book. A murder mystery. It keeps me moving when I work. All the adrenaline."

I pat the seat next to me. "Kathryn, come sit down. Let Rosa do what she does best. She's a pro at taking care of me."

"Thanks, Rosa. Everything looks and smells delicious. In all the excitement today, I realize I haven't eaten a thing."

"My pleasure. You two enjoy."

"Rosa, would you care to join us?" I've never shared a meal with her and the shock of my invitation is clear on her face as her eyes widen in surprise.

"Thanks, Mr. Kingsley, but I'm just going to put clean sheets on your bed. For later." I swear there was a wicked twinkle in her eye.

We dig into the small feast Rosa's made. I end up devouring several servings before I realize I've pretty much consumed the whole meatloaf, minus the small amount Kathryn ate. The mashed potato bowl appears empty now, too.

"Shit, I must have been hungrier than I thought."

"Hopefully, you aren't too full. I was thinking..." I feel her foot rubbing against the inside of my calf. "You might need to rest a bit before the detectives show up. Get your strength back and be on your full game."

I see desire in her bright blue eyes and know what she means by "rest." Yes, I think she's right. A rest sounds really good. Perfect, in fact, because fucking away today's hellstorm and getting lost in each other might be the best distraction.

"Whatcha say we have our dessert in the bedroom?" She answers my question with a slow smile that's full of promise.

Chapter 4

We make our escape from the kitchen and an overly enthusiastic Rosa who wants to serve us dessert, but we decide to have our dessert in the bedroom. As I close the bedroom door behind us, I realize that I have no clue how I'm going to make love to this woman, but I'll find a way. I'm already getting hard thinking about it.

"Adam?" My name rolls from her lips with a question that has only one answer. I marvel at her continued use of my name since she so stubbornly refused to say it before the shooting.

"Yes, beautiful?"

"I have an idea for some fun, and I think we both need it." I can tell she's plotting something as I see her wheels spinning. She stalks toward me and says, "It will require a few props, though."

"Oh, props?" I say teasingly while placing my arms around her. "I think I like the sound of that."

"You silly, horny man." She laughs and threads her arms around my neck. "We'll need just ordinary, everyday things."

"How ordinary?"

"Well... I have a tantric exercise for self-control where I help you learn to absorb and prolong pleasure. And it will work well with your injury."

"No pain and prolonging pleasure? Sign me up." She shakes her head, but I can't control the thought of being pleasured by her. Maybe that's the point she's trying to make here.

"I need six coins. They should be large ones, if possible." She forms a circle with her fingers to show me the size of coin she wants. "So, Mr. Billionaire, do you have any gold coins lying around the apartment?" With her other hand, she twists the hair at the back of my neck. Everything she does and says winds me up.

"Yes, I'm sure there are some in the cushions of my couch." I smirk and get a giggle out of her. "I also give them away in a swag bag to my guests as parting gifts."

"For your one-night stands? How very Derek Jeter of you." She sounds a little annoyed at me again. Seems I'm becoming a pro at drawing that response from her.

"Poor Jeter will never live that rumor down."

"'Poor Jeter'? You have to be kidding me? Who gives a woman he just fucked a gift bag with baseball swag in it? But, you—a billionaire—sharing gold coins in one would make sense."

"I've done a lot of crazy things I'm not proud of but giving hookups gift bags isn't one of them."

"I'm only half-kidding. Besides, I'm the first woman Rosa's seen here at your apartment."

"Exactly. Now back to those coins..." I turn the conversation around to more important things, like making my dick happy. "How did we get sidetracked on swag bags and one-night stands, anyway? I do keep a rare collection of coins stashed away in my safe."

"That's more like it." She grins, pleased that I have a few billionaire extravagances after all. "So are they in a panic room?"

"You're kidding me? I'm not that afraid for my life. I just have a safe hidden in the wall of my closest. Wanna see? You can help pick them out if you'd like."

"Why don't you go get them while I'm prepping the room for what I have in mind?"

I swear I feel my cock twitch at the word *prep*. "I'm on it. Six coins, right?"

"Yep. Give me a couple of minutes." She winks and I'm off to fetch those fucking coins. What the hell she needs six coins for is a mystery. But I'm game for what she's got up her sleeves and in her pants, literally. Who wouldn't be if he had the sexiest girlfriend in New York City?

I smile to myself at the word *girlfriend*. I don't think I've used that word to describe a woman since college. The couple of girlfriends I had back then came and went after a few weeks.

Removing a wooden panel in the back of my closet, I reveal the hidden safe. Peters made me put it in. I told him that the majority of my money is hidden in Kings stock, but he says someone of my caliber should have one installed at his residence. It's expected, I suppose.

The safe is biometric and opens by fingerprint recognition. After a quick scan of my prints, the lock releases with a ping. Swinging the door open, I see the treasures inside. Not much, really. Photos of my childhood that are priceless to me. They're safe here and also out of sight. Getting distracted, I pull out a picture of my mother.

I've kept these photos of her hidden away. Too many painful memories. But as I hold the image of her in my hand, I feel something different than the shame and remorse I've struggled with for years. Instead it's a longing to see her again. Something I never would have allowed before, but today I let the feelings invade every part of me. I swear my heart is about to explode as I remember back to the scene in the photo.

My high school graduation. I'm decked out in my cap and gown. Adorned with tassels and regalia showing all my academic honors. My mother never looked more proud as we stood side by side.

I close my eyes and let myself drift back to that day. I was awarded the most academic honors in my class and gave the valedictorian speech. I remember finding my mother in the auditorium after the ceremony, and she was smiling at me through her proud tears. She made me feel like I could do anything. Her love and encouragement gave me that kind of confidence.

I don't remember her ever smiling like she did that day. It gave me a glimpse of the joy snuffed out by my father when she left New York City. She always had an underlying sadness as her smiles seldom reached her eyes.

I place the photo back inside the safe and realize of all my possessions inside, this one is my most treasured. Shaking my head, I try to regroup and focus on the real reason I'm standing here, rifling through memories. As I'm about to begin searching for the coins, Kathryn places a hand on my back.

"Hey. I'm just checking on you. Have trouble finding what you were looking for?"

I wonder how long I've stood here going down memory lane. It seems like minutes but who knows?

"Sorry to keep you waiting. I was just looking at old pictures."

She peeks around me to see inside my safe. "What pictures?"

"Just some from my childhood." I find the custom-made wooden case for the coins we need tonight. As I grab the case, she places her hand on mine and stops me.

"I'd love to see those photos. Do you mind?" She moves to stand almost in front of me. I don't think there's any way to avoid sharing them.

"Sure."

Before the word has left my lips, she's pulling photos out of the safe. The one on top of the stack in the box is the graduation shot.

"Wow, Adam. Look how young you were... and handsome. Is this your mother?" Her voice fades as she mentions my mother.

"Yes," I whisper.

"She was so beautiful and looks so proud of you. She's smiling from ear to ear." Kathryn peeks up at me and searches my face for a reaction.

"My mother was even more beautiful on the inside than she was on the outside. She gave up everything for me. Honestly, I haven't gone through those photos in years." I decide there's no need to keep the truth from her. "It's been too hard."

"But you looked at them just now?"

"Yes."

"You sweet man." She reaches up on her tiptoes and I meet her halfway. Our lips connect for a quick kiss. "I don't think you would've been able to do this without the experience you had the other night."

"Me, neither." She lays her head gently against my chest, careful to avoid my side. I know the tantric sex a couple days ago freed something inside me where my mother is concerned. I can actually dwell on her memory without experiencing a crippling feeling in my soul.

"We can save these for another time. I think you need a little TLC." She places the photos back in the box. "What we need right now are coins."

"The reason I came in here." I move a few financial documents off the top of the custom-made case for my coins. I open the leather-encased top to reveal perfect rows of coins lying on red velvet. The coins are housed in individual slots.

"These are perfect." Kathryn traces her finger over the top of the silver coins. "And extremely old."

"They're Greek, around 500 BC. I bought them when I was on business in Athens." I take one coin from its resting spot. "They're knows as Athenian Owls."

"They're beautiful."

I place the coin in the palm of her hand. "Flip it over and look on the other side."

When she turns the coin over, a woman's face takes up the entire side. "Was this woman a queen?"

"It's Athena, the goddess of wisdom." I place five more coins in her hand. "I purchased ten of them on a whim, and I'm damn glad I did now. Very fitting, considering whose hands they're in."

"I love them." I watch, amused, as she continues to examine them. "They're going to be perfect."

"Said the wise woman."

"Follow me." She motions to me as she exits the closet. I quickly close the safe and trail behind with a perfect view of her sweet little ass.

Once in the bedroom, I noticed she pulled the long, gray, velvet curtains over the wall of windows while I was at my safe. There's still sunlight peeking through but the room is more subdued.

Kathryn also removed the bedspread and pillows from the bed, and only the sheets are exposed. It reminds me more of the cushioned mat she has in her harem tent.

"Where do you want me?" I'm unsure what she has in mind. Yes, I'm conceding control. After all, the coins are in her hands and I've agreed to play this game.

"I know your side still hurts, so I'm going to make this easy for you."

"You know I'm easy."

"The world knows *that.*" She winks at me. "Question is, can you stay still? That's what we're about to find out."

I've moved to her side by the bed. She places the coins on the nightstand and then begins to undress me.

"There are a few rules in this tantric game. Keep eye contact as much as possible. And definitely no closing your eyes. I don't want you escaping behind these lids." She gently outlines my brow with her finger. "And *no* talking."

"No talking?" Our previous Tantra experience was different from what she's doing now. I wasn't silenced and was free to ask her questions.

"Yes. Trust me. Having to exact intense control will add to the pleasure when I finally let you experience it," she says then begins to unbutton my shirt and kisses my newly exposed skin. All I'm left to do is trust her. What man in my shoes would do differently? I surrender to her. It feels good, different, and somehow freeing.

After unbuttoning my cuffs, she slowly removes my shirt. She's so careful with my side, I want to say thanks but think better of it. I've taken a vow of silence.

My shirt falls around my feet. My pants soon follow as they pool around my ankles. I'm standing in my boxer briefs with a very hard erection.

She places her hands on my hipbones and trails them down my legs. Kneeling in front of me, she looks up and smiles seductively. I run my fingers through her hair, hoping they convey what my voice can't.

After unlacing my running shoes, she helps me step out of them and then my pants. "Hmm, now the big reveal."

From below, she places her fingers on the elastic top of my briefs and slides them down my legs. My aching cock is free and pointing at her as if it's a homing device looking for its target.

"You're so chiseled." Kathryn places her fingers around me and brings her lips to the head of my cock. In one swift movement, she envelops me inside her hot mouth. Her tongue welcomes me as it swirls around the tip. I have to bite my lip from moaning as she bobs back and forth, sucking me between her plump lips.

She breaks away, and I catch myself before pleading for her to continue. "That's a little preview of what's ahead." She rises to her feet and releases my erection.

"Lay down on the bed." She pats the side of the bed, and I comply. "Perfect. Now place your arms at your side and keep them there."

Here I'm lying with my cock raised at attention. I'm completely at her mercy, and hopefully she's willing to give me some.

I watch her pick up the six coins with absolutely no idea what she's going to do.

"Make a fist with your hand." Standing over me, she covers one of my hands with hers. She squeezes tightly and my fingernails dig into my palms. I look down and see my hands in hard knots as if I'm ready to fight.

"Now make the same closed fist with your other hand, too," she commands. "Yes, like that. Keep them closed snug."

She begins to push the coins between my fingers as they're pressed together hard. If I were to loosen my grip, the coins would fall from my grasp.

"The trick to this Tantra game is keeping still. It will also keep your side from hurting, as well." She has a good point there. I haven't felt a bit of pain yet.

"Hold the coins between your fingers and keep your hands still. If you drop the coins or move your hands to touch me, I'll stop whatever fun I'm having with you and start over. It may not seem hard now, but believe me, as I get to work on your cock it's going to be difficult and will take all your strength to keep still." The sound of her saying *cock* makes mine twitch. I want to moan but somehow contain myself as her fingers blaze a trail down my arms. Her light touch feels so intense to me, I almost fear for what lies ahead. Almost.

"Are you trying to kill me?" Fuck, I just spoke my thoughts out loud. She moves her head in a tsk-tsk fashion.

"Hush." She brings a finger to her lips, and I nod my head in submission to her request.

"My mission is to bring you to life, not kill you."

Right now I've never felt more alive, thanks to her. I settle back and hold my fists as tight as I can, waiting for her next move.

She steps away from the bed, and I have a better view of her body as she unbuttons her dress. One by one they are freed, and she eases the silk from her shoulders, exposing a pale pink bra. The lace is so sheer I can see her hard nipples pressing toward me.

I run my tongue over my lips like a starving man. God, how I want her nipples in my mouth. Sucking, licking, twisting with my fingers. I stir and lift my left arm toward her but catch myself when she eyes me in warning.

"Oh, sweet Adam. I don't even have my clothes off yet and you're already moving and losing control. Be still."

She bends over and kisses me on the lips. I press back and our kiss deepens. Our tongues intertwine. It takes all I have to keep my hands at my side and my fists clenched. I can feel one of the coins starting to slip out from between my fingers as I struggle. Fuck. And as I feared, when I feel the lace of her bra teasingly touch my chest, one of the coins lands on the sheet.

She doesn't notice at first as our kissing continues. But she lifts her head, breaking our kiss and looks down seeing my guilt. Yes, not even five minutes into this game and I've failed. She begins to laugh, and I want to cry out in protest but don't.

"This isn't looking good." She teases as she runs a finger down my chest. "Should I put my dress back on and start over?"

I shake my head violently and she laughs.

"Okay. I'll give you *one* pass." She reinserts the coin between my fingers, and I now have a death grip on them all. I'll be damned if I drop another one. Hell, I got an A in quantum physics, so surely I can fight a little gravity.

She brings her hands to the belt on her dress, or more like the ribbon, threaded through the loops. She unties the knot and slips the ribbon out. Instead of setting it aside, she places the ribbon around her neck. The black ends hang down over her breasts like a scarf.

The rest of her dress falls to the floor, and I see her matching lacy, pink panties. Sheer and feminine with a touch of innocence, although thankfully for me, I know she's far from it.

I'm dying to remove the panties from her as I see her pussy barely hidden behind the lacy material. My impossibly stiff cock twitches as it begs for her attention, desiring to be inside her and thrusting away. I've never wanted to fuck anyone like this before. It's maddening.

She turns her back to me and unclasps her bra with her delicate fingers. Then continuing to torture me, she takes one hand and eases a strap down. Then repeats the same slow process on the other side. With her back to me, I'm about to throw these fucking coins aside, but she turns around right before I give in to my desperation.

Facing me, she holds the bra up over her breasts. With a little movement, she releases her fingers, the bra falls to the ground, and her breasts are free finally. I raise my head as if her exposed breasts are magnets, pulling at me.

"Be careful." She wags her finger seductively. "It'd be a shame to start over."

I behave like a good boy and stay still. I glance from her eyes to her breasts. I tighten my fingers around the coins as my hands ache to move and touch her. From the smile I see on her lips, I believe she's enjoying my struggle. I can't speak and beg for mercy, knowing that if I do I'll face a penalty, so I let my eyes do the begging.

She brings her fingers to my face and traces them across my lips. "Would you like a little taste? I don't want to be too cruel."

I lick my lips in answer, and *fuck yes* if she doesn't lean over and place a taut, hard nipple against them. I waste no time and suck her into my mouth, twirling and flicking with my tongue. Even grazing her slightly with my teeth. The whole time I'm reveling in tasting her, I'm also trying to keep those damn coins between my fingers. I don't think I've ever multitasked like this during sex before. But fuck, it's worth every ounce of work.

"I believe in equal rights," she says while bringing her other nipple to my lips.

I attack it, too, since I've always believed in equality for women. I'm looking up into her eyes as I tongue and tease her. The intensity we share makes me almost willing to release the coins and grab hold of her. I want this woman desperately.

She pulls away and I release a slight moan of agony, which produces a wicked smile from her. She's relishing in my discomfort, damn her.

"Now, it's time I attend to *you*." She slips the black silk ribbon from around her neck. One loose end ripples onto the floor. She brings her hand high over my legs and lets the end of the ribbon lightly touch my skin. I can barely feel it as she makes a path up my leg to my needy dick. The lonely thing twitches in response, and I push my hips forward without thinking. My side flares up with a sharp pain, protesting my sudden movement. I become still again, deciding to refocus on my fists as a way of channeling this sexual intensity I'm feeling. It's almost making me come unglued.

"Now for the fun part of this little game." She begins to loosely wrap the ribbon around my cock. It's not her hand, but I'll take any attention I can get at this point. She appears to be moving her hips to some hidden beat as she's twisting the black silk around me. I'm mesmerized as the tits I just tasted move and sway with her. I'm lost in sensation overload and mentally curse these damn coins.

Finally, there is no more ribbon left to twirl around me and only the head of my cock shows. I'm wrapped in silk. I swallow hard as she closes her hands around my ribbon-covered hardness.

She crawls onto the bed and straddles my legs, positioning herself over my knees. Her head is perfectly placed just inches above my cock. She lowers her head, and when she's only a tongue swipe away from the tip of my dick, she stops and eyes the coins.

"How you holding up?" She searches my face, likely seeing my misery and need for relief. "Such a patient boy."

With our eyes locked on one another I feel one of her hands moving up and down my silk-covered cock. My eyes roll back into my head and I moan. Her hand stills when I do. I mouth *sorry*, hoping she'll continue, and thank fuck she does.

When I barely thrust my hips upward to work with her motions, I fear she's going to stop but she has mercy and lets me slide again. Thankfully. Still moving her hand, she bends and licks the tip of my dick and I wince. This time I let out a moan of pain.

"Too sudden?" she asks and I nod. I love her hands on me but would rather have her mouth around me. As if granting my dying wish, she pulls the ribbon away, wraps her luscious lips around my cock, and sucks me fully into her mouth.

My fingers shake as I try to keep the goddamned coins from falling. I'd like nothing more than to hold her head and hair as she works me. But I can't risk her stopping. I really might die if she does.

Up and down she goes while I grip the coins tucked into my fingers tightly, praying she doesn't stop. That's all I can think right now. She's added her hand, and I feel something inside my gut tighten and the pain around my stitches adds to the intensity. Pleasure and pain.

I don't want her to stop. The sensations are like nothing I've ever felt before as my release builds within me and fights against my muscles that are strung as tight as a drum. It's as if she's killing me sweetly before I erupt.

When I'm on the verge of exploding in release, she pulls away, and I look at her with beggar's eyes, silently asking her to continue. But she doesn't and goes back to licking my dick slowly up and down while the release I was chasing subsides.

Over and over we waltz through this maddening dance toward my climax only to have her back off. I can't hold the coins much longer, my fists are shaking and my control is slipping, but miraculously the coins remain secured.

As she makes love to my cock, she peers up at me with her sex-filled eyes. Kathryn exposes and controls me with just one look, making me totally hers. Body and soul. It's an erotic sight as her lips and hand slide up and down my length. I get lost in the feeling until she begins to slow down...again.

Unable to speak, again I plead for mercy with my eyes. Thankfully she has pity on me and accelerates her movements. I feel my release beginning to churn in my groin. Her attention to my cock escalates as her hot mouth continues to devour and suck me relentlessly.

When my release hits me, I arch my back, pushing my cock deeper into Kathryn's throat. I break my silence and shout at the top of my lungs. All my senses are on overdrive. For me, it's an earth-shattering feeling, like a bomb being detonated. It feels like waves of heat are rippling through me from head to toe. My entire body is on fire as my cock continues to spasm in her mouth, but Kathryn works me even harder.

A part of me wants to pull her mouth off my dick, but the other wants to demand she keep going so the pleasure never ends.

The coins dropped onto the bed while I was coming, the thought of them and keeping a tight fist long forgotten.

"Oh. My. God." The words float one by one through my brain. Seriously, I have no idea what the hell just happened. Last week's intense release felt as if my chest was exploding when I came, but this time, I felt it through my entire body. From my fists to the soles of my feet. Maybe it was the fact that every muscle in my body was tensed as I held on to the coins. I have no clue, and who the fuck cares.

I'm out of breath and strength. It's as if she sucked it all out of me. Laboriously, I bring my hands to her head as she releases me and wipes the corner of her mouth. I can't help but appreciate the satisfied grin on her face. All the meaningless fucks I've had fade to nothing more than empty memories as my whole body is taken prisoner by this woman.

"Good God." She raises up on her knees, looking down at me with her bare breasts just out of my reach. Her pussy is so wet through her lacy panties and I know we're not done by a long shot. "Beautiful, I felt that everywhere."

"You're an easy Tantra lay." She kids with a wicked smile. "Usually it takes a while to have a full-body orgasm like you did."

"It was full of something, all right. I'm still coming down. The coin game worked like magic." She lifts herself carefully off my body, and I know what I want to do now. It's time to reciprocate.

"Take off your panties, babe." I love the flash of excitement in her eyes as she removes them.

"I want to have that sweet pussy of yours in my mouth. Move up toward my head and straddle my face. Tongue movement will not hurt my side one damn bit."

"Yes, sir." She scoots up and places her legs on either side of my face. They're high up and nowhere near my injury. I run my hands up her inner thighs and find her wet and swollen.

"Hold on to the headboard if you'd like." I watch her hands rise to her breasts and not the headboard.

"I'd rather play with these." She tugs at her nipples.

When I see Kathryn playing with her tits, my cock springs back to life. She's a fucking goddess with her hair around her breasts as she pinches and rolls her nipples. Her pale skin is luminous in the muted light and her curvy hips make me want to grab on and hold tight. Damn, I'm ready to devour her.

"Lower yourself, beautiful."

She eases herself down as I use my fingers to open her up to me. I find her clit, then wrap my left arm around her hip, keeping her in place.

I pull her toward my tongue, and the instant I make contact, I begin to make love to her. Flicking, sucking, and twirling. Watching her above me for signs of what she likes. Sucking seems be her favorite.

She must be getting close as she's now holding on to the headboard and gyrating her hips against my face.

Since she has support, I bring my left hand to her pussy and let my fingers explore, enter, and twist to find that one sweet spot. When I hit it, she moans with pleasure.

"God, Adam!" she cries out as the telltale signs of her orgasm show when her legs begin to shake. She gazes down at me, her eyes wild with scorching desire. I'm hard as shit knowing she's about to come on my tongue. Fucking stitches or I'd be fucking her, buried deep within hot heat.

"So close." She drags out the words in a moan.

She gets off a few seconds later when she throws her head back and brings the palms of her hands to her breast. My girl knows what she wants.

She arches back and pushes harder against my lips. I return her movement with a slight nip of my teeth, and her screams of pleasure follow.

As she comes back to earth and her legs stop shaking, she raises off me. This time I'm the one with the satisfied smile. I've made that sweet pussy mine.

Chapter 5

After having one of the most mind-blowing orgasm of my life, Kathryn and I collapse into each other's arms. She curls into my good side and rests her head on my shoulder. With a tender touch, I caress the soft skin on her hip as she drifts off to sleep. Her light, rhythmic breathing tickles my chest as she exhales from her parted lips.

I tried to nod off, too, but my mind won't shut down. I replay the day's events along with their possible outcomes over and over. The potential fallout in the press could really hit my company's stock. The old adage that "any press is good press" doesn't apply to Wall Street. Bad press is just that—*bad.*

My phone sits on the nightstand next to me. There are a million messages, texts, and missed calls I can no longer ignore. I slip away from the sleeping beauty tucked into my side, careful to not wake her up, and pull the sheets over her body to keep her warm. Grabbing my phone, I scroll through my messages.

It's worse than I thought. Tom, Patrick, and Meg are all proceeding at DEFCON 5. I'd rather return to bed with Kathryn, but I pick up my boxers, slide them on, and head to the master bath. My phone chimes with a new email. It's Meg; she's received word from *The Wall Street Journal* that the Securities and Exchange Commission plans to order an investigation after reported irregularities on Kings Capital stock.

It's becoming clear that a meeting tomorrow morning in my office with my senior executives is a top priority. We must plot a defense strategy and have a unified front for the media attacks that Kings will face. I quickly type out an email to Tom, Patrick, Meg, and our lead attorney, Ken.

After I answer a few more emails, I take a quick shower, dress in clean clothes, and return to the bedroom. Kathryn is still sleeping, her face so peaceful and beautiful. I don't want to wake her yet, but the dip of the bed as I sit down causes her to stir. Soon our time away from the world will be over, and we'll have to face the morning's events. The detectives are due here in about an hour, so it's time for her to get up from the warmth of my bed.

I brush the hair from her face as her eyes flutter open. "Hey, beautiful."

My words are met with a slow, sexy smile that unfurls my desire to take those sweet lips again, if only we had the time.

"How long have I been asleep?" She stretches on the bed and I bite my lip to hold back a groan as her perfect tits peek out from under the covers.

"A little over an hour, I think." I touch the soft round side of her breast, as I'm unable to keep my fingers away. "But the detectives will be here soon, so you better get up."

She pulls the covers over her head in a huff. When I yank them back down, I'm greeted with a mischievous smile and an exploring hand on my thigh. It appears the nap has reenergized Kathryn. Lucky me.

~

Kathryn and I sit on a leather couch in the wood-paneled office of my apartment. The room gives off a rich appearance and makes a statement of authority. It's the only place I would meet the detectives in my home. My attorney, Ken MacDonald, and Peters are to my left, sitting in club chairs, and appear prepared for the detectives' arrival. Due to the short notice of the interview, Ken has agreed to represent Kathryn. He felt that Marcus Rhodes, the criminal defense attorney who met with them yesterday, wasn't needed for this interview. One thing is for sure this time, the questioning will *not* be conducted at the expense of my dignity.

"Excuse me, Mr. Kingsley." We all turn to see Rosa standing at the open door. "Detectives Baker and Simpson are here, sir."

Rosa stands to the side, and the detective duo from yesterday appears from behind her. We'll see if their attitudes toward me have changed.

As planned, Ken walks to the door and greets them. Kathryn and I stay seated, keeping our distance. After all, this isn't a fucking social call.

"Good afternoon, gentlemen. Ken MacDonald." Ken gestures for them to enter.

"Good afternoon," replies Baker as he shakes MacDonald's hand. "Baker, and my partner, Simpson. Can't say it's good to see you again, though."

"Definitely not under the circumstances. This is obviously a difficult time for my clients as they've had an intense day."

"Your clients?" Baker furrows his brow.

"Yes, I'm representing both Kathryn Delcour and Adam Kingsley today."

"Got it." Baker's response is quick and curt.

The detectives stand in front of Kathryn and me. I should welcome them into my home, but I don't. Instead, I rest my hand on Kathryn's leg at the same time she moves to greet them. She side-eyes me in question before easing back into the couch. The intimate act with my hand doesn't go unnoticed. Baker shares a look with his partner. I'm pissed that they could have leaked the love triangle bullshit to the media, so I remain distant. I don't trust them one fucking bit.

"Good afternoon," I say in a frosty tone, reluctantly offering my hand to Baker and Simpson. I'm being explicitly rude by not standing, but I don't care. I give both men a very firm handshake.

"Good afternoon, Mr. Kingsley." Baker lets go of my hand and turns his attention to Kathryn. "*Dr.* Delcour, right?"

"Yes." Kathryn offers her hand to the two men in greeting.

The men's dour faces turn to polite smiles as both Baker and Simpson shake Kathryn's hand. Fucking Simpson acts as if he's going to bend down and kiss her knuckles. If he doesn't back off, he's going to meet mine. I don't recognize this jealousy. It's foreign to me because I've never known a woman I wanted to possess and own, ever.

"It's my pleasure, Dr. Delcour." Baker's gaze runs up Kathryn's long, crossed legs. It doesn't take much imagination to know what he's thinking about. Fucking slimeball.

"Let's get down to it. Gentleman, please take a seat." MacDonald points the detectives to a couple of chairs across from us. "First, I'd like to discuss the likelihood that your office leaked the motive for Simon Edward's mental breakdown and alleged shooting of my client."

"Pardon me?" Baker scoffs. "I'm not following you. Leaks?" Baker and Simpson's confusion is apparent as their jaws become unhinged. I'm watching Baker carefully for any cracks in his armor, any slip he can't conceal.

"Yes, the media is reporting the previous and brief relationship Mr. Kingsley had with Marta Llewellyn, Mr. Edwards's ex-fiancée. And I can assure you the leak didn't come from Mr. Kingsley or Kings Capital," Ken finishes and waits for either detective to speak. I continue to scrutinize Baker's face, but don't see anything resembling guilt in his expression.

"We didn't leak this with the media. Details will eventually come out in the press when the final report is filed, of course. Nothing can stop that unless a judge orders the documents sealed."

"So what guarantee do we have that what is discussed here today will not be leaked?" Ken's question presses Baker for a direct answer.

"I won't sit here and be accused of leaking this information by an attorney for a big shot executive. I haven't been promoted because of my loose tongue, just the opposite in fact." Baker huffs, sitting back in his chair, and I have to concede he appears to be speaking the truth. If it wasn't Baker or Simpson, then who leaked the affair to the news? Marta? Though that makes no sense at all since it casts her in a horrible light.

"Gentlemen, let's move on and get this interview rolling." I try to steer the meeting back to the reason we're gathered here.

"Yes, I'm sure you have more important things to do, Mr. Kingsley," Baker adds with a mocking smile as he glances at Kathryn. He's trying to get under my skin for calling him on the carpet, but I'm not taking his shit today.

"There's no need for smartass comments, Baker. You are a guest in my home, and don't you dare forget that." The smug smile dissolves from his face.

"Fine," Baker says, spitting out the word, and then begins interview.

"Your bodyguard, Jordan Hayes, briefed us on the morning's events, but we need to confirm everything firsthand with you to close our case. I'll ask the questions. Most of them are a simple yes or no. Pretty easy."

I glance at Kathryn, who nods at me, and then back at the detectives. "We're ready." I clasp her hand and weave our fingers together as she gives me a reassuring smile.

Baker dips his eyes to focus on the notepad he's holding. "So you and Dr. Delcour were exiting The Pierre together with your bodyguard, correct?"

"Yes," I reply. Ken advised us to say as little as possible, and I'm following his suggestion.

"Mr. Hayes mentioned you were heading to the office *alone*." I tighten my grasp on Kathryn's hand.

"That's correct."

"Dr. Delcour, where were you heading at the time of the shooting?" Kathryn seems as steady as a rock.

"To my apartment a few blocks away." Baker writes something down on his notepad.

"What time did you wake up?" Baker asks.

Really? What kind a silly question is this?

"I don't remember the exact time." Kathryn attempts an answers and turns toward me. "Do you, Adam?"

"Around eight." I'm ready to move to the next question—one with more depth.

But the mundane questions continue as the interview progresses. My nerves are frayed as is my impatience with these men. Until finally we get to the gritty part.

"So what were you doing when you first saw Simon Edwards, Mr. Kingsley?"

This answer will take more than a few words. "I was kissing Kathryn—excuse me, Dr. Delcour—good-bye when Simon jerked her away from me. It took me a few seconds to figure out it was him. He had bleached his hair and appeared crazed. He held the gun to Kathryn's head while he gripped her in front of him, using her to shield his body."

"He was talking the entire time he was holding me," Kathryn adds.

Baker nods at Kathryn and says, "What did he say? Did he tell you the reason he wanted to shoot you?" Asking Kathryn about the motive pisses me off; these questions should be directed at me. I'll be damned if she's going to be the one talking about his ex-fiancée and me. I've had enough of this simple, make-no-progress questioning. Also I don't really care to rehash the fucking motive as I know it's been established. I give Ken a warning look, letting him know I'm going rogue. I'm finishing this interview.

I butt in before Kathryn can answer. "Here's the rundown of what occurred: Simon grabbed Kathryn. He held a gun to her head as he threatened me. When I saw a police cruiser pull up to the sidewalk, Simon looked away for a split second and I ran at him, freeing Kathryn." Ken nods in approval; he seems to have had enough of this interview, too.

"We fought. Simon fired a round during the struggle. Luckily the bullet only grazed my side, but I fell to the ground from the shock and initial pain. Simon then pointed the gun at my head." I swallow, the memory still so vivid. "But Hayes shot and killed him."

I take a breath as Baker scribbles down my statement. I can't think of anything more that needs to be said. While I watch his pen fly over the paper, I can't help but get lost in my thoughts of the event—Simon holding the gun to Kathryn's head. The vision feels so real, it's like I'm seeing it happen all over again right in front of me.

But this time it's different. Simon's hateful eyes pierce me while he says, "Bang, bang. She's dead." I look toward Kathryn and hear the pop of gunfire before she falls like a ragdoll at his feet. I can even smell a hint of sulfur from the fired shot.

I nearly jump out of my skin as the vision disappears. I turn quickly to see Kathryn sitting next to me... alive, her brows knitted in concern as she searches my face. I realize I'm squeezing her hand painfully tight and mine is dripping with sweat. I'm relieved that the sick scene my mind just conjured up wasn't real. I shake my head to clear any remaining thoughts of Simon and concentrate on Baker, but I can't find the right focus. I decide this interview needs to conclude, since we've covered the important details. I take a deep breath as I rise from the couch.

"I believe we're done here. If you have any more questions for either of us, you can contact Mr. MacDonald. If you'll excuse us." I turn and face my attorney. "Ken, can you see them to the door, please?"

Ken nods while Baker and Simpson stare at me with contempt in their eyes. Kathryn stands up and moves to my good side. I take her hand in mine, and we exit the room. With no fanfare or time for them to protest, we're free of Baker and Simpson.

"What's wrong, Adam?" Kathryn looks up at me, worried. "You looked like you saw a ghost a minute ago. Were you thinking about the shooting?"

I can't fool a doctor of psychology; Kathryn was well-trained and intuitive.

"Something like that," I say, not letting on too much. My thoughts of Simon are nothing for her to worry about, so I change the subject. "And my stitches are bothering me."

"Are you sure you're okay?" She doesn't drop the subject even though I'm sure she knows I want to.

"I'm sure. I need to get some more pain meds, though. I think my body is protesting all the fun you had earlier." I wink and hope I've put this new line of questioning to an end.

A wicked grin spread over Kathryn's face. "I may have worked you over a little too much. I did pocket those coins, by the way." She winks and laughs teasingly.

"Thief." I tease back. "And believe me, beautiful... any pain is damn worth it. I just need my meds."

"I'll get you a drink and ask Rosa to make you something to eat. Those pills aren't good on an empty stomach. Be right back." I kiss her quickly in thanks and head to the bedroom. I sit on my bed and pop a Percocet from the bottle on my nightstand.

Determined to put that ugly vision of Kathryn dead behind me, I dig my phone out of my pocket and check emails on it while I wait for her. Everyone responded to my earlier email requesting a strategy meeting. One email catches my eye.

Meg, my communications director, wants to schedule a press conference Monday morning inside the lobby of Kings Capital's building. She believes a "hey, I'm still kicking and Kings Capital is fine" appearance from me is needed to suppress any Wall Street rumors of my demise. I agree with the request and tell her to arrange the one-ring circus for eight thirty sharp.

While I'm finishing up my email, Kathryn comes in, carrying a tray. As she nears me, I see what looks like chocolate cookies and two tall glasses of milk.

"Ah, more comfort food from Rosa. She knows what I love. I'm gonna get soft if I keep eating like this without working out."

"You're kidding, right?" Kathryn sets the tray on the bed, runs a hand over my bicep, and gives it a little squeeze. "Hard as a rock."

"For now. Let's take the cookies to the media room. We can watch a movie and get our minds off things."

"Okay. But no guns or bombs or action of any kind. Maybe a chick flick?" she says with a bit of lightness in her voice and a twirl of her fingers in my hair.

After this morning, I say something I thought I'd never utter in my life.

"Okay, I'll let you decide." Her face brightens up, and I wonder—who the hell am I? She's got me wrapped around her finger, and my dirty mind drifts to earlier in my bed. Kathryn's hand wrapped around me as she sucked my cock. I'm hard all over again. Well, a sappy romance should take care of that really quick.

Chapter 6

"I love that movie," Kathryn says, wiping what she's promised are happy tears from her eyes. I remove a few more from her cheeks with my fingers.

"Come here." She folds herself into my side, the good one, and gently leans her head on my chest.

"Is this okay?" She looks up at me with her shining blue eyes.

"You're fine. I think Rosa baked some magic in those cookies. I've felt better since I ate them." I haven't had any more creepy visions of Simon, either. A thought I keep to myself.

"Chocolate is the answer to the world's problems," she says very seriously. "*Really.*"

"If you say so, beautiful." I stroke her silky hair as she leans into me. "Well, I've survived *P.S. I Love You...* barely." She glances up at me with her brows pressed together; pretty sure she's offended by my remark.

"What do you mean by 'barely'?" she asks before her lips form a beautiful red pout.

I wink to let her know I was teasing. "It wasn't horrible. The acting was pretty good, actually."

Maybe it's just me, but I had the whole plot figured out after the first few minutes. But ten minutes into the movie, I checked out completely and ran over everything I have to do at the office tomorrow, where I'll be likely putting out fires all day.

The theme of the movie did stick with me: Meeting the right person and knowing there was something special there, an instant connection.

I could relate to this part because there seems to be the same kind of crazy chemistry floating between Kathryn and me. It reminds me of standing under those large electrical power lines. The ones that make that buzzing sound as high-voltage currents flow through them. You can feel the electricity humming in the air. That is Kathryn and me.

"Yeah, I guess it wasn't too bad for a chick flick."

"Not too bad?" She laughs, but more with me than at me. "I guess you really weren't the target audience anyway."

"I would have to agree. I can check 'Watching a chick flick' off the old bucket list."

"Funny." She moves to face me as we sit on the leather sectional in the media room. "Name one thing you'd like to do on your bucket list. I can't imagine a billionaire having too many things left on it."

"You'd be surprised. I've been focused on building Kings, but I've done a lot of traveling. Mainly for business with a few side trips here and there. There is one thing, though. I've never thought of it as a bucket list item, but I need to make it happen." I pause and look away, not sure I should share what is on my mind.

"What is it, Adam?" Her tone is quiet. The mood between us has become serious.

"I've never gone back to my mother's grave. The day I buried her was the only time. The thought of going back and facing what I did the day she took her life was too much." I bring my head up and see Kathryn's eyes filling with tears again. She knows what happened and understands the guilt I hold inside for not getting to my mother before she committed suicide.

"Her death isn't your fault. What she did was her decision," Kathryn says, Her voice, soft and caring, comforts me.

"I will never forgive myself for going off and fucking some flight attendant instead of going straight to see her. But I have to face the loss, to move on with my life. You helped me last week. Everything I buried with her, all the feelings, came out of me like an explosion."

Kathryn sits up on her knees next to me, pushes my hair aside, and kisses my forehead. "Sweet, sweet man. It's time you quit blaming yourself."

Her words are healing and help to soothe the ache in my heart. I don't know if the pain from my mother's death will ever go away, but I can face it now. That mind-blowing night of tantric sex forced me to open up and release some of the pain. No more stuffing it away. This woman and her crazy Tantra helped me. And dammit, I think I'm falling head over fucking heels in love with her.

"I think it's time I faced it and visited her grave."

"I'll go with you, if you'd like? This is the kind of closure you need to move on with your life. I have to believe she would've wanted it that way. The woman I saw in that photo loved you dearly."

"She did. I never doubted her love for me. Ever." I lean my head back and let the feelings I've suppressed fill me. I take a deep breath and raise my head up to face Kathryn. I can't help but feel anxious to actually set a date to visit my mom, but it's time. "I think you're right. I need to go, and with your support, I'll make it."

"Of course you will. You're Adam Kingsley, right?"

"Damn right." I bring her hands to my lips. She leans into me, and I bury my face in her hair, inhaling the exotic and feminine scent of her perfume. "Thanks, Kathryn."

"I need to tell you something, too. I was waiting for the right time, and now feels right." She sits back on the couch, placing her hands in her lap. "I got a call from Ollie this morning. Apparently he saw a news clip of the shooting on TV and it briefly mentioned my name. He freaked out and wanted to know the details. I didn't know what to tell him, really, but I had to be honest."

"So you told him we were together?"

"I did. But he doesn't know that you two are half-brothers." Kathryn searches my face, as if gauging my reaction. "I hope you're okay with it, but he's my oldest and dearest friend. I just couldn't go along with the press reports and lie. He'll keep it quiet. But…"

"But what?" I have a feeling I know what's next. Ollie is likely questioning her on why she's with a man like me.

"He isn't too thrilled I'm with you. You know he's in the same type of software industry as you are. Although he admires you professionally, he wants me to be careful. Ollie's just worried."

"As is everyone else in your life." I shake my head. Maurice at the restaurant, her friends at the fundraiser, and Ollie have all planted seeds of doubt about her being with me. "I can't say I blame them. Once the details from the police report come out, my reputation as a male slut will be worse."

" 'Male slut'?" Kathryn laughs.

"Yeah, it's Tom and Patrick's nickname for me. Make light of it now because it's just going to get worse." Hopefully I can protect her from the scrutiny of the vultures in the press. "Simon's motive for trying to kill me will feed the media. Sex mixed with a crime. Put a love triangle spin on it and it's the lead story."

"I guess so." A grimace crosses her face and I hate that I put a frown there, too.

"I'll do everything within my power to keep you from having to deal with any negative fallout. I'm hoping to curb the press on Monday morning by holding a news conference."

"I hate seeing all the lies affecting you and your company. I hope it goes well, Adam. After all, you're a victim in this whole ordeal, too." I appreciate her sympathy, but seeing myself as a victim is a stretch. Not that I deserved what happened, but I played my part in the whole fucked-up mess. There's no denying it.

"I would like to meet Ollie. If you think it's a good idea, I want him to know we're half-brothers. What do you think?" I swear my palms sweat at the thought of how Ollie will take that revelation. Fuck, how I hate sweat.

"I want you to meet him, too. He called me this morning before he flew back to San Francisco. He said he's flying back here next week for business. I think we should all go out for dinner. I'd like for him to get to know you and put all those male slut rumors he's heard about you to rest." Kathryn winks. I have to agree, because I want those rumors dead and buried, too.

"If you're okay to be seen with me in public and ready for reporters to hound you..." Before I can finish my thought, I have a brilliant idea. Goliath. He can be her bodyguard. I believe Goliath may be working for me a bit longer, after all.

"Of course I'm okay with being seen with you in public. Funny how everyone is concerned about us being together—except my mother. She's thrilled. When we talked this morning, I gave her a rundown of the last few days. I swear she was giddy. She wanted me to wish you a speedy recover, by the way."

"I have a soft spot for your mother. Always have. She's one hell of a lady and you're very much your mother's daughter, beautiful." She brings her lips to mine for a quick kiss of thanks.

"Her birthday is next week. How about instead of dinner with just Ollie and us, we all go and celebrate her birthday together?" Kathryn claps her hands, barely able to contain her excitement. "It's perfect. She will be your ally and help win Ollie over. Seriously, I can't think of a better plan. Where should we go?"

I think for a moment before the ideal place comes to mind. "The Core Club. I just joined there a few months ago." The Core Club is an elite, members' only club on Fifty-Fifth Street. Honestly, I was surprised they let me walk through their doors as a member since I'm the epitome of the *nouveau riche* bad boy. I suppose money and power have their perks and help cover up any misgivings.

"You belong there?" I think Kathryn's even more surprised than I am. "Not your typical meet, greet, and 'take a gal for a ride in the limo' establishment."

"No, it's not." I give Kathryn a timid smirk in hopes that I'm hearing a twinge of jealousy in her voice and not disgust with the player extraordinaire she once considered me. I push away the latter thought. "I don't go there often. I feel out of place. But the opportunity for me to be sponsored as a member came up unexpectedly, and I couldn't refuse."

"Why do you feel out of place? I've never been there, so I have no idea what it's like, but I've heard it's very exclusive."

"It is *very* exclusive, but it's more a retreat from the gritty life of New York. I've held business meetings there when I've needed to, but it's not really the hot spot for a single man. Mostly I try to impress clients or potential investors, but going there by myself makes me feel strange." I have difficultly describing what exactly makes me uncomfortable; maybe it's going there alone.

"Then next week we'll go there together, and you'll have a tableful of friends. Well, at least my mother and I will be, initially. Ollie's friendship will come around. Believe me. He's an only child and always wanted a brother or sister. Finding out he has a brother, even thirty-two years later, will make him happy."

"I hope you're right. I haven't been around any relatives for ten years. Even as a child, it was only my mother, a cranky old uncle, and me. I refuse to count the few brief encounters with my father. Thorpe wasn't family." Kathryn flinches at the mention of his name. "I get the feeling you don't care much for him, either."

"That's an understatement." Kathryn nearly spits her words. "He is a horrible human being."

I can surmise why she has such strong feelings for him, but I ask anyway. "It's the way he's treated Ollie and the fact that he's gay?"

"Partly, yes." Her beautiful face twists into a scowl of disgust. I've never seen this look from her before, either. "And now, knowing how he treated your mother and you..." Kathryn whispers. "It's deplorable. All of America sees him as this wise, New York City mogul."

"What he did to my mother was horrible, but what he did to Ollie, publically disowning him, is unconscionable." Kathryn nods, my statement on the mark. "Ollie and I really do have a lot in common. We're the children Thorpe never wanted."

"I think the common bond of having a jerk for a father will help Ollie forgive the rumors about you. I bet you two will become close."

"I hope you're right. So it's settled, then. I'll call and make reservations for us at The Core Club. They have some semi-private rooms mixed in with the main dining area."

I need to spend more time with Kathryn outside our apartments. Ava, her mother, is fun to be around, and I believe she genuinely likes me, but part of me is on edge about meeting Ollie. What do you say to the brother you never met? I'll have to rely on Kathryn and her mother to help win Ollie's approval.

"I'm excited, and after the last couple of days, we both need something fun to look forward to." Kathryn chimes in.

"I agree. And speaking of being excited..." Smirking, I place a hand on her cheek and trace her lips with my thumb. Kathryn's eyes darken at my touch, and that intangible connection between us heats up. "You have very kissable lips."

"So I've been told." She flirts back with me and moves forward so our lips touch.

Our kiss starts out slow but builds as my tongue finds hers. I grab the back of her neck and pull her closer, our lips pressed together almost painfully. I'm tempted to rip off her clothes and fuck her senseless.

"God, Kathryn. I want you so bad. I can't seem to get enough of you."

"I feel the same, but you need a gentle touch after all you've been through today. Something slow and easy tonight."

"God, woman. I'll say it again. You're going to kill me." I try to lift up the oversized T-shirt of mine she's wearing, but she pushes my hand away.

"There's plenty of time for me." She undoes the drawstring of my sweats and then glances at the door before looking into my eyes. "Rosa won't come back here, will she?"

"I hate closed doors, but we're fine. She keeps out of this area of the apartment unless I'm at work. It's an unspoken rule."

Seeming satisfied with my answer, Kathryn grips the elastic of my waistband. "Raise up a little for me."

I follow her request as she eagerly moves my sweats down. This woman knows what she wants, there is no denying it. With more room to move, she reaches into my boxer-briefs and palms me with her warm, soft hand. Her delicate fingers encircle my length. She uses her free hand to push my briefs all the way down to free my erection.

"Babe, slow down. Let me make this about you this time." I say.

Kathryn looks at me like I'm crazy and says, "Adam, it's been two long years. Let me have my fun."

"Who am I to argue." I throw my hands up and she goes to town.

She slowly pumps me up and down, and her movements do the trick; I'm hard as granite. I'm okay with her hands, but after having felt her hot mouth on me earlier, I'm aching to have my dick enveloped in that sweet mouth again.

Being the greedy bastard that I am, I place my hand on her head and give her a gentle push. A seductive smile greets me in response, the hint clearly taken. Kathryn lowers her head and her lips close around me.

I weave my fingers through her hair but don't push her or pull the strands. Her movements are her own, and I gladly let her lead. Since her pretty face is hidden in my lap, I throw my head back against the couch. Eye contact isn't needed for this session of pleasure as I get lost in the sensations.

Her wet tongue glides around the tip of my cock, eliciting pulses of desire throughout my body. Eager and wanton, she's helping me fuck away the terrible day we've had with each suck from her mouth and pump of her hand.

I adjust my position and push my pants further down my legs as she fondles my balls. She traces them with her fingers, slowly caressing and playing with them, driving me wild. The combination of her touches quickly brings me to the brink.

"Kathryn, I love your mouth. Fuck." I moan my words as the muscles in my legs begin to tighten, my release on the cusp.

Kathryn works harder, sensing I'm close. I practically jump off the couch when I feel the slight grazing of her teeth against my sensitive skin. "Whoa, baby."

And damn if she doesn't do it again. But fuck, I don't want to come yet, so I pull her head up from its position. She shoots me a confused look.

"As much as I love that sexy mouth of yours, I want to come inside your sweet pussy. So take off your clothes."

"Yes, sir," she says while starting to remove her clothes.

"Damn, right!" I roar while grabbing her T-shirt and pretty much ripping the damn thing to pieces. As soon as her bra's exposed, I dip my fingers into each cup and lift her tits so they sit high and perfect on the lace.

"God, that feels so good." Kathryn moans as she grinds her now-naked pussy all over my cock. She places her nipple against my lips and looks at me with her eyes half-open and full of passion. "Please."

I comply instantly, taking her nipple into my mouth and sucking it hard. I graze my teeth against her, returning the favor she bestowed on me moments ago. She moans louder in appreciation of what I'm doing. I continue to flick and nip as she squirms all over me, getting some friction against her clit.

"Oh, fuck! She throws her head back and cries out. "Yes, like that." She raises herself up just enough so my dick is positioned at her entrance. I feel a flash of pain when she touches my side, but I bear the discomfort as she slams herself down on my cock. The movement is so powerful that my breath leaves me for a few seconds.

Kathryn bounces up and down on me with rapt need. I cup her breasts in each hand and flick her nipples with my thumbs.

"How's that, beautiful?" I know the answer as she throws her head back. "Touch yourself, I'm getting close."

She snakes her hand between us. The feeling of her hand pressed where we're joined is beyond hot to me. I am trying to hold off my release as the erotic scene plays out in front of me. When I feel her legs beginning to shake, I give her nipples a little twist. I want the sensation to be strong enough to tip her over the edge, and thankfully it works as she starts to spasm around me.

"That's it, beautiful. Come around me."

I push up into her as best I can without too much exertion, my injured side already firing up in protest. Kathryn tightens more around me, furthering all the sensations and spurring on my climax. I remove my hands from her tits and cup her ass for better leverage. Finally we come together in mutual pleasure, and I spill into her through each wave of my release.

"Kathryn!" I cry out. She latches her mouth onto mine in a blistering kiss. I'm lost in her display of passion. No word or thought computes, only a feeling of ecstasy runs through me.

Kathryn's still wrapped around me as we come down from our high. She folds into my good side, smiling contentedly. I reach for the soft cashmere blanket on the back of the couch and tuck it around her.

She rests her head against my chest, and I lazily stroke the long strands of her hair before pushing it back behind her ear. She looks up at me, and I love what I see reflecting on her face, a look of peaceful bliss.

It feels great knowing I've changed with her help and crossed over the line. The line between knowing how to fuck versus how to make love. The difference rests snuggled in my arms as I've never held a woman tenderly like this after sex. She's my first.

"I'm completely spent," Kathryn mumbles against my chest. Before I can respond, my stomach rumbles, killing our moment.

"With my ear to your chest, your stomach growling sounded like a clap of thunder." She laughs while bringing her fingers up to caress the back of my neck. I shiver in response. "All this activity has left me a little hungry, too. Maybe we should think about something to eat."

"I agree. It's getting late and I'm starving." It appears that skipping dinner in lieu of eating cookies didn't quite work for us. "Let's give Rosa the night off. What do you say we order a pizza?"

"Do they deliver to penthouse apartments?" From the little twinkle in her eyes, I know she's kidding.

"This is New York City. I can get a pack of gum delivered if I want."

Chapter 7

I awake with a start from a nightmare featuring an irate, gun-toting Simon. My heart pounds like it's trying to break through my chest. I rub the sleep from my eyes and squint at the brightness of the room. The morning sun pours through the wall of windows in my bedroom. Usually, I close the floor-to-ceiling curtains before bed, but last night Kathryn and I fell asleep with the city lights dancing shadows across the room.

I try to block out my bad dream and instead gaze over at a sleeping Kathryn. She's moved to the other side of the bed, out of my reach. She's on her side, facing away from me with waves of hair spilling over her pillow. The view is wonderful. The covers lay low across her hips, allowing me to see all of her bare back. Damn, she's one beautiful woman. The curve of her spine. The dip of her waist. The swell of her hips. All combine to tease and taunt me worsening my everyday case of the morning wood.

Kathryn's like a magnet, and I make my way to her side of the bed so we're touching skin to skin. Trying not to wake her yet, I rest quietly next to her. She is warm and soft against me. After a couple of minutes, I can no longer keep my hands to myself, and I begin to trace large circles over her hips. The sheets give way and allow me to touch her pale skin.

After the first few circles, she begins to stir. Maybe I should've let her sleep, but I am a selfish man. I need her company before I start what will likely be the day from hell.

Kathryn slowly rolls over on her back with her eyes still half-closed.

"Morning." She stretches her arms up over her head. As she groans through her sleepiness, her breasts thrust forward when she arches her back. Temptation. This woman is utter temptation. On instinct, my fingers move to touch one of her exposed nipples. She peeks at me, giving me a very seductive smile for six o'clock on a Sunday morning.

"I can't keep my hands to myself. It's all your fault." I follow her curves with my finger to her other breast and lightly touch the nipple. It hardens under my touch.

"What did I do?" Her voice is raspy likely from a combination of arousal and the early hour.

"You fell asleep in my bed with nothing on. I believe that's a free pass for any man."

"Is that so?" She smirks while turning on her side to face me. She glances below my waist. I'm covered, but my erection isn't quite hidden as it pushes against the sheets.

"Well, what do we have here?" She grazes her finger over my needy cock, and her smirk turns into full-blown smile.

"It's the usual morning condition." I bite back a moan as her entire hand covers me through the sheet. This scene reminds me of the ribbon wrapped around me yesterday.

"How do you normally *handle* this condition?" I chuckle at her word choice.

"Pretty much the same way you're *handling* it. Although normally in the shower. Clean and quick." Kathryn starts a nice steady rhythm—up and down. Fuck, it feels so good.

"You know, Tantra teaches that lovers should spend a few minutes together each morning. It can be as simple as holding each other in bed and doesn't have to be all about sex. But I don't think it would hurt." Each morning? I don't think I can get any harder as I focus on her words.

"What a wonderful wake-up call. The more I learn about this practice, the more I love it. But you don't always have Tantra sex, right?" I've been confused on this point since we've mixed it up quite a bit.

"It's like cooking: Sometimes you make the effort to cook a five-course gourmet meal. And savor every bite, not skipping anything." While speaking, she removes the covers and brings her lips close to my cock. I think she's in love with it, and I couldn't make me a happier man. "Other times you're famished and just grab something quick to eat to satisfy your hunger. One takes time and preparation, where passion builds up slowly. The other is immediate, where passion makes you claw for more."

"Yes," I moan. It's the only word I can force out of my mouth as she licks my dick from base to tip. I understand the meaning of *claw for more* because right now I'm clawing at the sheets while she's making love to my cock.

"Experimenting with different types of sex"—she stops to lick around my head—"makes you appreciate it all. Variety is—"

"The spice of life." I finish her sentence for her. "Beautiful, you're driving me crazy. Let's continue what you're doing in the shower. I need to fuck you, and standing up might be best, considering my side.

"You feel up to it?"

"Wild horses couldn't stop me, babe. The shower... now."

"You're bossy this morning."

"I forgot to warn you. I'm not a morning person. Now move."

We rise, and I stand before my nightstand. I pop open my pill bottle, shake a couple of tablets into my hand, and down them with a little water from the glass next to my meds. I should be feeling fine in a few minutes.

I turn to see Kathryn leaning against the bathroom door. She's posed with her head held high, one leg bent, and her hands tucked behind her back. Her stance gives me full view of her fucking hot body. God, how I wish we could stay naked today and never leave my bed. Fucking duties and responsibilities.

I stalk forward, completely focused, never taking my eyes off of her. She has this sexy "come and get me" look in her eyes. She wants to toy with me. I don't think I'll be playing her game this morning, though. If anything, I'm going to be toying with her.

"Get in that shower. Now," I say and spin her around by the shoulders, spanking that sweet ass of hers.

"Oh," she squeaks and follows my orders to the shower.

I lag behind to watch her hips sway. All I can think is how I'm going to fuck the pain away under the hot water of the shower. Nothing's going to stop me. At this point, I'm pretty sure it's my cock leading the way.

She turns on the water and I watch it cascade over her body. The heat of the water warms her skin and turns it a blushing shade of pink. I slide my hands over her and follow the trails of water from top to bottom. They're streaming around her curves, dripping from her full breasts and rounding over her hips.

We gaze into each other's eyes, neither of us moving. I've grown accustomed to her desire to watch me, connect with me, and I am beginning to see why it's so powerful. Everything between us is intensified in the connection.

Kathryn lets her hands roam my body while I palm each of her breasts and flick her nipples with my thumbs. She bites her lips and lets out a quiet moan as I pull on her nipples a little more roughly.

She lowers herself to her knees on the tile. I place my hands in her hair and close my eyes as her mouth sucks me in again, totally in love with my cock.

"Damn, babe." She's fucking swallowing me whole. "That's it, yes!" I practically yell as she runs her tongue around me. I hold her head and gently push in time with her movements.

When she looks up at me, her wide blue eyes hooded with desire, I know I'm not going to last long. It's a powerful aphrodisiac—having a woman on her knees, giving me her all, and withholding nothing as she worships me.

Even though I don't want to stop fucking her mouth, I pull away. She appears surprised and disappointed, as if I've stopped her from carrying out an important mission.

"Stand up and place both hands flat on the bench." My demand is clear. "Bend over and don't say a word."

Kathryn eagerly does as I ask and finds the tiled shower bench.

I line myself up to her and caress over the round part of her ass. Pushing my cock between her legs, but not penetrating, I try to stimulate her clit.

"You want me, don't you, beautiful?" I tug her hair so she arches back.

"Yes, Adam, I want you." She wiggles her perfect ass over my erection. I thrust against her wet entrance and seat myself deep inside, buried to the base. The connection we have seems to multiply when we become one like this.

"Come on, Adam. Fuck me!" She tries to move back and forth on my cock.

"All right. Hold on, babe." I take her hips into my palms and grit my teeth. The pain in my side keeps me from thrusting as hard as I want, but I'm not going to let it stop me.

Skin meets skin as our moans of pleasure intermingle. The sound of the shower pounding the tile wall creates a natural serenade as steam rises around us.

As much as I want to keep pumping away, the pain I thought I could ignore starts to catch up with me. I know soon it will overpower my senses, and I don't want that to happen before we reach our climaxes. I'm on the edge as it is and need her to join me there.

"Touch yourself, baby. I need you there with me." Kathryn's hand disappears between her thighs, touching herself. She comes into contact with my dick as I thrust faster and harder into her.

This position offers me perfect access to a place that I haven't touched yet. Her little backdoor is totally at my mercy.

I wait until her legs shake before I delve into new territory. Knowing she's close, I press my finger into the opening of her backside. The running water trailing over her body makes my penetration easier. She arches back and cries out. Her release hits instantaneously with my exploring. I keep up a steady rhythm with my cock and finger as her climax keeps rippling through her body.

As her orgasm subsides, I feel mine starting to build around my balls. At the last second before I explode, I pull out of her and let my come spill over her ass. Pulse after pulse. I leave my mark only for it to wash away from the spray of the shower.

I turn her around, and she gives me a satisfied smile. "Damn, Adam." Her words are practically breathless.

"Damn right." I collapse onto the shower bench next to her and she cuddles up with me.

Somehow we need to make it out of the shower and get ready for the day ahead, but my body doesn't want to cooperate. It's happy to sit here with Kathryn in our steamy afterglow.

"I wish I didn't have to go into the office today." I lean over and kiss her forehead. "I'd rather stay home and play hooky with you, take you for a long walk through Central Park, and buy hotdogs for lunch. It's supposed to be nice out today."

"That sounds great, except for the hotdog. I refuse to eat street meat. You never know."

"You're pretty uppity, beautiful. Some of my best lunches have come off the street meat carts. There's one by my building that has its own Zagat rating. Scout's honor." I hold up three fingers and make the Boy Scout sign.

"You know, I've always been a sucker for a man in uniform." She winks.

"If we keep this up, I'll never make it to my first meeting."

"Would that be the end of the world?" she asks with a teasing grin.

Reluctantly, we finish our shower, and I dress for the day ahead. Kathryn stands before the vanity mirror, drying her hair... nude.

I want to sneak up behind her and cup her breasts while her hands are held high, styling her hair. If she doesn't put on the fucking clothes I had my personal shopper from Barneys send over last night, I'm going to end up taking her back to bed instead of meeting my team at the office.

I shake my head and try to remember my priorities, though I'm not sure what they are right now as she offers me a glowing smile in the mirror.

"Damn, you'd tempt the devil to leave his throne in hell, beautiful." She lays the hairdryer down on the counter and turns around to face me.

"That's the most unromantic line I've ever heard." Her eyes dance with humor. "Saving your wit for the boardroom, are you?"

I move a step forward and draw her into my arms, wanting one more touch of her bare skin before we part.

"Something like that," I whisper before inhaling her scent and burning it into my memory. I know it will take more than a little wit to conquer the week ahead of me. But having her in my life right now will make anything Wall Street throws at me bearable.

Chapter 8

Sunday was a blur as I met with my partners and fielded phone calls from top investors. They called with concerns and questions in addition to meetings with department heads who were looking for information to pass along to their employees. I spent yesterday at the office with barely enough time to piss as the pressures on me came from every angle. Not my idea of a restful Sunday, but I had no choice.

The rumors reported yesterday about an investigation became more than whispers when the SEC announced their formal inquiry surrounding the departure of Simon from the company around four yesterday afternoon. We weren't given an advance warning, either. A statement, only a paragraph long, went out over the news wires, sealing the deal and hopefully not our doom.

Fortunately the SEC's focus seems to be Simon, personally, and not our company as a whole. The misconceptions brought on by the investigation surrounding Kings will have to be fought long and hard over the next few days.

I spent all Sunday afternoon on the phone with investors in Japan, trying to squelch fears before the markets opened there. I was semi successful and Kings' stock is down less than ten percent in the world markets so far. Early trading on Wall Street has been brutal, and I fear the stock exchange might halt trading if things don't calm down.

The stock markets are nothing more than a legalized form of gambling. Investors gather data on a company and bet on the movement of its stock. If they see something unpredictable looming in the future, like an investigation, stockholders tend to fold their cards and sell. So I need to put on my best poker face and regain the Street's confidence.

Monday morning has come early for me since I didn't sleep a wink last night. My first public appearance since the gala where I met Kathryn is a scheduled news conference in the Kings Capital lobby at eight thirty, exactly one hour before the markets open.

What I say this morning could make or break the future of my company as well as the livelihoods of thousands of employees. To say I feel a little pressure is a fucking understatement, but I'm up for the fight.

I'm finishing my second cup of coffee when Meg, the smartest communications director in New York City, walks through my office door.

"Morning, Adam." She's in her usual chipper mood. I cock my brow. Her upbeat attitude never fades—she's always the optimist. Although I'm not convinced this day's outlook is so rosy.

"Morning, Meg." She pulls up a chair to my desk and places her laptop on the edge. She taps her fingernails on the desk as the laptop boots up. "Would you be more comfortable if we moved to the conference table?"

"No, this is fine." She begins typing away but continues to speak to me as her eyes are laser-focused on the screen. "You have the main talking points, right? Any thing you'd like to add?"

"No everything looks fine—short and to the point. The fewer words I speak, the less likely I'll be hung by them." This comment makes her raise her eyes and quiet her fingers. Her face reflects concern, too. "My worry isn't what I'm going to say but what questions the news hounds will ask me. I fear the conference will go from questions about Kings to personal questions about Simon and the crazy belief that I was involved with his fiancée."

"I sent out the press release yesterday, covering all the same details you plan to bring up today. The best way to curb unwanted questions, especially the ones related to Simon, is by feeding them misdirecting answers. A distraction, if you will. Gently leading them astray."

"Agreed." I know the game. I have to stay on point. One question handled wrong could be disastrous.

"So, what have you heard from the first round of the financial shows on CNBC this morning? Please summarize." I wave my hand for her to begin.

Meg stops clacking her nails on her keyboard and folds her hands together on the desktop. She closes her eyes and takes a deep breath, as if to clear her head before she begins. "You want the brutal truth?

I don't make a move to answer her, but Meg knows better than to wait for my acknowledgment. She continues. "They've focused on the affair. I hate to say it, but it's the sex part of the story that's making the most news impact."

"Of course it is," I say with feigned amusement. I sit back in my chair and rub my temples, hoping to ease the tension.

"I believe your fight is whether you have the Street's backing as the head of the company. No one has criticized the value of the company and its subsidiaries overseas. Unfortunately, you have become the main topic of interest."

"That's what I thought." I fight off feelings of personal defeat and breathe deeply, hoping to expel my fears. "Are Tom and Patrick here yet?"

My friends, the other founders of Kings, have agreed to stand by me at the conference. A show of solidarity and, fuck, I think I'm going to need it.

"Yes, I spoke with them both before coming to your office. They don't plan on stepping up to the microphone, though. The show's all yours." She stops and looks me dead in the eye without blinking. Her pause seems to emphasize the importance of what she says next. "I know you can do this, Adam."

"Thanks." I hope to God she's right. "Let's get this show on the road."

We rise, leaving our laptops but taking our phones with us. While heading to the door, something feels off to me.

"Hey, would you give me two minutes?" I glance at my watch, knowing we have ten minutes before the scheduled start of the news conference. Meg plans to introduce me, Tom, and Patrick.

"Sure, we have time." She glances at her own watch and then up at me with an understanding smile. She must see the cracks starting to appear in my armor, but she doesn't mention a thing.

"Thanks, I'll be right out." I open my office door for Meg and shut it behind her.

Grabbing my phone, I call the one person I can't seem to get off my mind.

"Hey," Kathryn answers after the second ring. I have nothing of real importance to say to her, but I need to hear her voice before I head downstairs and face the inquisition since the last time I spoke with her was yesterday morning.

"Good morning, beautiful. I hope I'm not calling too early." I find myself smiling for the first time since Eddie dropped her off at her apartment yesterday on the ride to my office.

"Morning, Adam. It's fine. I've been up for a while. How'd your night go?"

"Long. Boring... and lonely without you."

"Same here." I know when we've been apart, it feels like something is missing

"I'm sorry about last night. I was really hoping to get away and meet you for a late dinner." My overseas calls went on through the night as I chased the sun's dawning on different countries when their markets opened.

"I understand. What time is your news conference? It's this morning, right?" I mentioned my planned strategy to her last night when we texted between my calls.

"Yes, everything is set up in the lobby. They're waiting on me to come down. I can take a couple of minutes, though, and make the media sweat it out. It should be live on CNBC if you'd like to watch." I cringe the second after I say this because I fear what the reporters will ask. But a part of me would like to know she's watching and perhaps cheering me on.

"Of course I'm going to watch. I just turned on the television." I picture her sitting on her comfortable couch surround by all those pillows. I'm tempted to ask her what she's wearing but think better of it. I need to stay focused, but even in a moment of stress, I can't curb my need for her.

"It could be brutal today..."

"You're going to do great. Just be your cocky self." She laughs.

"Speaking of..." I clear my throat, and my mood lifts hearing her laughter over the phone. "My cocky self really wants to see you right now." She laughs even more. I smile, imagining her face full of mirth, and wish to God I could be with her.

"I'm glad you're in my life." The confession slips from my mouth before I have time to think.

Kathryn doesn't take a second to answer. "I feel the same about you." She breathes into the phone as if the admission is just as heavy as I think it is.

There's a pause between us.

"Are you okay?" She breaks in before I can. "You're talking pretty deep for a Monday morning."

"You picked up on that." I figure speaking in jest would mask my neediness for her. "I'm all right and better get going, but knowing you're out there watching me helps."

"Good luck, Adam."

"Thanks, beautiful. I love you... your... ah... support."

"What was that?" she said with a hint of sarcasm in her voice.

Jesus Christ! Did I just almost tell her I love her? All of this stress is getting to me. I haven't spoken these words to anyone since the day I left my mother's grave. But they rolled off my tongue without a thought. Maybe it was my heart, not my head, speaking?

"I said support, I love your support." I wipe a small bead of sweat from my brow. "Gotta run, beautiful. I'll talk to you later. Bye."

With a chuckle Kathryn says, "I'll talk to you soon, then. And Adam, don't forget there's more important things in this world than money and power." Her words aren't harsh or preachy. I want to argue that I have thousands of people relying on my performance today and their welfare depends on me, but she ends the call before I can say anything in return.

Deep down, I know she's right. In the end, all the money I've amassed and the power I've brokered on Wall Street haven't made me a very happy man. Now I see my gains and power as a shallow soulless pool filled with wealth and extravagance.

I place my hand on the doorknob of my office door, close my eyes, and try to gain focus before I head out. Once I'm on other side of the door, I see Meg and Goliath are talking with Mrs. Carter, my assistant, by her desk.

With my presence known, Mrs. Carter greets me, worry etched all over her face.

"Good luck, Mr. Kingsley." Her voice is weak, but reassuring, and there's a worried look in her eyes.

"Thanks." I tip my head toward her, and with a slight nod, I acknowledge Goliath.

"I want you to stay here during the news conference," I command so there is no confusion.

I don't want him guarding me in my own building. I don't like the message that would convey to the media, and besides, I've always thought bodyguards seemed pretentious. And I sure as hell don't want to be labeled that today.

Goliath squares his jaw, clearly not happy at my directive. "I'm just following the orders Peters set out."

"And I'm trumping those orders." My decision stands and I look around for Peters. He was with me all Sunday night and this morning, but I haven't seen him since he stepped out for a smoke an hour ago.

"Speaking of Peters, where is he?" I glance between Mrs. Carter and Meg in hopes they know. "Have either of you seen him?"

"Did I hear my name?" Peters chimes in right after my questions, his face impassive as usual. "I just came up from downstairs where Mr. Duffy and Mr. Jacobson are waiting for you. The media is all setup. We only allowed seven outlets and chose Reuters for the main newsfeed."

"Perfect. But no protection." I nod at Goliath and leave Peters no room to argue when I say, "Let's do this."

Meg follows us into the elevator, texting something on her phone and then stowing it in her pocket. "Adam, my assistant just confirmed that everything is in place."

When the doors to the elevator open to the lobby, Tom and Patrick are waiting for me. Both men are stern as they stand together, looking like pillars of strength. They are the true rocks of Kings Capital. Not me. I was fucking away the success I'd been given, and Simon was too fucked up. Tom and Patrick deserve so much more than what I'm putting them through.

"Thanks for being here for me today." I hold out my hand to them, trying to convey my gratitude for standing next to me now and over all the years. Yesterday, I sat them and Meg down to confess all the ugly shit about my time with Marta Llewellyn. Even though Tom already knew about Marta, he still hadn't known the details and I didn't spare any. Meg was a bit flabbergasted that my actions went so far, and Tom and Patrick looked upon me with a new level of disappointment.

"Adam, like we said yesterday, we need to band together right now. We're lifelong friends, not just business partners. I think I speak for Patrick in saying we're here today as your friends."

"You don't know what it means to me to hear you say that," I say. Patrick clamps his hand on my shoulder.

"Now it's time for the show." Patrick ushers us forward.

"I suppose it is." I lead the way down the long hall toward the main lobby.

Although I can't see the crowd that has gathered, I hear the faint buzz of voices as we near the area set aside for the conference. With each step, I securely slide on my game face. Head up and shoulders back. I am proud of the company's accomplishments, and I'll be damned if my stupidity and Simon's insanity will bring it down.

All the good-luck wishes I've received are great, but it's time go full press.

The crowd of reporters and cameramen turn in my direction as we round the corner. Meg comes from behind us and stands in front of the bank of microphones, gesturing for the crowd to settle down. The calm that follows is eerie and not the norm for the bustling lobby.

The wall to my left is lined with employees, many of whom have been with Kings Capital since the start of the company. I stand by Meg as she acknowledges them with a slight wave of her hand, and they spontaneously begin to applaud. All their smiling faces are trained on me.

I smile, touched by their loyalty. I nod in thanks, trying to make eye contact with as many of them as possible.

Their praise emphasizes why I need to knock this interview out of the park. Nothing less than a grand slam will suffice here. These men and women are dedicated employees who have mortgages, rent, and families to feed.

Wires and cables from the podium run across the pristine marble floor and wind through the feet of news crews. I notice seven different mics clipped to the podium. One for each news crew in attendance. I glance outside the building's front glass window and see a satellite truck parked in front of the building, signifying that my words will be instantaneously heard across the globe in real time.

I scan over the reporters with confidence as Meg begins a brief introduction since there's no need for fanfare. "Thanks for joining us today. Adam Kingsley, the CEO of Kings Capital, will be speaking to you and answering your questions. He will give a brief statement, followed by a short question and answer period."

Meg turns to me and steps away from the podium, leaving me the floor. I walk forward with Tom and Patrick trailing close behind. They stand a few feet to my rear, presenting a united front. For some reason that gives me strength.

"Good morning. I'd like to begin this news conference by thanking the dedicated employees of Kings Capital here today." I extend my hand to the direction of my employees standing against the wall. Peters is among the crowd of employee onlookers, which I find odd since he's an independent contractor for me, personally, not Kings Capital. He gives me a thumbs-up as our eyes meet. His gesture makes me smile for some strange reason.

"And a big thanks to all the employees of Kings spread out across the globe." I'm sure these employees are watching me, too, and hoping I can erase the doubt surrounding Kings.

"Kings was founded by four young men, fresh out of college. Two of them, Tom Duffy and Patrick Jacobson are here with me." I pivot to the side and motion toward them. They smile at the crowd cordially. I return to face the front and continue. "Through hard work and dedication, our company has grown to be a worldwide force in software security systems. We pride ourselves in being the impenetrable firewall against hackers for the world's banking systems."

"One of the founders, the late Simon Edwards, was relieved of his duties at Kings Capital last Wednesday." I pause here in respect for Simon. I was advised to skip all mention of his death during my statement and only discuss it if a reporter brings the subject up. Why give the media any more ammunition to use against me.

"Due to the SEC investigation, we cannot discuss the reasons for his departure at this time. Now for your questions."

There, that wasn't so bad. I spouted off the rehearsed speech perfectly. But now the reporters go wild with a barrage of questions as cameras flash and blind me.

The first familiar face I see is John Stanford from CNBC. I point to him in hopes his question relates to business and not the insane rumors of a love triangle.

"Mr. Stanford." I train my gaze on him, trying to show strength, not weakness.

"What is your response to analysts who feel your leadership here at Kings Capital is in question?" Stanford ends by flashing a fucking gotcha smirk. Asshole.

"My leadership has brought Kings Capital to where it is today."

I have a little nugget of information that I was waiting to disclose, and I can't think of more perfect time to release it.

"Just this morning, I was contacted by *Fortune* magazine. They notified me that Kings Capital is now a Fortune 100 company. I can't think of a better answer to your question. Everything Kings has achieved to date has been under my leadership as CEO, along with my partners Tom Duffy and Patrick Jacobson standing behind me."

I allow Stanford a couple of follow-up questions. Thankfully they all center on the Fortune 100 news. The phone call from the magazine may be enough to save my neck. As Meg said earlier, it's all about giving distracting answers to the tough questions.

After Stanford is finished grilling me, which I successfully survived, I turn to the ball-busting reporter for the *Wall Street Journal*, Lauren Nettles. She's an attractive brunette I'm convinced has a fondness for leather and whips.

"Ms. Nettles." I point to her and brace myself for her questions. She moves closer to the front of the group, and I get the feeling she's inspecting me for sweat. She'll find none, though. She wets her hungry lips before she speaks. I worry she's hungry for blood—preferably mine.

"The witness who was allegedly held hostage by Simon Edwards Saturday morning outside The Pierre was identified as Dr. Kathryn Delcour. A reliable source has said you two are romantically involved. Can you comment on your status with Dr. Delcour?"

Well fuck me seven ways to Sunday. Who the hell are these so-called sources leaking all kinds of inside information? My thoughts go back to the two detectives and our conversation Saturday. They know all about Kathryn as well as Simon's motive for trying to kill me.

My hands start to shake and I feel my temper rise. I'm close to giving in to my anger, but I try to bury the building rage as best as I can. Blowing up at this woman is not an option, especially on camera.

Out of the corner of my eye, I see Meg scurrying behind the group of reporters, out of their view. In her concealed position, she mouths the word "distraction," trying to get my attention. I take a deep breath and try to remember what's important in this heated moment—protecting Kathryn.

I put on an airy smile and say to Ms. Nettles, "Dr. Delcour is a close friend. I have been a supporter of her mother's charity, The Swanson Foundation, for several years. Recently, I attended their annual gala and was able to contribute five million dollars to build a hospital in Africa."

I quickly disengage with Ms. Nettles and ignore her. Turning toward the other side of the group, I call on the correspondent from CNN. I can't remember his name off the top of my head, so I quickly peek at the cheat sheet in front of me.

"Corey Evers," I say as if I knew his name all along. He checks to make sure his cameraman is ready. Looks like all cylinders are firing, so here we go.

"I'd like to follow up on the last question you didn't answer." Oh, great, a fucking wise ass. "Was Simon holding Dr. Delcour hostage in response to your affair with his ex-fiancée, Marta Llewellyn? An eye for an eye, perhaps?"

"Kathryn—" I curse under my breath because I used her first name. "Dr. Delcour had never met Mr. Edwards.

And I would like to clear up one important fact concerning the ex-fiancée—"

A movement next to Evers draws my attention and I lose my train of thought. To say I'm stunned at whom I see is an understatement. It's Marta, as in Simon's fiancée Marta. I remember her face from the photos the detectives had shown me.

The same creepy smile from the photos is plastered on her face. Unnerved that Marta has come to the press conference, I turn my attention back to Evers in hopes that no one saw the slight breach in my calm demeanor. I wipe at my brow.

I chance a glance back at Marta to see her chuckling at me. What a cold, heartless bitch. Her selfish actions and our unfortunate situation—however unbeknownst to me—drove Simon to the brink. I return my gaze to Evers and hope I can hold my shit together, but when I look in his eyes I swear his face has becomes Simon's. The same face that stared up at me, lifeless, a couple of days ago.

I feel like I'm definitely losing my shit. I reach for the water bottle on the shelf inside the podium, twist off the cap, and draw back some of the water. I close my eyes tightly; this isn't real. When I open them again, my vision falls upon Evers. It's truly him this time, not the mirage of Simon I swear was there a second or two ago.

Evers appears concerned for me as he stills. I steady myself by leaning my body on the podium. I manage to plaster on my standard, charming, offensive smile. Others in front of me return the smile, mostly the women. Their response confirms that I have likely overcome my out-of-character fuckup. So I immediately return to the answer I was spouting, although I refuse to glance Marta's way. The fucking nerve of her showing up here. I'd like to know how she got in with the press.

"I met his ex-fiancée, Marta Llewellyn, briefly last June. It was our first and only meeting. Additionally, our meeting in the Hamptons occurred before she met Mr. Edwards. You can confirm this with her since she happens to be standing right next to you, Mr. Evers." An audible gasp echoes in the open lobby as all heads turn toward Marta.

I have to say that was one distracting answer. Meg is by my side again, and I shoot her a fast wink, proud of myself. She appears to be pretty damn pleased, too.

"I appreciate you coming today and giving me the chance to put to rest several rumors surrounding me and Kings Capital. Kings is stronger than ever and will continue to be a leader in the software industry." I bow my head and glance down at the podium and wait a couple of seconds before continuing. When I raise my head, I'm serious as hell.

"On a personal note, I'd like to send my condolences to Simon Edwards' family. Thanks again."

Before leaving the makeshift stage, I spy Marta once more in the crowd. Several of the reporters have converged upon her. She looks panicked, and a wicked chuckle escapes me. Slowly I'm becoming a believer in the concept that what goes around comes around. Karma is certainly a bitch.

Perhaps the few flashes I've seen of Simon illustrate my own guilt from my past—my own karma. One thing is for sure; the visions scare the shit out of me.

Tom and Patrick walk up, pat me on the back, and congratulate me on a job well done. I appreciate their continued support and lead the way back to the elevators. Several reporters yell questions at me while I make my retreat. They likely feel snubbed, but I didn't purposefully ignore them. The interview was clearly finished, in my opinion. I left with the focus off me and instead on the unwelcome visitor, Marta Llewellyn.

The crowd of employees congratulate me on doing a good job. I offer words of thanks and shake several outstretched hands as I pass by.

"That was an incredible performance," Meg says as we stand and wait for the elevator with Tom and Patrick. I breathe a labored sigh of relief.

"As long as it was good enough to quash the rumor mill; that's all I care about."

Peters joins us as the elevator doors open. I give him a piercing stare once we are all traveling up to my office. I am having trouble containing my anger at seeing Marta in the lobby, and I believe he knows it. He leans against the wall in an attempt to put some space between us but he can't escape.

"So, would someone please tell me what Marta Llewellyn was doing in the lobby?" Tom, Patrick, and Meg all look as confused as I am, but Peters doesn't. I continue to stare hard at him until he spills what he knows because I'll bet money he knows how she happened to be at this press conference.

"She works for the *Financial Times*. I just spoke with a couple other journos in the lobby, and since the *Financial Times* was one of the seven groups invited to be here, she got a press pass." Peters says.

"Well, I guess it helped me in the end. But Peters, I want you to get a restraining order on her ASAP. I don't want her popping up in my life again. Let's hope a public restraining order scares or embarrasses her enough to stay away from me." I rest my head back against the elevator wall and close my eyes.

"Unless you're physically threatened by Marta, it will be almost impossible to get a restraining order," Peters comments, and I know what he says is a fact. I'm personally offended, but she's not a real physical threat to me.

"Well then, increase the building security and make sure Hayes knows her face down to the tiniest freckle. Because I don't want her near me ever again." I spit out my demands while still leaning against the wall.

I still have the troubling and lingering question of why my mind keeps flashing scenes of Simon alive and real right in front of me. I feel like I'm going crazy.

I take a breath so deep it reaches my toes and wish I could follow Dr. Payne's advice to take off a few days. I simply can't afford to abandon the people relying on me right now. I open my eyes and shake off my concern as soon as the elevator stops and the doors begin to slide open; I have more important worries today.

Chapter 9

My workweek has been hell. I have spent every hour—waking and sleeping—behind the doors of my office, pouring over reports and stock price fluctuations and calming worried investors. After a while, my surroundings feel like a cave, even with the panoramic views of New York City out the massive glass windows. I've let the business of Kings Capital control my life over the last five days, and finally I'm going to get out of this place. I shoot off a few more emails before I wrap things up for the day.

It's been one damn emergency after another since the press conference on Monday. Kings stock has fared well, by not plummeting into an abyss.

Even with the favorable report, I've been swamped trying to do everything within my power to wipe away the tarnish left by the Simon scandal. The worst was a fire I had to put out in Japan in the wee hours of the morning. A major investor had been inches away from canceling a deal with us. Then a newspaper in Sweden reported that I was resigning from my position as CEO. The list of shit I've dealt with is long and exhausting.

The only bright spot has been my occasional text or phone call with Kathryn. One night we tried to have phone sex, but I was interrupted by a news alert in Singapore. My business obligations have held me prisoner and kept me from her all week. However, tonight will be different. I plan to take her out for a nice dinner at one of my favorite spots on the Upper East Side; I just need to call her and confirm the details.

I hit the intercom. "Mrs. Carter, can you come into my office, please?"

It takes less than a minute for her to walk through my door. There are dark circles under the poor woman's eyes, making her lack of sleep apparent, too. "Yes, Mr. Kingsley?"

"You've been working almost as many hours as I have this week. Go home, get some rest."

"Thank you, sir." She exhales a long sigh of relief. "Are you sure that you don't need me for anything? I hate to abandon you. I've never known another human being who's worked as hard as you."

"I'm sure. Please go home and enjoy your weekend." I shoo her toward the door, but she doesn't budge... yet. "How about this? You do me one last favor, and then you *have* to go."

"Anything for you, Adam." I swear she stands up taller when I mention another duty. I need to send her on a long vacation when things cool down a bit more because she's one damn invaluable employee. "What do you need me to do?"

"I need a reservation for two at Hospoda. Let's say around eight." I glance up at the ceiling and smile as I imagine escorting the lovely Kathryn to this unique Upper East Side restaurant. Connected to the Bohemian National Hall, it's one of my favorite places to dine, but for once it will be for pleasure, not business. "Tell them to book half the restaurant for me."

"You and Kathryn?" Mrs. Carter snickers behind a knowing look but wipes her grin away when she realizes she may have overstepped her bounds. "Sorry for presuming, sir."

"Yes, the infamous Kathryn."

On Monday, I sent Kathryn a bouquet of long-stemmed red roses. I had Mrs. Carter order them and asked that the card attached be signed, *"Yours, Adam."* The gifts continued all week long with Mrs. Carter helping me choose them each day. I had precious seconds to spend on the task, so she'd place a choice of two or three things in front of me. I have to say, Mrs. Carter helped me woo Kathryn in style.

"Got it." Mrs. Carter adds a smirky wink. "What time do you want Eddie here?"

Oh yes, Eddie, my driver. I've had him chauffer Kathryn around the city since I've been cooped up in the office. It's kept him happy and not twirling his keys. He seems to have quite the crush on her, too.

"Have him pick me up in fifteen minutes. He can take me home first, and then we'll swing by Kathryn's on the way uptown—around seven thirty."

She nods, but the smile falls from her face. "Will you promise me one thing?"

"Of course, Mary," I say without thinking. Mrs. Carter wouldn't ask something of me I couldn't do. After her service this week, how can I deny her request?

"Get some sleep tonight." She speaks to me in a motherly-fashion. "I know you haven't seen her all week..."

When her voice tapers off, I realize what she's implying. Me. Up all night with Kathryn. Making love. It's one promise I truthfully may not be able to keep, but I'll promise her anything at this point. I just want to send a few emails, go back to my apartment, and lie down for about an hour. Followed by a nice warm shower and then pick up Kathryn for dinner. Those are my best-laid plans for tonight.

And speaking of getting laid...

"You have my word." We share an understanding as I give her a wink.

"Good. It's not physically possible to keep up the kind of schedule you've been living this week." She straightens her skirt and turns, speaking as she leaves. "Well, have a wonderful weekend. All the details for tomorrow's Fortune 100 reception and meetings are in your calendar. I'll be available if you need any last-minute help."

"I'm sure I'll be fine." Tomorrow there are all-day meetings with the other Fortune 100 companies, followed by an evening reception. My company has made its first appearance on the list at number ninety-nine. At least we made it over the threshold.

The bright spot in tomorrow's all-day affairs is the lovely woman who's agreed to attend with me. It will be our first official outing as a couple. Since the heat has died down on me concerning the shooting last week, Kathryn and I are coming out with our relationship.

"Have a good evening, Mr. Kingsley," Mrs. Carter says. I think she's finally ready to leave. God knows I am.

"Thanks. Same to you." She walks out the door and I return to my laptop to send out my last email. I'm not crossing the threshold of my office the entire weekend once they close behind me.

As I'm pressing send on the final email of the day, someone knocks on my door. I roll my eyes half in frustration, half in laughter.

"Come in, Mrs. Carter." I glance up from my laptop as the door swings open, and I'm surprised at the sight before me.

I shake my head, wondering if my tired eyes are playing tricks on me, but I'm definitely looking upon one of the most beautiful sights I've ever seen. Kathryn greets me, her full lips turned up on one side, and I've missed them just as much as the gorgeous woman attached to them. My mind drifts off to the thought of her red lips wrapped around my hardening cock as I sit paralyzed in my chair.

"Sorry, dear, overworked Adam. Mrs. Carter's already left for the day. It's just you and me. No more papers to push or calls to be made." She pulls the door shut behind her and locks it.

I can't mask my smile when she faces me, her demeanor serious as if I'm in trouble. She stalks toward me, wrapped in a khaki trench coat.

I decide to play it cool and go along with her whatever game she's playing. "Did we have an appointment today? I don't remember seeing your name on my calendar."

"Oh, I'm on your calendar, all right. I just asked Mrs. Carter to keep our little meeting to herself. I wanted the element of surprise." She stands in front of my desk, way too fucking far away from me.

I place my hands on my desk and rise from my chair, unable to resist the magnetic pull between us. I want this woman now. Fuck my lack of sleep; I want her scent all over me.

"Stop." Kathryn points her finger at me and motions for me to sit back down. I acquiesce but counter with a question.

"What is my reward for sitting back down? It better be good because I want to kiss you until you can't remember your name. Tell me. I am this close to getting back up and doing just that."

She trails her finger along the desk as she circles toward me. Everything about this woman screams seduction.

God, what I want that finger to do to me, and what I want my hands to do to her. She halts as she reaches the last corner of the desk. I have a notion to reach out, grab her, and pull her onto my lap, but I'll give her a few seconds before I pounce on her.

"So this is where you've been holed up all week." She sweeps her arm to the side, gracefully showcasing the room and my rather plush surroundings. "Quite the place you have here, Mr. Kingsley."

When she calls me *Mr. Kingsley*, all I want to do is swipe my arm across the desk and push the clutter onto the floor. Then I'd place her on the desktop and strip off her coat.

I reach for her but get my hand slapped as I near the hem of her coat. "What the fuck? You're killing me, baby."

"Please be patient. I promise to make it worth your while," she says. There is no doubt who's holding all the cards tonight. She knows the power she has over me. The odd thing is I'm perfectly happy to be under her control.

I allow my gaze to travel up her long legs, to her belted waist, and finally to the curves of her breasts. They all add up to one awesomely fuckable woman.

"Oh, I'm not letting you out of here until you do," I say, even though I'd be willing to yield to her wishes in the end.

She sits on the edge of the desk and crosses her legs. They're long, toned, and end in sexy red stilettos. The lobby guards probably thought she was a "working girl" as she walked to the elevators. The thought makes me chuckle.

"What's so funny?" Kathryn leans back on her hands, toying with me as she licks her cherry-stained lips. "Was it something I said?"

"I was just thinking about your hot ass walking across the lobby and what the guards must have thought." Inching closer as she sits in front of me, I place my fingers on her leg and trace a small pattern on her smooth skin. "A beautiful woman in a tightly drawn trench coat arriving at closing time wearing red fuck-me heels. I'm sure there were stiff cocks in the lobby after you walked by."

"I *was* asked on a date before I made it to the elevator." She throws her head back, and a smirk carries up to her eyes. I know she's teasing, but I feel like a territorial animal at the thought of some other man coming on to her.

"They'll be lucky to keep their jobs." I roll my chair so I'm between her legs. I part them with my hands, dragging my fingers up her inner thighs. The feel of her soft skin makes me briefly close my eyes. It's this contact I've been missing this week. "I don't want anyone talking to you like that. It drives me fucking crazy."

She parts her legs further as I reach the top of her thighs. I continue my path and touch her uncovered pussy. "Shit, Kathryn. You don't have anything on under this coat, do you?"

"Nope, all I'm wearing beneath it is my perfume." She loosens her belt at her waist and lets it fall away. It's my turn to lick my lips at what I'll soon find before my eyes.

Kathryn works the buttons of her coat open and parts the sides, leaving them gaping for me. Her sex is on full display, enticing me. I haven't had her since Sunday, and it feels like an eternity. I'm a thirsty man seeing an oasis ahead of him, and without a thought, my fingers wander over her abdomen until my hands are finally cupping her breasts.

"How I've missed you this week." I get up and push back my chair until it collides with the window behind my desk.

"Have you now?" She pulls me by the lapels of my suit jacket. I'd forgotten about her penchant for lapels. "Show me," she whispers and bites her lip.

"With pleasure." I descend on her, crazed with animalistic desire. I'm soaking up the smell of her as she wraps her legs around me, pulling me closer. Shalimar and sex. Intoxicating.

I find myself rock hard and push against her body. The coat she's wearing has to go. I don't want any barriers between my hands and eyes and her body.

"I've never had sex in my office before." I spread my hands over her shoulders, letting the coat fall to the desk. Lightly I trace my fingers down her arms.

"Really?" she asks with an arched brow.

"I don't fuck my employees, and I sure as hell have never brought a random woman up here."

The slender curve of her neck beckons me, and I kiss along her throat to her ear. I place the lobe between my teeth and gently tug as I find and explore her wet pussy with my fingers. I circle her swollen clit, and her body arches into mine with her tits pushing against my chest. Bending down, I tongue her taut nipples before sucking them into my mouth.

"Feels so good. How I've missed this." She moans while she gyrates her hips in a continuous rhythm with my fingers.

Something in her words sting. It was slight but something I'm not accustomed to. She's missed *this*? Or has she really missed me? I can't believe how my life has changed in the span of ten days. This thought would've never even crossed my mind before I met her.

"Have you missed this?" I push my fingers inside her and twist as my thumb presses against her clit. "Or have you missed me?"

We both still when our eyes connect. My body tenses as I await her answer.

"I missed *you* first and foremost. Although your fingers do come in a close third." She drops her gaze down to where my fingers remain inside her. When she looks up at me, the desire in her eyes is scorching. "Second only to your talented tongue."

She pulls me forward and grabs my hair before she crashes her lips to mine and sucks on my *talented* tongue. I can't seem to stop my lips from curling up into a smug smile, knowing I'm more to her than I thought. If my dick wasn't so fucking hard, I'd check to see if I was still a man because I'm starting to sound like a character from that horrible chick flick we watched last weekend.

It's time to assert that I'm a man—her man—so I push away a few objects that are on the desk behind her. "Lie down."

She complies, dangling her legs over the edge of the desk. She lies before me, bare from head to toe, only a diamond solitaire necklace shining at the base of her throat. I fixate on the lone object as it rises and falls with each breath.

The square cut of the diamond reflects the evening sun from the windows, and I can't help but touch the brilliant stone. I guess the weight to be around three carats.

She seems protective of the necklace when her fingers join mine to touch the diamond as if she's ready to pull it from my hands or hide it from my sight. Immediately I know who gave her the piece: her late husband, Jean-Paul.

"It was a gift from him, right?" I ask through gritted teeth, wondering if he might be on her mind when she's with me.

"Yes, my engagement diamond." She lowers her eyes. "I was in a hurry to leave my apartment and meant to remove it. I wasn't thinking."

"Look at me, Kathryn." My voice drops an octave with my demand. She peeks at me, distress clear in her eyes. It cuts me to the bone because she's not fully over this man.

"I'm sorry, Adam." Kathryn tears up, and I fear it's worse than I'd thought. "I will always remember him. But right now, make me forget."

"Well he can't be here... between us," I say, grabbing hold of the delicate necklace. I pull hard, ripping it from her neck in one quick movement.

Her eyes are wide with shock as she brings her hands up to her throat and feels for the necklace. I open my hand and reveal that it's in my possession. "I can't replace him and will never try. But I will make you mine."

I fling the necklace away as if it's a deadly poison. We both watch as it hits against the wall. She turns back toward me with fire in her eyes.

"Why did you do that?" she questions.

"Because I'm making you mine," I growl while cupping her ass and pulling her hard to me.

A look of surrender passes over her face and she murmurs, "I am yours."

"Hold on tight. This won't be sweet lovemaking. No, beautiful, you've never been fucked like I'm going to fuck you now."

I tear my clothes off, literally. The metal of the zipper releases with a protesting sound. Seams rip and buttons fly as my clothes fall to the floor. Getting inside this woman is my single focus, along with fucking away the memory of any other man.

I look down at her as our need for each other builds. There's a haze of desire in her eyes as if she's on a high. With her legs spread and ready, I position myself and plunge into her with one movement.

"Who is inside you, Kathryn?" I shout while pounding into her with each and every thrust. At first her moans are the only response to my relentless pace.

"You are," she answers with a weak quiver.

"That's damn right." I clench my jaw.

All my strength channels into my hips, so I can plunge deep inside her. The force pushing me is my need to claim her—her mind, her body, and her soul—because I know her life has room for only one man, me. Holding on to her hips, the push and pull of our bodies melts into one hot mass of flesh.

"Harder, Adam," she cries while reaching to touch me. I fold over her body and claim her lips with mine.

Clutching her shoulders as an anchor, her legs wrapped around my waist, the force of my movements is raw and untamed. Want satisfying want. Need meeting need.

After a few more deep thrusts, her legs begin to tremble. Knowing she's close pushes me closer, too. She needs to come now because I can't hold back my climax. I am on the verge of a release that I won't be able to contain.

"Come for me, Kathryn." I pant into her ear while grabbing even harder onto her shoulders as I drive into her a couple more times. She'd fall off the desk if I wasn't holding her so tightly.

"God..." Her one word turns into a cry as she finally surrenders. I slow my pace and feel her tightening around my cock. My body responds to hers, and I'm leaning over the edge of a cliff, ready to fall with her. I want nothing more than to stay buried inside her as I come, but I pull out at the last second.

Pumping my cock, I explode all over her tits. God, it's so fucking hot to see her covered in my release. Her bliss-filled eyes observe the act. She's wearing a part of me now. Nothing from him remains on her body. A proud and twisted smile crosses my face, one of satisfaction and possession.

I collapse to my knees, genuflecting before Kathryn in a simple act of worship. The sex goddess stretched across my desk deserves nothing less. I lean my head against the inside of her knee and press soft kisses to her skin with a whisper touch.

"Kathryn." I speak in short breaths as air returns to my lungs. "That was one hell of a fuck." Caressing her legs, I return to a standing position, looking down at the painted beauty beneath me. Taking my discarded shirt, I wipe the evidence of my orgasm from her breasts.

"Yes. Fucking for a release." She gives me a lazy smile, confirming that I am the only man on her mind. An achievement that I plan on continuing. "I take back my criticism of it."

"As you said, there's *gourmet sex* and then there's *satisfying a hunger* fucking. And beautiful, when you walked into my office, wrapped like a perfect package for me, I was famished. Craving only you." She wraps her legs around me where I stand. If I wasn't exhausted from lack of sleep, I'd press for round two.

"I've been craving you all week." She rises to sit before me. Proud as usual, though nothing covers her body. "And it's been a long week for both of us."

"It's ending with a definite touch of heaven." I lean forward and kiss her lips. "Let's go shower and wash the week away. I have other plans tonight, and I want to get out of this place."

"Those plans of yours—" She's hesitant, which makes me fear she may cancel on me. My smile falls and my disappointment must show. "*Wait*, we still have plans. I've just changed them up a bit with Mrs. Carter's help. Dinner will be served at my place tonight. Your assistant and I have become close friends this week."

I'm surprised by this revelation. "Friends, huh? Mrs. Carter failed to mention this little detail to me. I had plans for our first date tonight."

"Our dinner date will be private. Eddie is picking up a lovely dinner from Sant Ambroeus. Compliments of Maurice." Could I have possibly won over the hardnosed Maurice?

"So Maurice is fixing dinner for two? Does he know I'm the other member of your party?" I search her face only to see a pleasant smile.

"Yes, he does." A thought flashes through my head. Is my portion safe to eat? He did say my cards were marked, and Kathryn came close to being shot due to her connection with me. "I'll take a bite of yours first," she adds with a wicked laugh, and I'm convinced she can read my mind.

"You must have ESP." I gently tap her temple. "But I'm curious how you and Mrs. Carter became close enough to conspire together for tonight. When she left, I was certain my plans at Hospoda were set in stone."

"She had to contact me about a delivery that went a little awry." She blushes a rare shade of pink for my bold Kathryn. "There was a mix up with the La Perla delivery."

"Oh yes, La Perla." I smirk, remembering how Mrs. Carter helped me purchase a sheer bra and panty set from the lingerie boutique on Madison Avenue.

Mrs. Carter suggested the place and seemed very familiar with their selections. I wound up giving her the final say-so. Discussing intimate undergarments for Kathryn made me hard, but uncomfortable discussing them with Mrs. Carter. It was quite the conundrum. I live a block away from the store, but I've never had a reason to darken its doorway, although the window full of lace finery would beckon me whenever I walked by.

"I thought about wearing your gift today, but I decided you might appreciate this better." She drags a finger down her body from the lovely valley between her breasts to her waist. "I believe I was right."

"Yes, anything other than the coat would've left you overdressed." I scoop her up into my arms and find her lips with the hope of leaving her breathless. We press together, and her body softens into mine. "Back to those plans..." I mutter.

"Well, I've promised you some Tantra lessons." Now she wears the smirk. "Don't get me wrong, I love the sex we had..." My muscles twitch as she glides her hand up my arm. "But I want to give you a special massage tonight. Work this wild week out of your system."

The muscles in my body unwind at the mention of easing the week's tension in her harem tent. "Tantra and a massage." I gather up our clothing and throw it over one arm. "Off to the shower." I pat her sweet ass after she gets up.

"The doors over there, right?" asks Kathryn. I nod toward my private washroom. As we near the wall that stilled the diamond necklace, she walks over and bends to pick it up. She picks it up so quickly, I almost miss the movement.

"Did you forget him for the moment?" I tilt my head back toward the desk.

"I did, for the moment. And truthfully, I've been letting go of him since I met you." She stands on her tiptoes and gives me a welcomed kiss. I exhale a slow breath that's mixed with relief and thankfulness.

I open the door to my suite and wait to enter as she passes by me. I can't hold back my smile knowing the promises she's made for the night ahead. The only obstacle will be my exhaustion and whether I can push beyond it and stay awake.

Chapter 10

Kathryn and I hold hands across her dining table. We can't wipe the satisfied smiles off our faces. I survived the food supplied by Maurice, although Kathryn did take a bite of my entrée to prove it wasn't poisoned.

"You'll have to give my regards to Maurice on an another great meal." I push my plate to the side and close my hand around hers.

"We should stop by for breakfast in the morning. You can thank him for yourself." She leans toward me. That undeniable pull draws us together again.

With a quirk of my lip, I say, "I think that could be considered an invitation to sleepover." I smile, seeing a twinkle flash in Kathryn's eyes.

"I think at this point that's a given. Unless you have other plans." I love how this woman can throw it right back at me. God, our verbal foreplay is such a fucking turn on. Because conversations like this invariably will lead to a raging erection along with a desire to ravage her body.

"Yes, we have moved beyond silly juvenile games." A fact that pleases me, and one I have rarely experienced before.

"I'm too old for games." She blows out a quick sigh. "Frankly, you are, too, Adam."

"I agree. The events over the last couple weeks have taught me this, and you've helped me through them all. Only a fool would deny it."

"We've both been through a lot." She gazes down at our hands with a pause. I can almost hear the gears grinding away in her head "The list is long. Hiding out in my apartment and having guns pointed at both of our heads for starters. Not to mention the intrusive media coverage. Though thankfully the media realized how secluded I am in my apartment and moved on to other stories. They can't chase boring. All in all, you really know how to show a girl a great time."

"Boring? You? Never. But any one of those points should've scared you off me, but you've stayed... and here we are." My last words are nothing more than a whisper.

"Yes, here I am." She rises from her chair. I pull on her hands as she walks around the table and bring her to my lap.

"Yes. Here with me." I kiss the top of her head as she folds into me and I hug her close. Burying my face in her hair, I breathe in. I close my eyes as a long-forgotten feeling of contentment overwhelms me. Belonging. Purpose. These words mean permanence to me.

"Are you doing okay?" Kathryn's knitted brow and observing eyes work as a truth serum. "You've worked like a machine all week. No sleep."

There is only one person who could have told Kathryn about my lack of sleep since I had intentionally kept it from her to avoid any worry. "Mrs. Carter," she says, confirming my hunch.

"Is that right?" I laugh. "What other secrets did Mrs. Carter share?"

"This whole billionaire thing is a ruse, and you're really a spy like James Bond." She punches my shoulder hard. I retaliate by beginning to tickle her. My mother coined the term *hickle*, which means a hugging tickle. Kathryn gets lost in a fit of giggles as I play along her sensitive ribs like a piano.

"Stop. It. Adam!" She squirms against me, causing my dick to stir and salute. My innocent *hickling* appears to have backfired since I'm experiencing the torture, too.

"Okay, but only because you're making me as hard as a rock." She quits moving that sweet ass but places a hand over my crotch

"Just checking," she explains with a shrug, and I quietly moan when her hand presses against me.

"I haven't given another person a *hickle* since my childhood." I stroke her sides, grazing the outside of her breasts.

"A 'hickle'?" She places her hand on the side of her neck.

"Not a hickey." I smirk, although the thought of marking her is tempting. "It's a term my mother used when she combined her hugs with a tickle."

Kathryn moves on my lap to straddle me so we're face-to-face. "Oh, Adam. That's so sweet." She runs her hands along my jaw to the back of my head, twisting and pulling my hair around her fingers. I love it, so I close my eyes and enjoy the sensation. I'm relaxed and sated; there is nothing more in this moment I need than Kathryn. I have to fight my exhaustion because if she keeps this up, I'll be asleep in no time.

"You know what you just did?" she asks. I open my eyes and gaze at her even though my lids feel as if they weigh ten pounds. "You shared something with me that had to do with your mother. A memory surfaced, and you let yourself enjoy it. When was the last time that happened?"

I scan through my memory and come up empty, with the exception of an event a few days ago.

"Last weekend, when I held my mother's photo. It's the only time over the last ten years I've allowed myself to remember the good times. And there were many."

"Of course there were. Having them pop up like this one did is good." She bends down and kisses me but pulls away before I can take it further. I wanted more. I always want more.

"Thank you, baby," I murmur.

I'm not feeling tearful, only grateful to her since she's the one who's helped me face the past I'd stuffed away. Grateful she's in my life. Grateful I can go back to my childhood memories and... feel. The emotional novocaine that hindered me has worn off. The numbness is gone, and I hug her to my chest. In a short time, she has brought me back to life. Kathryn hugs me back, soothing us both as she rocks me.

After a few minutes, she sits up, rises to her feet, and holds out a hand. "Come with me. You need to rest, and I planned a little something to help you get a good night sleep."

"Lead the way, beautiful."

My body aches, and my legs feel like dead weight. Nothing stops me from following Kathryn's beaconing smile.

We stop at her office, or my term for it, her harem tent. Kathryn stands in the doorway.

"I think you're too tired tonight. It's best if I give you a massage in bed. I'm bending the rules, but once I'm finished, you may be too tired to move."

"Damn, what kind of massage is this?"

She releases my hand and trails her fingers up my arm, pressing gently into my flesh.

"The kind of massage that will leave you spent. Especially in your condition." She steps closer to me when she speaks. "Head to my bedroom. Let me get a couple things, and I'll meet you there. And get undressed." She reaches up and kisses me, and then traces my jawline with her lips from a tender spot under my ear to the tip of my chin.

I dutifully obey her commands and shuffle off to her room. I begin taking my clothes off on my way. In her room, I toss my shirt on the bench at the end of her bed. I rid myself of everything but my boxer-briefs and turn around when she waltzes into the room, carrying two items. A candle and a small bottle of oil.

Kathryn sets her treasures on the nightstand. She flings back the cover and top sheet from the bed and throws them onto the floor. For a petite woman, her strength can't be denied. She packs power in her curves.

"Lie down on the middle of the bed." She runs her finger under the elastic waistband of my briefs, her sexy assertiveness making my cock twitch. "And take off everything."

I peel them off and climb on the bed as ordered. The second my back hits the bed, I sink down into the soft sheets and close my eyes. If left alone for two seconds, I might be out for the night. The thought of missing out on her massage forces me to open my eyes as wide as they will go. I'll be damned if I'm going to fall asleep before her massage.

"Good." I hear her approval before I see her standing by the bed. Her clothes are gone, and the La Perla lingerie I purchased adorns her body.

"Holy fuck," I mutter. The deep blue lace matches her eyes. The contrast of the dark shade and her pale, luminous skin arouses me, and I find myself itching to caress her body. "Join me, beautiful. You look good enough to eat."

A devilish smile spreads across her face, mirroring mine. My arousal stands at attention with the hope of what's to come.

"Lift up your head." She rests a pillow underneath me. "Bra on or off for this?"

"What kind of question is that?" She chuckles at my reply and toys with the straps before finally letting them fall down her arms. "Seriously, you look as sexy as hell, but I'd rather have you bare."

"Fine." Kathryn maintains eye contact while removing her undergarments. "In the end, most men prefer lingerie on the floor."

She winks and sashays back to the bed; her tits bounce as her hips sway. Without a thought, I wrap my hand around my cock.

"Hold on." She eyes me as I try to curb my need. "Hands at your sides and relax. You need patience. Tantric training rule number one."

I slap my hands down to my side and follow her every whim. "Such a spoiled man." She waves her finger at me in warning and then leans over the nightstand. A red votive candle sits inside a clear glass tumbler. She picks up the lighter next to it and lights the candle. The flickering flame grows tall and a stream of smoke rises.

"I'm trying to be patient but you're a fucking goddess, and as you can see..." I say while directing my gaze down to my raging erection. "I'm having a hell of a time."

She places her finger over my mouth. "Hush. Please, relax."

Kathryn sits next to me on the bed. I inch my hand toward her hip and steal a touch of her skin. "You really have trouble following directions, don't you?"

"Yes," I concede while lowering my eyes. I quickly return my gaze to hers. "With you naked before me and my dick eager to be buried inside you, I have no control." I let my fingers ease over her hips toward her sex. But she catches on fast and places her hand over mine.

"You're incorrigible." Her reprimand precedes her sweet laugh, and she stills my hands. "Let me wash away the week."

"I'm all yours." Truer words have never been spoken. As much as I want to possess her, the evidence speaks for itself. She owns me completely.

Kathryn kneels next to me on the bed and takes the bottle of oil off the nightstand. She raises the bottle above me and tips it so that a thin stream of oil flows from the opening. She dribbles the oil down one arm and then another. Next she zigzags the liquid across my abs while being careful of my stitches.

"How's the injury?"

"Forgotten." I hate lying to her, but truthfully, the shooting still haunts me. The few hours of sleep I've had this week have been disturbed by troubling dreams where Simon is very much alive and taunting me.

"Not buying it." She shakes her head at me. "But for now, it's my mission to erase everything from your mind."

Kathryn continues trickling a path of oil down my legs. As I look down, every area of my body glistens, with the exception of my cock. The damn thing feels needy and lonely.

"I want to see your reactions and you to see mine. So make eye contact with me as much as possible. Keep your hands at your sides, but unlike our coin fun, keep your muscles relaxed."

I nod because not agreeing to this is laughable, and she runs her hands up my arms, rubbing the oil into my skin.

Our eyes stay connected, and I love how her entire body moves up and down in sync with her hands. She puts her all into the massage. Straddling my waist, she brings her hands to the top of my shoulders, and spreads her fingers over them. My muscles turn to putty under her touch. After she spends several minutes working and digging, the built-up tension leaves me.

"That feels wonderful," I moan and she answers with a brilliant smile. "Your fingers are magical."

Continuing over my chest, her hands flutter down my abs. My breath hitches when Kathryn pushes herself over my straining dick. Instead of pressing against me, she lays her body entirely over mine.

Body to body, the oil covering me now rubs all over her. She gently slides up and down the length of me in sensuous movements. Her eyes are on fire, burning away any other cares I have in the world.

She travels along my body, her glorious tits rubbing delicately against my chest. It takes everything I have to not touch her because it's the most erotic thing I've ever seen. The view of her sliding over me... well, I've never imagined anything like this in my wildest dreams. And I've had some pretty fucking wild dreams.

Now that her body is slick, she maneuvers her legs between mine and pushes them apart. She sits up on her knees and drags her oiled-covered hands over my legs. Starting at the top of my feet and then moving to the sides of my calves, she spreads the oil. I want to close my eyes and absorb the feeling, but not watching this beautiful woman in action would be a crime.

Stopping to massage my thighs, Kathryn kneads the muscle with the heels of her palms to release any tension. Right now, I'm so loose; I could melt into the sheets.

After a couple more rounds from my feet to thighs, she pauses at the side of my hips. I glance down at her lingering touch, and she tsk-tsk at me for breaking eye contact. Her lips turned up in a slow smile. She is clearly in control here.

I lie still in surrender, giving her free rein. After managing all the issues and carrying the burdens of my company this week, it feels good to just fucking let go.

"You're finally starting to relax," she says, showing that she has once again read my body.

"Yes," I mumble because even my jaw appears to be on shutdown.

"Good. Now, you're ready for the fun part of the lingam massage." There is a hint of mischief in her eyes She's fully aware I have no fucking idea what she means. She takes the oil bottle from the nightstand and pours more into her hands.

"No clue, baby." My voice slurs as I force my slack jaw to move.

"That's tantric for lingam or penis massage." That got my slack jaw moving in response.

"I thought you might like that." She chuckles while I nod eagerly.

Scooting closer to me, but still between my legs, Kathryn crisscrosses her legs and lifts mine to rest over hers. Her shins are touching the backs of my thighs and my ass. This position leaves my cock and balls vulnerable to her as if they're being served on a silver platter.

The process begins with long strokes up my thighs that end at my waist. She's careful to miss my stitches, ending her ministrations just below them.

"Adam."

"Yes?" My voice is nothing but a whisper.

"Look into my eyes." I comply. "And breathe a little deeper." I begin to exaggerate each intake and exhale, hoping to meet her approval. "Yes, like that. I'm going to mirror you."

As I inhale, Kathryn exhales. A complementary rhythm continues as her hands explore me, inching closer to my length.

"My touches are an act of devotion," she explains. What does that really mean? Devotion of my cock? "This is more than sex. Tantra defines my gentle touch as honoring you and your body."

"I'm fully in, beautiful," I rasp as her hands wander over my skin.

Our breathing mimics each other's once again, her hands moving closer to where I need them. I feel them near my balls, and my cock twitches.

"Oh God." My moan betrays my impatience.

"This will not be quick. So relax and enjoy." The twinkle in her eye makes me hope I survive.

Kathryn never looks down at her fingers. They move on their own, knowing and searching me. She centers on the area below my balls and inner thighs. Although her touch is sensual, it feels like more than just sex. I can tell she wants me to feel something more. I think it's the *honor* part she mentioned.

While pressing her thumbs in the sensitive area below my balls, her other fingers extend over my sac, caressing and fondling me. There is no hurry, just Kathryn giving me pleasure. She doesn't bring her touch directly to my cock, but rather returns to my inner thighs and repeats her motions all over again. And again. Occasionally, skimming my erection as her fingers manipulate me.

I want to move so badly, and I can't stop myself when I do. My hips start making tiny pulses toward her. Not quite thrusts, but forward movements, in hopes of hurrying her along. Finally she does what I'm desperate for—she encircles my erection.

One hand starts at the base and rises to the head, followed by the other. My muscles tighten and a release builds from deep inside of me, making me quake.

"Not yet," Kathryn tells me. I want to believe her voice was my imagination. But when she removes her hands from around me and starts her manipulations all over again, I know the words spoken were hers.

"Fuck!" I cry, hoping for mercy, but she denies me and continues on.

"Pleasure will build and plateau. Then build again."

My body fights within itself. I'm in the crosshairs between pleasurable relaxation and physical exhaustion. A toxic mix like I've never experienced before. Determined to survive at the hands of this siren, I steel myself to focus on the pleasure.

On the third or fourth cycle of her tantric massage—hell, I've lost count—I begin to understand what she said about plateaus. It's as if she's making me climb a sexual staircase, taking me upward, floor by floor, with the true destination somewhere above me.

Even though I'm flat against the bed, a part of me reaches for something, seeking a higher place. The whole fucking experience is a rush. It's not the emotional high from our first tantric time, but a sensory high.

"Floating yet?" Her question startles me back to reality. Floating describes everything I'm feeling. I nod because speaking would require too much of me at the moment.

"Good." She sounds pleased. "Close your eyes. Imagine this bed is a pool of water and you're floating in the warmth of the sun."

Closing my eyes, I feel as if I'm propped up, buoyant and relaxed beyond measure. Once again she starts a pattern, but this time she's more determined and leads me on without a pause.

Tremors start in my legs. I blink quickly to see her look of satisfaction. Without speaking, her hands strokes harder, firmer, and unrelenting.

Fucking finally...

"Close those eyes now." Her voice weaves through me as I follow her directions.

Higher and higher, I chase my release in my mind. With my body shaking, every thought and feeling converges on my cock as she works me with her hands.

The buildup gathers inside me, pulling its strength from each cell like the reverse of a bomb exploding outward because all my energy pools together. As I feel myself reaching toward some violent release, Kathryn calls me back.

"Adam, Adam," she pleads, but I'm unable or more likely unwilling to respond. "Open your eyes if you can."

The second I flash my eyes open, she wraps her soft lips around the head of my cock. All the sensations collide together as she sucks me until I explode.

"Fuck!" I shout, arching my back and hitting the back of her throat. She swallows around me.

Spasm after spasm rattles me until I collapse. She lifts her head and releases me from her hot, wet mouth.

"Never..." The word lazily falls from my tongue. I can't speak anything else yet. Hell, I don't even know my own fucking name.

"Never... experienced an orgasm like that, right?" She guesses correctly with a smug smile. Not only is this woman quickly becoming my world, she's finishing my sentences, too.

I can't even move my limbs. The week's exhaustion I've held at bay can't be stopped and I close my eyes. She pulls the covers from the floor over us and cuddles up next to me.

"Sleep, Adam. Sleep." I fall into a welcoming abyss before the sounds of her voice disappear.

Chapter 11

I'm ripped from my sleep from a nightmare fresh in my mind. Another dream about Simon. Sitting up in bed, the covers fall into my lap. I gaze at the woman lying next to me. Kathryn doesn't stir from her slumber as I throw my legs over the side of the bed and walk to the windows. The pre-dawn view of Central Park looks so peaceful, the only ounce of serenity inside this beast of a city called New York. A shiver runs through me, the dream chasing me even now that I'm fully awake. I stretch my neck and roll my head, hoping to God all the tension from the week hasn't found its way back to me, but it's a stupid thought because it has.

"Dammit," I say under my breath and run my fingers through my hair. My mind keeps taking me back to the shooting. Even in my waking hours, I can't seem to escape it. I relive the shooting even in my stray thoughts. Like a scary flashback when I least expect it. During a conference call yesterday with our division in London, I swore I heard Simon's maniacal laughter. I shut the call down without giving an explanation. I probably upset the London crew, but I didn't care. I needed to escape, much like I do now.

That London call was only a part of it, though. Every night this week I've had reoccurring dreams about Simon. This one tonight was the worst yet.

Simon held the gun to Kathryn's head and pulled the trigger, much like the daydream I had before. However, it wasn't a quick thought flying through my head. It was like a movie playing in slow motion.

The sight of Kathryn in my dream, lying dead on the ground instead of Simon, was horrifying. I shudder and fight a sick feeling, remembering the blood and the emptiness in her eyes. The fire she consumes me with was extinguished like a candle's flame. Everything I love about my beautiful Kathryn was gone.

I place my palms against the cool glass, needing to feel something... anything. I glance back over my shoulder at Kathryn and know I can't return to the bed because the dream has me fully awake. She needs to sleep, and I need to leave the room.

I feel around in the dark for my clothes. Once I find my jeans, I slip them on, quietly open the door, and head down the hallway to the kitchen. Maybe a drink of water will cool me down.

After I fell into a sex-induced coma, Kathryn must have turned off most of the lights because only a solitary lamp in the living room remains lit. I enter the room and gaze over the photos and albums on her bookshelf. Like jewels peeking out of an open treasure chest, the mementos on display beckon me.

I didn't fail to notice a decanter on the shelf of something I'm sure would numb my thoughts. I pour three fingers of the amber liquid into a glass and sip. Scotch. A very good one, too.

I scan the photos as I drink. I saw many of them the night I hid out with her. Her late husband, friends, childhood days with her family. No matter the photo, in every one Kathryn stands out with everything fading into the background. Her presence steals the attention away everywhere she goes.

A few of the older albums stand against each other. I run my finger along the spines until I stop on the last one. Her wedding album. I resist pulling it down because I don't want to see her with him. Knowing he held her heart hurts mine, and I'm already feeling tortured tonight.

I choose another one, grab it along with my drink, and head to the couch. I switch on the table lamp next to me so some of the darkness fades. Sitting down and getting comfortable, I drink some more before opening the photo album. Between the photos and the liquor, I'm hoping to get my mind off the reason I'm up in the middle of the night and not wrapped around Kathryn.

The outside of the album is worn at the edges. I can only gather that someone has viewed it many times over the years. I grab hold of a padded corner and lift the cover.

The first page contains clippings from the 90s. All of them cut from *The Daltonian*, the newspaper at Kathryn's private school, The Dalton School. The second page is dedicated to Kathryn's athletics. Tennis, squash, and lacrosse photos show Kathryn in action.

I chuckle, realizing that all these sports require a stick and a good strong swing. If only there was a picture of a young, beautiful Kathryn dressed in a short sports skirt, my night might turn around.

The photo that captures her perfectly is one of her lacrosse shots. Her hair is pulled back in a long ponytail and tossing in the wind. A look of sheer determination defines her face as she scoops the ball with her stick.

Turning further into the album, there are a few shots of her and Ollie. One in particular makes me smile; Ollie and Kathryn dressed formally and standing posed arm in arm. They look like two young kids playing dress up. Ollie's wearing a tuxedo Armani wouldn't sell to his worst enemy, and Kathryn's formal attire seems more appropriate for a woman twice her age. I laugh at the picture of these two seasoned socialites apparently ready to shed their formal attire for jeans. If I had to guess, it looks like they went to prom together or at least a dance of some kind.

A page later, Ollie and Kathryn are dancing together in a line dance. Someone had written the word *Macarena* on the photo. I throw my head back and laugh, remembering the old song and its crazy dance steps.

"Damn, that song was nuts," I mutter to myself.

"Who are you talking to?"

I nearly throw the book across the room at the sound of Kathryn's voice. She's standing in the doorway to the dark hallway, leaning against the wall with one hand propped on her hip.

"Shit, you scared me." I close the album and take a deep breath. "You could have warned me that you like to sneak up on people."

She emerges from the darkness and into the room. She's wearing a black silk robe loosely tied at her waist, her hair a mess of curls that makes her even sexier than ever. From the prominent outline of her nipples, she doesn't appear to have put on anything underneath the robe. I look to heaven because she's a naughty angel sent to rescue me.

"Sorry to scare you." Her eyes dip to my lap. "What do you have there?"

Sheepishly, I hold up the book since I'm long past trying to hide things from her.

"I was curious," I say in my defense. "I don't normally go poking around people's things..."

"Relax, Adam." Her voice holds a hint of laughter. "I think I'll join you."

A wave of relief washes over me as I pat the cushion next to me. She walks the length of the room but stops as her eyes land on my drink.

"Awfully early for a drink." She takes the glass and swirls the liquid around. She brings the glass to her lips and swallows a large portion. "When in Rome." She sets the glass down on the side table and licks her lips. I'd love to pull her into my lap and lick those lips myself.

"Yes, when in Rome." She sits next to me and curls her legs to the side. I draw her near, wrapping my arm around her shoulders. "I enjoyed seeing you in high school. I'm certain you were the center of all the boys' fantasies."

"I wouldn't know." She shrugs.

"Why's that? Guys had to chase after you. God knows there weren't any girls like you in my high school."

"Ollie and I hung out all the time. We were inseparable, and everyone thought we were a couple. But we were connected at the hips not the lips."

We both chuckle, and I hug her closer to me.

"Ollie didn't or couldn't let Thorpe know he was gay." The sadness in her voice told me that what Ollie had gone through with our father was despicable. Thorpe was a fucking bastard.

"Thorpe found out later, though?" I'd been curious what happened between them. There were rumors but nothing was publicly confirmed, and I wanted the truth.

"Yes, and I'll never forget it. It was the summer before our second year of college. Ollie was back from Stanford, and we were spending every waking hour together. They got into a horrible fight, and Ollie came out of the closet without meaning to let it slip out."

"Were you there?"

"Yes." I waited for her to continue. She searches my face for a reaction, as if she's deciding what to say. "The whole incident revolved around me to some degree."

"What do you mean?" An uneasy feeling comes over me as she moves away from me and turns her body to directly face me. She takes a deep breath and steels herself.

"I haven't told you this because I know you already hate your father." The blood in my veins begins pumping a little faster.

"What haven't you told me?" I try to conceal my impatience, but she visibly pulls away from me even more. I take her hand in mine to keep a connection.

"I need you to promise me one thing before I start to tell you." Her tone is serious, and my palms begin to sweat. Like a premonition, I know in my gut what I'm about to hear isn't going to be good.

"I'll do my best." It's a promise I'm not sure I can keep. The lightly suppressed feelings for my father bubble to the surface.

"I'm serious. Part of me doesn't even want to tell you. It was so long ago. But..." she stops, and I clench my jaw, trying to contain my frustration.

"For fuck's sake, Kathryn." I quit my rant when she flinches from my harsh words. I don't want her retreating from me; instead, I want the exact opposite.

"Sorry." I hold my hands up in surrender. "I'll be good."

"Okay, but if you interrupt me or freak out, I'll stop." Damn, she likes her control. I hope that I can control myself.

"I'll do my best."

She takes another deep breath and begins. "I was nineteen at the time. For years I'd felt uncomfortable around Thorpe—"

"What do you mean by 'uncomfortable'?" The words are out of my mouth before I realize it. Her mouth pinches and her eyes narrow at my question.

"Seriously, Adam. One or two sentences and you're already blowing up?" She begins to rise from the couch, and I grab hold of her hand.

"I'll rein it in. Please..." She stares at me, examining me for a chink in my armor. What she may not know is she's my weakness, and I'm not sure that will change.

"I'm warning you. One more chance." She holds up one finger, and I take her hand to kiss the back of it. I hold her hand against my chest.

"For a few years, I'd catch Thorpe looking at me, or rather leering. Our families vacationed together in the Hamptons. Thorpe and my father were business associates, and Ollie's mother and mine were in the same social circles. When Thorpe would look at me, he looked too long."

A shiver runs through her body and I rub my hands over her arms.

"I tried to distance myself from him when we were in the same room. I'd wear a jacket, hunch my shoulders, or pull my hair over my face. I made myself invisible." I cringe at how she must have felt.

"Ollie knew me too well and soon caught on. He watched his father in disgust, but I begged him to say nothing. He was already hiding so much from Thorpe. He didn't need more trouble."

"One afternoon, I was over at Ollie's brownstone. It was rainy out, and we decided to watch a movie. This was before Netflix so Ollie went down the block to get a movie. I stayed and channel surfed until he got back."

She takes a breather and her eyes dip down. I can feel her working up to tell me something difficult. I want to hold her, but I don't think it's the right time for that.

"I was on the main floor when Thorpe came home. I tried to be quiet, but he heard the television on and walked into the room. I froze as our eyes met. He wanted to know where Ollie went. With the way he was looking at me—like a predator about to capture its prey—I could only whisper that Ollie ran out for a minute."

Finally she lifts her eyes, tears brimming. A single tear falls down her sweet, sad face, and I wipe it away with my thumb. I leave my fingers on her cheek as I try to caress away some of the pain.

"Oh, babe," I murmur, trying my best to not sound like I'm about to explode. My anger toward my father has reached a new level.

"I don't want to go through a play-by-play of what happened." I ache when I hear the pain in her voice, but it does nothing to lessen my hatred for my father.

"I don't know if I could stand it right now, either."

"When Ollie came home, Thorpe had me pinned to the couch with my hands clasped over my head. My shirt was torn and my bra was showing. I was kicking and screaming, trying to defend myself, but I wasn't any match for a man twice my weight. I was just a kid at the time, a virgin. And I was scared to death he was going to rape me."

"Ollie grabbed Thorpe by the back of his shirt and threw him off me." She removes her hand from mine and draws her knees to her chest. I continue to rub along her arm, wanting her to know she's protected and safe with me. But I'd really like to wring the neck of the disgusting piece of shit that is my father.

"Things from there were blurry. I thought Ollie would kill him. Ollie pushed Thorpe into bookshelves, which caused everything to tumble down on them. The fighting escalated when Ollie grabbed him by the collar and pulled back his fist, so I actually tried to defend Thorpe by putting myself between them. I couldn't allow Ollie to destroy his life by going to jail. Thorpe hardly touched me really."

Hardly touched her? There is nothing, not even my promise to Kathryn that can hold me back any longer.

"Like hell! He tore your clothes. You were exposed to him, right?"

She nods but remains quiet.

"So what happened? Ollie better have finished him off. Did the police find out?" My hands shake just thinking how my beautiful Kathryn was violated by Thorpe. A sweet young woman, victimized.

"Ollie's mother came home and heard yelling. I remember her standing in the doorway. She was holding her chest with one hand and onto the wall for support with the other. When she called out that she was about to faint Ollie ran to her, and I was left standing there by Thorpe, holding my torn shirt closed."

She buries her head in her knees and pulls her legs in tighter. Her shoulders shake as she sobs. I gather her up and hold her to me like a small child.

I whisper soothing words, letting her know I'm here for her. My heart shatters as this strong woman falls apart in my arms. We remain in this position long after her crying subsides. I don't want to push her, but I need to know more if she's willing to tell me.

"You asked about the police..." Her quivering voice rips me apart, and I want to avenge her pain. "When Ollie and my parents all got involved, the whole thing got worse.

"What do you mean? I can't imagine how things could get worse."

"When I could get away, I ran from Ollie's. I was a disheveled mess when I got home. You've met my mother." I nod and imagine what Ava Swanson thought when her beloved Kathryn showed up in that state. "I was too upset to hide the truth from her. She saw my clothes and at first thought some random stranger had attacked me. But Ollie came barging through the door a minute after me."

"So Ollie left his mother and father and came after you?" I was really starting to like my half-brother.

"Yes." Kathryn shares a watery smile. "He called out to me, and I went running to him. My mother followed me, in tears, too." She glances at my glass of scotch. "Pass me your drink, please."

I hand her the glass and she slams down what's left and wipes her hand across her mouth. I'm tempted to pour us more, but there isn't enough scotch in New York City to calm my rage against Thorpe.

Then it hits me. The Fortune 100 reception is tonight, and he'll be there. *Fuck.* I can't tell her now, but I will have to at some point. She needs to know. Maybe she shouldn't even go.

"So my mother called my father, hysterical. I was hysterical, too—only Ollie was calm. Although deep down I know he was livid. His muscles were rock solid when I leaned into him."

Kathryn draws in a breath and continues.

"When my father didn't come home right away, I began to worry. My mother did, too. She tried him on his cell phone a few times, but nothing." I picture her huddled with Ollie, traumatized. The anger builds in waves as my mind wonders.

"Then Ollie's mother called our house. I'll never forget my mother's face as she listened on the receiver." Kathryn breaks down in tears. It's killing me to watch her in pain.

"My father." The words are spoken through her sobs. "He went to see Thorpe. They got into an argument." I fear for what's ahead as she cries on my chest. I know her father died the summer before she went away to Paris. It was sudden, as per the background report by Peters. A heart attack.

"He died in the foyer. Heart..." She can't say the word.

"Shh," I whisper while rubbing her back, trying to absorb some of her pain. "I know, babe. I know."

"Ollie wanted to call the police, but with my father dying..." She sniffles and wipes at her tears. The puzzle pieces are coming together. The death of her father was too much for her to bear. If Kathryn had chosen to press sexual assault charges against Thorpe, the public attention and media circus would've been ugly, accusing, and damaging to everyone involved, innocent or guilty.

The pain and personal cost would've been too great. So she ran, just like my mother did. I understand it because Thorpe owns this concrete jungle. The power he wields in this city resides in the gutter with the vermin he calls his friends. They're thugs and bullies just like him, gaining an edge by knowing another man's weakness. The world has no idea who this man really is, but I think it's time they find out.

Knowing Kathryn's father met an early death and the thought of her having to flee to Paris in such turmoil— both because of my father—stokes my already simmering hate for the man. How many others like us has this man destroyed or tainted?

The muted rays of early dawn appear through the window. I hold her and savor my time with her while I plot to annihilate my own father.

I need to plan an attack where it will hurt him the most: his pride. He struts around this city like a peacock, touted as the mascot of Manhattan, but the devil couldn't find a better recruit for Team Hell.

I lean my head back on the couch, tired from everything but still riled up from Kathryn's confession. I squeeze my eyes shut to block out the fury that is rising up in my chest, but the only thing I want is his blood. I hear a faint whisper that resembles Simon's voice. I know my mind is playing tricks on me again, but I strain to make out the words as they repeat in the dark distance.

Destroying a man for revenge. You're no different than me.

I pop my eyes open.

Holy fuck! I'm startled beyond reason because there is a hint of truth in what I just heard. I would love to see my own father ruined, but death would be too quick. He needs to suffer in shame somehow, be humiliated. I'd have no remorse or tears for his demise.

But I'm not like Simon; I'm not seeking revenge for myself. Instead I'd be avenging the woman I love. Damn, is it love? No other word can describe what I feel for her, and I can't deny it a moment longer. I've fallen in love with Kathryn. This remarkable woman in my arms is the one. I lay my cheek against her head, very comfortable with the fact that I'm not afraid to admit I'm deeply in love with her.

I wished my love for Kathryn could lessen the revengeful urges I have toward my father, but nothing is going to make them go away.

My father will pay. He hurt two beautiful young women, Kathryn *and* my mother. He drove them from this city, away from their lives.

They are the only women who have held a place in my heart. One was lost, the other I've just found.

Chapter 12

The sun shines brightly into the room. The shadows of the night have disappeared, but the darkness of Kathryn's confession still lingers with me. Nothing will make me forget the knowledge of what Thorpe did to her. Nothing. As each minute has passed by I've buried the anger inside, but the desire for revenge grows stronger, settling into my bones.

Kathryn and I are still huddled together on her couch. She fell asleep as the soft pink sky turned blue. I refuse to move or speak and risk waking her.

Sometime later, a sleepy Kathryn peeks up at me. Her eyes are swollen and red-rimmed from crying. My jaw clenches and releases as the reason for her sadness flashes through my brain again.

"Good morning, beautiful." My voice is raspy and dry from the scotch. Brushing a strand of hair from her face, Kathryn smiles. It reaches her eyes, genuine and full of emotion and a welcome change from a short time ago. "You seem happier this morning."

"I am." She hugs me tight. Her touch is intimate and caring, with her arms around my bare chest, but not sexual. It's more like a thank-you. "I've wanted to tell you about... him." I can see the internal struggle in her eyes before she mentions last night's topic. "Having you know is a weight off me, but I have a feeling it isn't for you. I've had years to process and heal."

"You guessed right. While I've sat here holding you, I've wondered how I can hurt him for hurting you."

"Revenge?" She searches my eyes.

"Yes, revenge for you *and* for my mother." The thought of these two women being his victims serves to multiply my determination to make him pay. I want him broken, left with nothing.

"I was young. Ollie was young. My father died when he confronted Thorpe." She moves out of my lap and sits next to me on the couch, her eyes steady on mine. "My mother and I were a mess. Ollie would've had to testify against his own father on my behalf since he actually saw what happened. With Thorpe's connections, any judge or jury wouldn't be hard to pay off. No one would win except him. So I backed off and vowed to never think of the incident again."

"I'm so sorry, Kathryn." I bring her hand to my mouth and kiss her knuckles. "You are such a strong woman. How can I stop the hate and desire for revenge?"

"When I met Jean-Paul." The late husband. I wonder what role he played in her healing. "He told me something that changed my life. He was a carefree man. The stereotypical skier type. Daring, looking to get the most out of every minute he was alive. Jean-Paul said that the human heart doesn't have room for both hate and love. It's one or the other."

"But surely he hated what Thorpe did?" I can't imagine a man who loved Kathryn would blow off her attack so easily.

"He hated what happened and probably hated Thorpe, too, but he didn't dwell on it or want to get even. He told me love was the only way to heal from what happened. His favorite line was, 'Hate is a disease, but love is its only cure.' He was a pretty wise man."

I mumble, "I can't think that way. I have to be honest."

"I had a few years of sorting through everything before I met Jean-Paul. Give it time, Adam. But his words are true." She pulls one of her hands from mine and circles it over my chest before stopping in the center and pressing down. "This heart can't be divided."

There is truth to what she's saying. But I can't let it go until Thorpe pays a hefty price. I want him humiliated, and then I'll work on the love in my heart part.

"Enough of this heavy stuff." She moves forward to the edge of the couch. "How about some coffee?"

I take a deep breath because I have more *heavy stuff* to tell her. "I need to talk to you about tonight."

"Tonight, as in the reception?" She sits back.

"Yes." I dread having to telling her this, but she must know. "Thorpe will be there tonight. I had no idea what happened to you, or I would've mentioned it before now. I thought you didn't like him because he rejected Ollie for being gay."

Kathryn closes her eyes slowly and dips her head. When she raises her eyes to mine again, she looks resolved. "I want to be with you, Adam. I do. He knows who you are, right?"

"I believe he does, although we've never spoken besides a short hello. He doesn't want anything to do with me because I'm a reminder of a mistake he made."

"I suppose we both are, aren't we?" Kathryn sums up our stance in Thorpe's life perfectly.

"Yes we are. I wish it was something we didn't have in common." I caress her cheek and let my thumb run over her lips. When she leans into my hand, I relish her subtle sign of affection.

"Me, too. But I don't want to run from the past. I want to live in the present with you, so I'm going."

"And the future?"

"I'm hopeful," she replies in a singsong voice while rising to her feet, pulling me forward with her. "But for now, my future depends on coffee."

"Lead the way." I trail behind her and tap that sweet little ass before she gets too far ahead of me. "Caffeinate me, woman."

She giggles and runs toward the kitchen with me hot on her trail.

After downing a cup of coffee, we head back to her bedroom. I haven't glanced at my phone since last night, and damn, it feels liberating. But I can't push off work entirely.

I rummage around in the duffle bag I brought with me. My office suite resembles a mini-apartment, and I stock it with a full wardrobe and essentials because I stay overnight frequently. Last week it was every fucking night.

I have scores of emails that need attending. One after another, fires still smolder from all the bad press I've battled. Perceptions have improved, though, but need more work. I hope tonight's reception highlighting Kings as a new Fortune 100 company will help lift any lingering worries about our strength.

I fire off a text to Peters, telling him to meet me at my office before he heads to the meetings related to tonight's event. He responds immediately with a yes.

Today's meeting with him will be personal and regarding one person: Xavier Alexander Thorpe. My teeth grind together at the thought of him.

"Is everything okay?" Kathryn stands beside me and places her hand on my arm.

"Just fine," I respond quickly, not wanting her to pick up on my stress. "I'm meeting Peters in two hours." I stash the phone back in my duffle and turn my attention back to her.

"I'm curious about this Peters. Who exactly is he?"

"I met him when I came to the city. We lived close to each other in Brooklyn and hung out at the same pub. It was way before I hit the big time." I fondly remember my shitty studio apartment. The experience makes me appreciate where I am now. "I wasn't taking much of a salary those first few years. We reinvested every dollar back into the company. Peters works as a gatherer of information. A much-needed profession since Wall Street covets information above all else. He started working for me about nine years ago. Now I'm his only client."

"Oh, so he doesn't work directly for Kings."

I don't want to tell her why he's more a personal employee than a corporate one for me. I'm not sure she would understand the need to have help from an insider who knows this city and those who run it. Both legally and illegally.

"He's more of an independent contractor."

"Got it. He knows where the bodies are buried." She teases me with a wink.

"Something like that. Let's hit the shower." The subject of Peters fades away, thankfully.

"Yes, my hair." She weaves her hands through the wild strands. "It's out of control."

"Nah, I love it." I pull her close while grabbing her hair in my fists. A carefree giggle escapes Kathryn's lips. I smile and kiss her mouth.

"Stop!" She tries to wiggle out of my arms, but I hold her tighter, not willing to let her go just yet. "Morning breath."

"It wasn't bad," I say and lick my lips to examine her taste on them. "A mix of coffee and scotch."

"Well, at least we match." She pulls her fingers through my hair, twirling the ends.

"We do. So no more protests." I place one arm behind her knees, and with my other one supporting her back, I cradle her in my arms.

"What are you doing? Put me down." She laughs and smacks me.

"This." I dip my head down to hers and kiss her hard. This time she joins me and our tongues meet. What a fucking awesome way to greet the day.

I travel down her neck with my lips, and she welcomes my approach by dropping her head back. I walk toward her master bathroom and as I approach the shower, I lower her legs to the floor.

Neither of us is wearing many clothes. Kathryn has her robe, and I've got on jeans. "Undress for me, beautiful." I am starving to see her bare flesh again. I crave this woman's touch and body.

"Ditto."

With her clothes discarded on the floor, I can't keep my hands at my side, and I cup her firm breasts. Her nipples are already hard and firm and become even more so as I caress them. She steps closer to me and wraps her arms around my waist, making our connection stronger.

"Get in the shower." She raises her brow at my demand. "Now." I lift my brow back at her, and she gets my drift. She smiles and follows my orders like an obedient student. But the real Kathryn peeps out behind the fire in her eyes.

"Yes, sir," she quips with a short giggle. Her words remind me of our last encounter in the shower. After her tears, I love seeing her playful like this. I push the thoughts of Thorpe's attack away as soon as it comes to mind. That fucker won't ruin this moment for us. He's stolen enough already.

"Showers bring out your submissive side, and I totally approve."

"Do you like bossing me around?" She looks over her shoulder at me while turning the showerheads on full force.

"Well, I am used to telling people what to do. But honestly, I'd rather share the moment with you versus control it." I have no idea where that came from. Usually I control everything about my interactions with women.

Interactions would be the key word here, not relationships. What Kathryn and I have goes far beyond a mere interaction. When I analyze my treatment of women prior to Kathryn, I can't deny it was based on complete selfishness. A twinge of guilt grabs me and twists.

"I'm not sure what you've done to me, beautiful, but things have changed for me." This isn't an easy confession.

"You've let yourself feel." She looks me directly in the eye. No wavering. But can such a simple act really bring that type of head-spinning change? Perhaps it's true. I had controlled my feelings with a tight fist, and once they were set free, my icy heart thawed. Her passion drew me to her like a moth to a flame, and I can't pull away.

She eases herself under the spray of warm water, and I'm in awe as it streams down the length of her body.

"You know, you're a wise and beautiful woman." I let my hands wander over her body, mirroring the water's flow. "And I'm one lucky bastard to be here with you."

"Yes, you are." She points her finger into my chest.

"Rather confident in yourself, huh?" I toss her attitude right back at her, and she coyly nods. "Well you should be. I've never met another woman like you."

"Just remember that when one of your backseat warmers shows up somewhere."

"Ouch! That hurts." I place my hand on my chest.

"Good."

"You know you're special to me. Let me show you." I grin.

She opens her eyes a little wider while she looks up at me. That small change reveals so much to me. Trust and anticipation.

Placing my hands at her waist, I gently push her back against the tiled wall. I slide my hands down her body as I kneel before her.

With one of my hands anchoring her hip and the other behind her knee, I have one simple command. "Your leg over my shoulder, beautiful."

She complies and I worship.

Chapter 13

I open the door to Sant Ambroeus and follow Kathryn inside the restaurant. I won't be joining her for breakfast but want to make sure she made it here safely. During the short drive over, I prepared myself for meeting Maurice again. Our first interaction left me labeled a womanizer, and I was warned I better not use or hurt Kathryn. He also mentioned that my cards were marked. This time the circumstances are different, I hope.

"Ms. Kathryn." I hear the voice of Maurice before I see him.

"Good morning, Maurice," Kathryn responds in cheerful greeting.

He sees me as he comes up to Kathryn and kisses her cheek. His bright smile fades as he glares at me over her shoulder. They part, and I take a deep breath before extending my hand because I feel like I'm here to convince a "father" that I'm not so bad after all.

"Maurice," I say and stick out my hand. He looks me up and down before taking my hand. I squeeze his fist in return, trying to show him that my confidence isn't in question. The same confidence that has helped me win many a deal in boardrooms and over business lunches in restaurants like this. Let's see how it works on him.

"Mr. Kingsley." Maurice eyes me over the spectacles perched low on his nose. "I see you survived your little lovers' shootout, as the papers say. The other guy wasn't so lucky."

"Maurice, please," Kathryn whispers sharply. "He saved my life. And please don't believe what you read about Adam."

146

Maurice steps back and appraises me with his arms crossed over his chest. "You saved her?"

"Yes." I wrap my arm around Kathryn and pull her toward me. I kiss the top of her head so Maurice can understand the depth of my affection. Kathryn gazes into my eyes as I pull away. No one can confuse the intimacy we share with just one kiss. Not even Maurice. I want to him to know that my feelings for her are genuine. "But I think it may end up being the other way around in the end."

Maurice looks between us and chuckles. "Yes, I believe you're right. But remember our conversation from before."

I tap my finger to my temple. "I won't forget." How could I? He pretty much threatened me with bodily harm if I hurt Kathryn.

"Adam has behaved, Maurice." She squeezes his arm in reassurance. "But I appreciate your concern for me."

"We enjoyed dinner last night." The meal he sent us was nothing short of delicious even if I was afraid he poisoned the food. "But I'm afraid I can't stay for breakfast with Kathryn. I have a meeting in a few minutes, and my driver is waiting for me outside."

"What a shame." I'm surprised at Maurice's lack of sarcasm. Perhaps I'm winning him over after all. "Here. Please take a muffin, and I'll have my Sofia pour you a coffee. Cream and sugar?"

"Thanks so much. Just cream." Maurice grabs a muffin out of the counter display and hands it to me. His wife Sophia stands a few feet away from us, and I watch him pantomime pouring coffee into a cup after he turns to face her. She nods and scurries away.

After removing my hand from around Kathryn's back, I reach into my pocket and pull out my money clip. I remove a hundred and hand it to Maurice. He looks at me with a questioning eye. "It will cover Kathryn's meal and my breakfast."

"Adam, you didn't have to do that, but thanks." I know she could buy the entire restaurant breakfast, but I want to pay for her. I'm old school in believing that providing for her needs should be my responsibility.

"Yes, he does," Maurice answers with a stern voice. "A man must take care of his lady, right?"

"Exactly," I reply. "I plan on doing just that." If she only knew what I'm going to plan when I meet with Peters in a few minutes. The end of Xavier Thorpe's reign as king of this city. He tried to harm Kathryn and in my eyes, killed her father. I'm sure there are countless other lives he's left in tatters, and it's a sin that he's not paid for his crimes. Instead he's been allowed to walk free to continue fucking up other people's lives. It's just another way to take care of her and one that would win Maurice's approval.

Sofia brings a cup of coffee to go and shoves it into my hands. "Here, I have other customers to serve." It may take some time to win her over.

"Thanks for the coffee, Sofia." I give her my signature smile—the one that often stunned women's panties off. She snorts and walks back into the kitchen.

Kathryn hides her smile behind her hand while Maurice looks after his wife proudly.

"I must attend to my customers, please excuse me." Maurice nods at me.

I hold up my coffee. "Thank you again."

I turn toward Kathryn. "I really need to get going. Eddie is waiting for me." When she pushes out her bottom lip, I pull her to my side and whisper in her ear. "Sorry, beautiful."

"I understand." She nestles into me, and I hate that I have to leave. "What time tonight? For the reception?"

"The cocktail starts at seven." I stare straight into her eyes before asking her a question. "Are you sure you're okay with going tonight? Thorpe will be there front and center. He'll be in his element."

"I want to be by your side tonight. We can't avoid him forever, and I sure as hell don't want him controlling our lives." But then she adds with a smirk. "Just make sure we don't sit at his table."

Her humor and stubbornness make me smile in return. "I agree. And no worries about seating. I requested a table some distance from him. I'll be at your apartment at six thirty."

"I thought I'd be arriving by myself since you have meetings there all day." Her eyes dance at me in approval.

"You're kidding me? What man would allow *you* to walk in unescorted at tonight's reception? Besides, it will be our first formal outing. The press will likely go nuts when we walk the red carpet."

"Our relationship should raise a few eyebrows."

"Yes, it will. Especially since I skated around the question of whether we are together at the press conference." I have one more request before I leave. A simple wardrobe decision on her part. "Speaking of the red carpet... wear something that matches your lipstick."

~

Peters arrives on time for our meeting. He knocks on my office door as he walks into the room. I'm seated at the conference table, not at my desk, with my sleeves rolled up.

"Morning, Mr. Kingsley." Peters is carrying a computer case and wearing a fierce look of determination. He sits down in his usual chair by my desk and opens up his laptop. He presses a few keys, and he looks up at me, ready to engage. "Let's hear what's up. Thorpe, correct?"

"Yes, you've been collecting information on him for years. I need to add up what we have because there's a score I want to settle with him." I clench my fists on top of the table because there is nothing else I can do when I think of Thorpe. Especially when I remember what Kathryn told me last night. I have to concentrate to loosen them and remain composed.

"What kind of score?" Peters is paid to know all my secrets. He's my crypt keeper—a paid vault to hold all kinds of information. He's one of the only people I trust with everything. The million-dollar apartment I purchased for him here in Manhattan helps keeps the vault sealed, too.

"He hurt someone I care for deeply." I spit out my words. "And was never held accountable for his actions."

"Someone you care for deeply?" He meets my eyes with a knowing look. "Are you talking about Kathryn Delcour?"

"Bingo!" I slam my hands against the shiny wood table, unable to contain my fury, and Peters jumps. "He has a long-standing, uncollected debt with her and her family."

Peters nods, understanding. "Okay, how bad of a hit do you want him to take? Slightly wounded?" He glances at my now-healing side. "Or a mortal blow?"

"Mortal. The last nail in the coffin. In the business sense, that is." I must have looked menacing because Peters stares back at me, startled.

"Thorpe must've done something beyond his usual bullying."

"His actions caused Kathryn's father's death and made her flee to Paris." My head pounds as anger fuels my beating heart. "What do you have? We need a trump card."

A light of understanding shines in Peters' eyes. "Oh, the reason she left for Paris. The missing puzzle piece you asked about."

"Yes, the piece is found." I tap my fingers on the table. "So, let's have your best."

"There is a real estate deal he's developing in Jersey. A massive commercial development. Remember it?" Peters asks with a hint of excitement while leaning toward me.

"Yes, the economic zone in Camden," I say and Peters nods, confirming my answer.

"I've heard some rumors about the millions of dollars Thorpe has invested being used for other real estate deals. Peter to pay Paul, as it goes. He's trying to prop up some bad deals, it seems, and I have some proof of the transactions."

"Okay, so he's moving funds around." I wonder how hard of a hit that would be. "I need more details."

"He appears to be funneling investor dollars into another project without their permission."

"I like the sound of this. It's got scandal written all over it." I silently create *The New York Times* headline when it reports Thorpe's demise. I try to contain my excitement, but fail miserably.

"Looks like you want me to pursue this avenue," Peters states the obvious.

I rise out of my chair and walk toward the windows, looking out over the Hudson River. The next words I speak will give the okay to destroy my own father. I swallow hard, but my answer comes easily when I picture a young Kathryn and what he put her through.

"Do it." I make the command while turning toward Peters. "But nothing illegal or potentially illegal on your part. Or at least don't get caught."

"Give me until Wednesday. What are your plans after you have all the damaging info?" Good question.

"I want to reveal what I have on him to his face. I want to set up a meeting, and I want you to attend with me. No one directly employed with Kings should be there. This is personal."

"So a meeting." Peters scratches his head.

"You said you'll have the information lined up by Wednesday, right?" Peters nods. "So when I see him today at the Fortune 100 meetings, I'll ask if I can meet with him Thursday morning. Bright and early before the markets open. It may be a long shot that he'll agree, but I'm going to give it try."

"Sounds good. I'll leave you this information." Peters retrieves a few papers from his carrying case and spreads them out on the desk. "I will only document what I find on paper. Nothing via mail or text to avoid an electronic trail."

"Smart." I take a page off the table and pick it up. "This is easily shredded."

"Exactly. Electronic trails are forever." He closes his laptop and shoves it into his case. "I better get to work on this project. Good luck with Thorpe today."

"He's the one who will need the luck. Maybe we should call back Hayes, just in case my temper gets the better of me." Hayes returned back to Washington, DC, since things with the media have calmed. I imagine standing near Thorpe and being unable to resist the urge to take a couple of swings. And I smile.

"Not a bad idea." Peters has had plenty of opportunities over the years to see me explode. "You have to play it cool, though, if you have any chance of him agreeing to meet with you."

"I know. You're right. I'll ask him while there are others around. He'll be more likely to say yes, and I'll be less likely to punch his fucking face in."

"Sounds like a plan." Peters throws the strap of his bag over his shoulder. "Well, I'm off. Remember no texts on this subject. Paper and actual phone calls only."

"Got it." I place both of my palms on the table and lean forward. "I'm going to enjoy watching him squirm."

"Me, too," he says with a chuckle. "Hell, you've had me watching and working on a way to get him for years. Maybe I can take a vacation now."

"You help me pull this off and I'll pay for you to take a trip around the fucking globe."

"I'll hold you to that." He stretches his back before walking toward the door. "I sure as hell need time off."

"You and me both, my friend." I clap my hand on his shoulder and he makes his exit. When the door closes, I turn and scan the view out my windows. Concrete and steel buildings, fortresses of power, stretch across the sky. I smile, knowing in a few days one man's empire will come crumbling down. A pile of lies settling into dust.

It's time to make my way to the meetings for the day and work on that Thursday morning request.

I grab my phone from my pocket, bring up Eddie's number, and press call.

"Yes, sir," Eddie answers.

"I'm ready. Out front in five." I take a few seconds and browse through the papers Peters left me. Bank balances and money transfers coordinate with payments to corresponding developments. How they hell did Peters get his hands on these? The only answer is that he's an investigating genius.

I need to tuck them away somewhere safe because I sure as fuck can't take them with me today. Walking to my office suite, I find the painting that hides my safe. Just like the one in my apartment, Peters demanded I install this one, too. Damn glad he did.

A quick scan of my thumbprint and the lock clicks open. The space is empty since I like to keep my personal documents at home, but it's been waiting for something special like these papers. I can only find one word for them: priceless.

~

The last meeting of the day is coming to a conclusion. The group of men and women surrounding me has earned the right to be called Wall Street's elite. I am a newcomer to this group. The new, young punk on the financial block. Most of them have been in the trenches longer than I've walked the earth.

They've weathered the economic ups and downs. Survived the good and bad press, too. Needless to say, I've tried to listen and take notes as their wise advice and economic predictions circulate around me.

But one voice in the meeting has made my blood boil. Thorpe. Fortunately, this is the only time today I've had to see his smug face. It's no secret to him that I'm here. The only secret—to anyone outside of him and I—is that I'm his son. The bastard's bastard.

He walked into the room and scanned it, instantly finding me in the crowd. Our eyes locked and we exchanged the usual head bob. The only form of communication we've had in public.

Today, his pompous arrogance enraged me and was too much to handle. When a subject was introduced, he shared his opinion without fail. Everyone looked at him in awe as if he was the man with all the answers. A few journalists joined us and eagerly typed his every word into their laptops.

After listening to his pontificating for almost an hour, I found myself itching to get up from my chair, grab his tie, and strangle him with it. Murderous thoughts that helped satisfy my fury kept speeding through my head.

I need to rein myself in and gather control over my emotions. I've yet to speak with him and request a meeting for Thursday. Appearing calm and conciliatory will be the best approach.

Taking slow, deep breaths like Kathryn has taught me, I begin to calm down. Even the tightly screwed muscles in my face loosen as I remember her soothing touch.

As the meeting's leader officially dismisses the gathering, Thorpe rises from his seat and converses with a CEO from the food industry. Not his usual audience or victim.

I force myself to move toward him as I continue my breathing. The closer I am to being in his presence, the tighter my fists become. I need to release them before they give me away. I need to act natural and mask my hate behind a smiling face.

I close my eyes briefly and exhale. With a subtle shake of my head, it clears and my fists relax. I focus on the end result because it's my only chance of success.

"Good afternoon, gentleman." I introduce myself to the two men in front of me. The words leave my lips without a twinge of anger. This successful first step spurs me on.

I'd expect nothing less. His voice unnerves me, and I stuff my left hand in my pocket because I want to punch his egotistical face. It will serve as an outlet to my anger during this conversation. "I don't believe we've formally met."

No we haven't, you bastard! is what I really want to say. However, I take the hand he's offered and shake it. "Mr. Thorpe." I retract my hand and wipe my palm on the outside of my suit jacket.

His eyes follow my movements then return to my face, amused. My face remains impassive under his scrutiny. So far all my anger stays contained.

"Adam Kingsley," the gentleman to my left finally speaks up. "Pleasure to meet you. I'm Jon Canton of Mason Foods. Congratulations on Kings Capital making the top 100."

"Nice to meet you, and thanks. We barely snuck onto the list, but we're here amongst the greats." I turn to Thorpe as I finish my sentence. He's continuing to eye me, waiting for my next move. Here it goes. "Mr. Thorpe—"

"Please, cut the formal bullshit." I'm taken aback by his brusqueness. I glance at Mr. Canton, whose eyes are wide in shock. Terse is an understatement for Thorpe's tone. Rude would be more fitting. "Just call me X."

"As you wish, X." I smile, successfully hiding my previous desire to throttle him. The chance of publicly squashing this arrogant jerk calms me. There is something to be said for having the last laugh. "You mentioned today that you're looking for companies to help develop areas that are still struggling with the economy."

"Yes, we have a development in Camden, New Jersey that will change the face of the city." He sticks his chest out, and I wait for him to start beating it. "I've succeeded as a real estate mogul here in New York City, so it's time to spread my talents around."

"I was interested in hearing about the strides you're making, too." Poor Mr. Canton tries to interject himself in our conversation but is quickly brushed aside when we ignore him.

"I'm curious to learn more. Possibly become involved on a corporate level." I speak with mock enthusiasm, but the source of my upbeat mood lies in setting a trap for Thorpe.

"Honestly?" Thorpe appears astonished and a little leery of my interest.

"Yes, I'm interested in finding out more details on how partners can invest." I chuckle to myself at this gross understatement. "I'd like to meet you one morning this week. Early Thursday, if that works for you."

"All right, Adam. I'm not sure what you're trying to pull here, but I'll bite. Thursday works. Seven a.m. sharp." He straightens his back, becoming more rigid, and reaches out his hand to me once again. "Gentlemen." He shakes both Canton's and my hand before turning on his heel to leave. His quick departure doesn't leave us any time for a proper response.

"Well that was one damn intense conversation." I'd momentarily forgotten the man next to me as I watched the devil himself walk away.

"Pardon me?"

"You and Thorpe. Are you sure you've never met before?" Mr. Canton is one intuitive son of a bitch. He could see that something lies deeper between Thorpe and me.

"Never officially. But we do know one another from a long time ago." Mr. Canton accepts this explanation with a simple nod. "Well that might explain the fencing match I just observed." He laughs at his own joke. But I suspect his comment is more to ease the tension in the air than an attempt at humor.

"He might have been in danger if I'd been armed with an actual sword." I throw out a little laugh so my seriousness appears to be in jest.

If Mr. Canton only knew the truth.

Chapter 14

"Hi." Kathryn's voice is soft when she answers my call.

"Hi, beautiful. I can't wait to see what you decided to wear to the reception tonight." Eddie and I are on the way to pick her up at her apartment. "I'll be there in five minutes."

"I matched my lipstick as you requested." She purrs into the phone and I imagine her licking those red lips.

"I thank you in advance." I grin at her feistiness.

"I'm ready, so I'll meet you in the lobby." She doesn't sound apprehensive about tonight, which sets my mind at ease. Her attendance should be her choice, not done to please me. Coming face-to-face with Thorpe after what he did to her takes strength, and Kathryn has that in spades.

"Perfect. See you soon." I end the call and start another one.

"Evening, Mr. Kingsley," Peters answers before I hear it ring. He must have been waiting for my call.

"We have a meeting for Thursday. Thorpe seemed leery of me. I expected nothing else. I told him I wanted to discuss the development in Camden. As an investor, of course."

"Smart. To be a fly on the wall for that conversation." He chuckles.

"My performance was going to go one of two ways: stuffing away my anger or hitting him in the jaw. I think I won an Oscar."

"You must have. I have been pressing my sources for more information. I think you'll be pleased."

"Let's meet on Monday morning around eight. We can go over what you've found."

"Yes. See you then, Mr. Kingsley." I end the call as Eddie slows the SUV in front of Kathryn's building.

"Be right back with the lady, Eddie." I exit the SUV a second after the wheels stop turning. Walking past her doorman, I nod my head and he responds with a smile. I want to tell him to get used to me because I plan on being in Kathryn's life for some time. Actually, I have *no* plans of not being in her life, ever.

Ahead of me, Kathryn is standing next to the lobby desk. My forward motion comes to a complete stop as I process the entire package before me. Kathryn is in a red halter dress. Her hair waves around her bare shoulders, a perfect contrast against her pale skin. I itch to have my fingers in her hair... and panties.

She is a naughty goddess whose beauty radiates around her. My pulse races as I step quickly to her.

"Hot damn," I blurt out once I'm able to touch her. Taking her hand, I spin her around. Her dress flares as the air catches it. A red, silky circle floats between us. The front dips dangerously low and ties behind her neck. I can't imagine she's wearing a bra. Knowing that undoing the straps behind her neck will leave her bare before me causes my cock to harden. I'm not sure how I will make it through the night.

"You like?" She bites down on her ruby lips while toying with the knotted strand of pearls lying in the valley of her glorious tits. I have to shake my head before answering her.

"Like? That word inadequately describes my feelings." I lower my lips to her ear so I can whisper my next comment. My eyes close as I savor her scent and ride its high. "Love, or perhaps lust, is a better word. Because I want to lay you down on the desk next to us and make you mine."

I detect a slight shiver as my lips skate over the skin behind her ear. While kissing the tender area, I take her into my arms. "I don't know if I want other men to see you looking the way you do tonight. I can't imagine their thoughts will differ from mine."

"Not all men are sex-driven animals like you." She pulls away so that I can see a teasing smile play across her lips.

"When they see you"—I run my hands down the sides of her dress, ending right above her sweet ass—"dressed like this, they'll have no choice. It's fucking involuntary."

"Oh, that sounds serious. Even dangerous." She runs her fingers under the lapel of my tux. Her light touch is sweet and familiar. "I should go change into something else. My mother left a caftan at my apartment—"

"Beautiful, you'll do no such thing." I release her but stay at her side with my hand on the small of her back. The tips of my fingers make contact with the soft and silky exposed skin. "I prefer to have you by my side dressed like sin so I'll be the envy of every man, and who knows, even some women tonight."

"Oh, I get it. I'll be your sexy accessory. Fitting for the cocky playboy." She rolls her eyes as she lists my less-than-stellar qualities. "Maybe I'll just pretend you're my boy toy. I do have a thing for men in Armani. And besides, I'm older than you."

She steps out of reach and covers her shoulders in the black wrap that was slung over her arm. "Coming?" She beckons with a come-hither look. I'm pretty sure she knows I'll follow her anywhere.

Eddie stands beside the SUV, waiting for us as we approach. When he waits for me, he never leans on the car like other drivers. He emulates a soldier's stance. But cracks start to surface as we near him. His eyes are on Kathryn, which isn't a shock under normal circumstances, but completely understandable considering what she's wearing tonight. I glance down at her to see a beaming smile targeted right at poor Eddie. Yep, he's a goner, too.

"Good evening, Eddie." Kathryn stops and kisses his cheek before entering the open door of the SUV.

"Ma'am," Eddie mumbles under a shy grin.

I follow behind Kathryn as we slide into the backbench seat. We sit on either sides of the vehicle with a body's space between. As much as I'd like to have her body next to mine, I'm thoroughly enjoying the view of Kathryn from head to toe.

I reach across the seat for her hand and rub my thumb over her soft skin. "You really do look beautiful tonight." Raising her hand, I pepper light kisses over her knuckles. And between the kisses, I decide to express what I'm feeling about her.

"I've never felt this deeply for anyone in my life. Having you here with me is my greatest accomplishment."

"Well, thanks for half of that compliment," she says with laugh. "Being an accomplishment isn't on any woman's list, though."

"Fuck, that sounded like shit." I drag my fingers through my hair, wondering if I am truly fifteen instead of thirty-two. "Poor word choice. From the moment we met, the deck was stacked against me. You were warned to stay away, and I've been trying to win you over ever since." I hope my explanation makes sense to her. She doesn't respond right away, and my nerves start to fray. One of my heels begins to tap against the floorboard as I wait.

"Relax," she says, and instantly my worry subsides. "I know what you meant. But it's not about winning me. It's about caring for me—another human being. Do you understand?"

"I think so."

"Your other conquests..." I cringe when she brings up my haunted past, the ghosts of other women who've sat in the very seat she occupies. "You won them for a night and checked them off your list of instant gratification."

"Ouch." A stinging realization hits me as I imagine how long that list is. Miles long. "I can't argue your point."

"Exactly." She tightens her fingers around mine. "Winning me over isn't another notch on your bedpost, it's about sharing ourselves and experiencing our time... together. In the bedroom and out."

She unbuckles her seatbelt and slides over the seat beside me. Her fingers find my hair and twirl the ends. The intimate touch relaxes me and makes me putty in her hands. She could ask for anything at this moment and it would be hers.

~

As we near The Standard hotel, the venue for tonight's reception, the SUV hits the bumps of the Meatpacking District's cobblestone streets. The jarring movements signal we're only a block or two away. Outside my window, I see the sidewalks brimming with the usual Saturday night crowd.

"We're getting close," I tell Kathryn. "I want to ask you one more time before we exit the SUV. Are you sure you're ready to face Thorpe?"

"Will I ever be *ready* to face him?" She hesitates for a beat. "No. But when I came back from Paris, I knew I'd eventually run into him. I worried that I'd see him for the first time by myself." She angles her body toward mine, her front touching my side and her eyes staring straight at me. "But I'm not by myself. I'm with you. Someone else he's wronged. We make a united front."

"Both our parents were destroyed by him. Mine over time. Yours in an instant," I say as she looks down when I mention the loss of her father. I place my finger under her chin. I need to tell her my next statement while looking at her. "We are two of his wrongs that will make it right together."

Leaning over, I kiss her forehead and let my lips linger there for a moment. "If you need to leave at any time, just say the word."

"Thanks, Adam." Her eyes soften at my affection. "I've thought about it today. Even talked with my mother about it. I believe I'm as ready as I'll ever be."

"Pardon, sir," Eddie calls from the driver's seat. "The red carpet entrance is on the Washington Street side, correct?"

I break away from my moment with Kathryn. "Yes, next to the Biergarten. You should see the limo line soon." I peer out the front window as we head down Thirteenth Street.

Once we stop in the line, Eddie climbs out of the SUV and opens the door for us. I exit first and offer Kathryn my hand. The stiletto heels she's wearing are no match for the uneven bricks on the streets. I have a mind to scoop her up in my arms and carry her inside. But she'd protest, I'm sure, and the paparazzi that have gathered would love to caption that photo. I settle for a firm arm around her waist where I'm practically lifting her as she walks. She eyes me as her feet leave the ground.

"So, you're helping me float into the building? Nothing unusual about that." She jabs my ribs, and I loosen my hold, but only slightly.

"Look down around your feet." I point down. "Heel-eating cobblestones." She peers down, then back up. We both crack up laughing.

A group of paparazzi are huddled close to the small red carpet area. I take Kathryn's arm in mine as we approach. Our connection shows the world we are very much together. She peeks up at me with a timid expression. An expression new to her face.

"Your first red carpet, right?"

She nods.

"They will shout questions. Demand answers. We'll walk right past them with smiling faces because they're good at finding that one frowning photo and using it." Her uncertainty disappears like magic. We're in this together. "I'll give them a little wave and tilt of the head. Some sort of acknowledgement. They hate to be ignored."

"So a smiling and polite snub?" she asks, summing it up perfectly.

"Exactly."

A few more steps and we're in the line of fire from their cameras. Flashes go off. I hear the buzz starting around us as reporters realize who's approaching them and cue their cameramen.

"Mr. Kingsley!" The first shout of my name comes from the pack. "Over here, Mr. Kingsley." Now the entire chorus joins, off key.

I turn toward the first voice yelling at me and plaster a smile across my face. Kathryn leans into me slightly as if she's trying to hide away. Truthfully, I wish we both could, so I hug her arm tighter. But I need this publicity prance in front of the media. It will add to the work I've done this week toward trying to restore confidence in my company.

"Who's that with you tonight?" The questions remain unanswered as I refuse to do the media's job for them. "What is your response to Simon Edwards' family? They blame Kings Capital for his suicide."

That question nearly causes my smile to slip and my steps to falter. This question, if true, contains facts that I haven't heard. Simon's family? I've seen this type of dirty journalism before. Emotional lies to get a rise out of you.

Still grinning from ear to ear, I stare down the journalist and give her a wave of my hand, acknowledging her presence but ignoring her questions. My actions need to show that all's well in Adam Kingsley's world and that I'm bulletproof. Literally.

"Almost at the finish line," I mumble under my breath to Kathryn.

"Thank God," she whispers in return.

Once inside the doors of the hotel, with the cameras and shouts far behind, we look at each other and let out a sigh of relief. "We survived." I take her hand as we make our way to a bank of elevators. "Press exposure is a necessary evil for me. You've been lucky as an unknown heiress."

"I think my lucky streak might be over. I'm no longer unknown." She winks. "A side effect of being attached to you."

"Attached." I roll that word around on my tongue, savoring the sound and what it means coming from her. "I like that."

"I have no doubt," she mutters. "Where to now?"

"The event is up a few floors, but I'd like to take you on a little detour." A slow smile forms on her lips. "Appears you're game, too."

"Sure," she says, picking up her step. "You're not talking about a coat closet, though? Getting caught in some form of undress is the last press you and I need."

"No, beautiful. But that does sound tempting." We stop before the elevators and wait our turn. "I'm taking you to the top."

"Another line you give the ladies," she says with a wink. "Actually, I've always wanted to visit. The Top of the Standard, right?"

"Yes. The Top. It's a favorite of mine." I hesitate and start to second-guess my idea. There could be women there I've known... intimately. But the earliness of the evening was on my side; most of the women I've met there tended to show up late and fully juiced up. Since it's only seven, I should be okay. I hope.

"A favorite of yours?" She eyes me skeptically.

"It is... or was my favorite watering hole." Kathryn's eyebrows lift as she eyes me through her lashes.

"Was?" She smirks. Can't fool this wise woman one damn bit. "So this is where you'd round up your nightly fun?"

"Hey, maybe this was a bad idea." The line for the elevators has thinned, and we're being signaled by staff to enter a car.

"Nope, I wanna see your sex stage, so to speak." She stands taller as we enter the open elevator door.

"All right." I gulp and press the button for the top floor. Everyone gets off on the third floor where the reception will be held. Only Kathryn and I remain in the car as it heads up to the top.

"Come here," I say, motioning my head to the side. My coaxing works as she falls into my open arms. "You have nothing to worry about."

Kathryn's lips curl into a smile. "But you do." The slight squint in her eyes delivers a warning that I'll heed.

"This is true," I say.

She places her hands flat on my chest and slowly slides them up until they're laced behind my neck. Our position and her plunging neckline give me a perfect view of her breasts. I reach inside her dress to fondle the fullness of her breast and feel only skin, no lace or silk beneath.

"You're not wearing a bra, and I like it." There is not enough fabric on the top of her dress to cover straps or hooks.

"No," she whispers. My fingers find her pebbled nipple all ready for my touch.

My cock hits high above her hip. I place my free hand on her ass then push her against me. Her eyes widen when she feels my arousal. "See what you do to me, beautiful." Our lips connect and our tongues touch as my declaration fades away.

The sound of the elevator opening steals the moment from us. We pull apart but don't fully separate from one another. I drape my arm around her possessively as we exit onto the top floor.

We turn to our right and I immediately regret this little detour. At the reception stand is a former hookup of epic portions. She was part of a bondage *ménage à trois* that started in this very bar. I brought Tom here one night for drinks before he was married. He left alone, but I stayed.

I consider pulling Kathryn back onto the elevator and leaving, but she gazes out the window in awe. The clear glass wall gives a view that stretches out over Manhattan. The twinkling lights of the city shine bright.

"Adam, this place is stunning," she proclaims while tugging on my arm.

Before I can speak, Ms. Bondage sidles up to me.

"Adam Kingsley." Her tone is sarcastic and pointed. The hand placed firmly on her hip accents her displeasure. "You remember me, don't you?"

I dig down deep in search of the best bullshit smile I can find. "Of course. It's been awhile. How have you been?"

"Fine," she says. "I wasn't sure."

"This is Kathryn Delcour, my girlfriend." My introduction is met with a wry smile from Kathryn. I don't have to explain anything to her; she knows this woman and I have a *past*.

"Hello." Kathryn greets Ms. Bondage with polished breeding. "And you are?" Thank fuck. The pressure of remembering Ms. Bondage's name is taken care of for me. But Kathryn's side-eye tells me I owe her. Big.

"Ashley Marshall." Ms. Bondage rubs her wrists in what has to be a phantom memory of our night together. My cock hardens like a fucking traitor. "My sorority sister and I were here a few months ago—"

I interrupt Ms. Bondage before she can utter another word. "Please tell your friend hello for me." Now comes the lying through my teeth part. "It was a nice to see you again. If you'll excuse us."

I grab Kathryn's hand with every intention of heading toward the bar. She responds to my escape with a giggle as I drag her away.

"Uh. Okay, sure." Ms. Bondage speaks to our backs as we leave.

Once we've cleared The Top's doors, the bar in front of us becomes my target. I want something strong. Shots, preferably.

"I need a drink."

"Hey, Adam?" Kathryn addresses me as we near the bar. "I know who she was and it's okay."

"Seriously?" There's no way what she had to endure was okay. "You don't deserve to have my trysts shoved in your face."

"Adam—"

"First I need a shot. What do you want?" I tap on the counter and alert the bartender. He raises his chin, letting me know I've been seen.

"Whatever you're having." She shakes her head with a half-smile.

"I brought you up here for some liquid courage and fun before we're forced to be in the same room as Thorpe. Instead you met Ms. Bondage." I clamp my mouth shut, wishing that nickname hadn't slipped out. "I mean Ashley."

"Ms. Bondage." She chuckles. I expel every molecule of air inside my lungs, because she's amused instead of pissed. Which is good but still embarrassing.

"Yes." I hang my head. "If you want the details, I'll tell you. Why hide the fact that I've fucked around this city like a dog in heat?"

The bartender makes his way to us, finally. This conversation will require a drink in each fist.

"Good evening," the bartender says. Squinting, I try to place him, or remember a name. Nothing. He gets the drift. "What can I get you... two?" He looks at Kathryn and gapes like a stunned fish.

"We'll have three shots of your best tequila. Two for me and one for the beautiful lady." Kathryn looks at me in approval. "What would you suggest?"

"Since you have the lady with you, I'd choose the Casa Dragones. No after burn and very smooth." The bartender's suggestion sounds perfect. I don't want Kathryn's mouth on fire... yet.

"Great. And don't forget the limes," I say before the bartender heads off to fetch our drinks.

"Here you are in your tux at a bar." Kathryn skims over me with a twinkle in her eye. "A top leader in the financial world, and we're doing shots."

The bartender sits the shots and limes down in front of us. I reach into my pocket and throw a couple of hundreds on the bar. "Keep the change."

"Wow, thanks." He walks away, looking like he won the fucking lottery. I grin, knowing my simple act of generosity made a difference in his life.

"Now back to that man in a tux and leader of the financial world," I say sarcastically. "He'd like to make a toast before we slam these down."

I pick up a glass and hand it to Kathryn along with a slice of lime. "I can't remember the last time I slammed a shot." She raises the glass with the lime in her hand. Wearing a contagious smile, she giggles under her breath. I'm powerless to her, of course, and return the smile.

"Here's to meeting you. Best damn thing that's ever happened to me." Our glasses clink, and Kathryn follows my lead as I toss back my head and down the smooth tequila.

"Wow," she says between panted breaths. "My mouth is on fire." She uses a hand to wave some air into her mouth.

Shaking my head, I can't help but laugh at her cute display.

"Here." I take the glass and lime from her hand. "Let me help."

Her eyes widen as I pull her flush against me. Bending down, my lips meet hers. Our tongues lazily play together in a hot kiss tasting of tequila and lime. My lips leave hers sooner than I want, but we're at The Top, standing at the bar. Not the best place for full-blown PDA.

"Better?" I peer down at her flushed face and hope the color comes from my kiss, not the tequila.

"Whoa." She whistles. "Better but still breathless."

"Good." I down my second shot and take her hand in mine. "Let's head to the reception, beautiful." She gives me a firm nod, and we're off to the monster a few stories below.

Chapter 15

Kathryn and I take the elevator down to the third floor after our little escapade at The Top. We are both a little buzzed from the quick intake of alcohol, but nothing sloppy, I hope. After all, the crowd assembled tonight for the meet and greet reception contains the elite and well-groomed of the world. Not a place to show up drunk, but a liquor-induced relaxed would be very acceptable and quite the norm.

We circle around the reception area, hand-shaking and hobnobbing like pros. Various men walk up to greet us. I believe they're hoping to gain a closer look at Kathryn's cleavage as their eyes hardly leave her breasts. They avoid looking at me because I'm rather dull in comparison to the beauty at my side.

I possessively stroke the skin on her shoulder in a silent declaration that she's mine. They admire her and envy me as though I hold the keys to the gates of heaven. And for me, she's as close as I'll get to that ethereal place.

Since I stepped into the room, I've searched for Thorpe. Once I spotted him, I zoomed in on him like radar locking on a target. We haven't made eye contact yet, but I'm bracing myself for the moment when we do.

Kathryn and I move about the room, avoiding the fucker at all costs. Thorpe moves right, we move left. He steps forward, we retreat. Kathryn has no idea I've been maneuvering our position as we go from one introduction or conversation to another on purpose. Tonight, I'm her protector. No one will touch her but me.

Conversations in the room center around numbers, profit and losses, and the hope of a strong economic recovery. The kind of talk that makes the mind wander after having a couple drinks with a beautiful woman at your side.

"I have a brilliant idea. One more drink and we head out for some real food." I've made my appearance at the reception, and the finger food they serve at these events wouldn't fill a mouse. "The fried kind."

"Greasy?" she asks, her eyes wide and hopeful.

"The best the city has," I say. "The Shake Shack or bust."

Kathryn laughs. "I haven't indulged since I moved back from Paris. So I'm all in. Why don't you get another drink while I visit the ladies' room."

I scan the people in the room and spot Thorpe several feet away from us—the closest he's been to us all evening. An escape to the bar and restroom would be smart since they're both in the opposite direction from where he's standing. I have a feeling seeing Kathryn and I together works as a repellant to keep him at bay. After all, he's fucked us over on a very personal level. Even here tonight, he's likely fucked over someone else in this room, and they're too chicken shit to stop him. Not me, though.

"Sure, I'll fetch us a refill." I nod in the direction of the restrooms. I know their placement very well... for several reasons. One for the purpose they were built for. Another to get a blow job after an event cleared out for the night. "But please wait for me right outside the door. I don't want you wandering around without me."

"Yes, sir." She salutes before turning down the short hall to the restrooms.

"Right here, Kathryn," I call behind her, and a teasing smile greets me when she looks over her shoulder. I point to the ground at my feet and mouth the words, "right here." She gives me a quick thumbs-up before disappearing behind a door.

I hurry to the bar so I can get back by the time she's done with the restroom. The second I make eye contact with the bartender I call him over.

"Two more, please. Glenlivet and your best chardonnay."

The bartender nods, grabs some empty glasses, and turns to fill my order. As I wait, the hair on the back of my neck prickles as the weight of someone's shadow falls on me. The counter-to-ceiling mirrors behind the bar show me exactly who's there.

Shit.

Thorpe. I swear his presence is like a dragon on my back.

"Adam." His use of my name causes my stomach to clench. I lower my head and close my eyes before turning around to address him. I dig deep to bring up a blank mask. I can't betray my true feelings of disgust when I face him.

"Xavier," I deadpan.

"So... Kathryn Swanson?" He speaks with a poker face similar to mine. A chill runs the length of my body when I stare into his cold, blank eyes. Nothing. There's nothing behind them at all.

"Her last name is Delcour now," I tell him, but I want to move the subject on to something else. If he keeps discussing Kathryn, my fist will end up on his jaw. "What can I help you with?"

He throws back his head and laughs as though I amuse him. "Okay, sport. I see that's one topic you'd like to avoid." My balled-up hands begin to shake, so I tuck them in my pockets for safety. "I need to change the time on that meeting you requested. Wednesday at two works for me."

My time doesn't matter apparently. He couldn't give two fucks. He sees himself as the Master of the Universe.

173

I have no idea what my Wednesday afternoon schedule looks like, but nothing will keep me from seeing him, presenting him with the glaring evidence of his illegal activities, and then funneling the information to the hungry press. Once his misdeeds are disclosed, they will eat him up like a school of piranhas.

"I'll make it work," I say sternly.

"All right, but I'm not sure what you're up to." He moves closer to me before he speaks further. "I'm very leery of you, son." He says son likes it's a dirty word. "So I'm going to have my attorney at the meeting."

The balls on this man are like boulders. "I'm not your son and never will be." I spit the words out, a purely involuntary reaction. "Never call me by that term again. And so we're clear, I will be bringing someone, too. If you don't mind." Whether he agrees or not, Peters will be with me on Wednesday. I'd never go into the lion's den alone.

"I suppose," he answers with a sneer. His hatred of me is deep-seated. I'll never be anything other than a mistake to this man.

Thorpe glances over toward the restrooms. Kathryn stands near the spot we were supposed to meet, but a group of men has circled around her. I can only see glimpses of the red silk of her dress and the dark swirl of her hair.

"Enjoy your evening," he hisses through his clenched teeth. I swing my gaze to meet his, and I know he's referring to her. Thorpe melts into a crowd of men before I can respond or get my fists out of my pockets.

I turn around to face the bar and knock back my new glass of scotch. I decide it's time to rescue my woman from the pack of dogs sniffing around her, so I push off from the bar and head in her direction.

Her seductive smile pulls me across the room, the powerful connection humming between us fueling my every footstep. I am going to steal her away from this crowd and kiss her lush, red lips because the last place she needs to be is in Thorpe's line of sight. He doesn't deserve to even look upon her shadow.

As I make my way across the ballroom to her, several faceless people try to get my attention. I nod some vague sort of acknowledgment and continue my path to Kathryn. Finally, I'm at her side and address the men huddled around her.

"Good evening, gentlemen." I place my right arm protectively over Kathryn's shoulder and draw her to my side.

I bow my head to nuzzle her neck, and each man draws back from the tight circle around Kathryn. In an effort not to alienate them all, I shake a couple of hands and suffer through some awkward introductions meant to be an apology for encroaching on my territory.

"Beautiful, are you ready?" She grins up at me, quite amused by my little pissing contest. "If you'll excuse us, gentlemen."

A chorus of good-byes surrounds us, and we quickly acknowledge them before turning toward the door. I pull out my phone and text Eddie one word. *Ready*. It's the only indication he needs to pick us up.

Once we've cleared the group, Kathryn gazes up at me with her brows knitted together. "I saw Thorpe talking to you, so I stayed away. What did he say?"

"I have a meeting with him on Wednesday," I mutter in a low voice, hoping it will soften the impact of my words.

"Did you say a *meeting*?" Her eyes are wide with fear.

"Yes, it has to do with some business he's conducting in Jersey. He mentioned it today in one of the meetings." We walk into the waiting elevator alone, and I push the button for the lobby. "But there's nothing to worry about over this."

"I can't believe you're meeting with him. After all we did to stay away from him tonight... It makes no sense. I don't feel like you're telling me the whole story here."

She moves away from me and places a hand on her hip, and dammit, I know I've ignited her fire now.

"Nothing good can come from meeting with him or trying to get revenge," she says. I flash her an innocent look at that word. "Believe me. He squashes people like bugs under his feet."

"Oh, beautiful. Trust me." After moving to her side, I thread my fingers through hers and bring them to my lips. "Please."

"I do. Just be careful. Can you promise me that?"

"Being careful around Thorpe is a necessity. So yes, I can promise you that." I cross my heart, but I hate that I'm lying to her. It's a necessary evil, though. "And I'm not going alone to the meeting."

"Hayes?" she asks with her forehead drawn.

"Yes." If I tell her Peters will be joining me at the meeting, she'll know there's more than business involved. So I keep his attendance quiet and change the subject fast. "All those men around you. Does that happen often? Something I should be prepared for?"

Kathryn's cheeks pinken, and she elbows me in the side. I flinch, pretending it hurt.

"Oh, cut it out. That was good your good side. What about that display of testosterone back there?"

I bend down to whisper in her ear just as the door to the elevator opens. "Pure and simple, those men wanted to take what is mine." I bite down lightly on her earlobe, marking her, and a tiny whimpered sigh escapes her lips.

Chapter 16

"Back to The Pierre, sir?" Eddie looks at me in the rearview mirror.

"Not yet." I glance over at Kathryn to confirm our previous discussion. She nods with an eager smile. "My woman wants The Shake Shack."

"The one on Columbus, correct?" he asks before merging into the street's traffic.

"Yes, that's the one." I pat Eddie's shoulder from the back seat and sit back next to Kathryn. "Eddie used to take Tom and me there when he first started working for me. We'd go when we needed something to soak up the booze late at night. That was before he met his wife, Lois."

"Oh, so you used to carouse around with Tom?"

"During our twenties, I used to hit the club scene with Tom. Patrick, our other partner, married right after we started Kings. But Tom didn't meet Lois until after Kings hit the Fortune 500 list three years ago. That's when I hired Eddie." I glance at the rearview mirror and see Eddie's smiling mug reflecting back at me. To think about it, this is the first real conversation he's ever heard from the back of the SUV. Hell, it's one of the first times I've left the privacy divider down. How things have changed.

"I see. So after Tom met Lois, you were unleashed to roam around town. No one to act as your conscience." Kathryn analyzes the situation perfectly, as usual.

"Yes. " I remember back to the times he pulled me out of bars before I was able to find a woman to wet my dick. I think he half fell in love with Lois as a way of escaping our nights out. "Tom kept me somewhat in line."

" 'Somewhat'?" she scoffs and then laughs.

"Come here." I pull her closer to me. "Cliché as it sounds, I think those days are over for me. Wait, I *know* they're over." I lean down and kiss her head as she cuddles into me. "Can people really change?"

"I don't know if you changed, Adam. I think it's more likely the real you is finally starting to surface." She wraps an arm around my waist and hugs me tight. I close my eyes and revel in her touch. "So who did you hang out with after Tom starting seeing Lois?"

"No one, really. I pretty much just went from one dinner or charity event to another." The nights all blended together back then. It played out the same way: drink some scotch, eat some food, and find some woman to fuck. "Nothing really stood out."

"That sounds horrible." She grazes her lips across my neck at my collar and loosens the bowtie until it's hanging free. The buttons at the top of my shirt are next. One by one she undoes them, and her lips follow her fingers down my chest. "Psych 101. You were lonely and used sex to fill the void in here." She taps her finger against my chest and climbs onto my lap where I cradle her in my arms. The place she belongs.

"You're right," I tell her because it's the truth. My life today is nothing like my life a couple of weeks ago, before I met Kathryn. And how I felt then can't compare to how I feel now. Our lips touch for a soft kiss, one meant for comfort versus passion.

"I worry about you going to see Thorpe on Wednesday. After all these years, why now? Was it what I told you about him and me?" She asks me the one question I don't want to answer.

"It will be a quick visit, I promise. Just to discuss his business in Jersey." I omit the dark details behind the meeting because I know she would disapprove of me seeking revenge. When the anvil falls on Thorpe and his empire, I don't want to miss seeing it hit him hard. So my disclosure of his wrongdoings has to be in person.

"Okay, but I can't shake the bad feeling I'm having right now." She gazes up at me with pouty lips. The kind of look that could make me promise her anything.

"Everything will be fine." I caress her cheek and slip my fingers in her soft hair. "There's another Thorpe I'm meeting on Wednesday night, right?"

She perks up in my lap, and the melancholy mood fades. "Yes, I can't wait. It's more than a birthday celebration for my mother. It's the meeting of two long-lost brothers."

I cringe when I think about Ollie's current opinion of me. He respects me in the world of business, but worries I'll break Kathryn's heart. "I'm more concerned about meeting Ollie than the meeting earlier in the day with our asshole of a father."

"Ollie's going to love you. You're pretty irresistible like that."

"The charms I've used to win you over would be lost on him," I say while tickling her side. "From the articles I've read about him, he seems like a no bullshit kind of guy."

"That would describe him pretty well," she says. "He's flying in tomorrow and wants to meet me for dinner. I think I should tell him about you then. Are you all right with that?"

"I think it's best to tell him beforehand. Springing it on him over dinner on Wednesday could ruin your mother's birthday. And I don't want that to happen to her."

"Me, neither. I'll talk to him tomorrow night. I don't normally bring up his father when we talk, so it might be best to have him over my apartment for dinner. It could be a tough conversation for a lot of reasons." She bites her lip in worry and I hold her a little tighter. "But I think he'll be excited he has a brother when it's all said and done."

"There's something about us both being shunned by the same man that could bring two brothers together. Although I find Thorpe's rejection of Ollie worse. To have a father practically disown you in the public eyes is beyond cruel."

"Ollie rejected Thorpe first…" She takes a deep breath before continuing. "After everything happened with me."

"True," I say, trying to remain calm, but in reality I'm fired up. "I'm glad you had Ollie to get you through that time."

"That summer was hell for sure. We both lost our fathers in a way. Although Ollie's loss was by choice." She stares out the window with a grimace, likely remembering those ugly times.

"Yeah." I agree as the SUV stops at the curb in front of The Shake Shack. "Looks like we're here," I whisper, breaking through her pensive mood. She gazes at me, and my heart warms when I see a small smile forming.

"I have no clue what to get. It's been years since I've been here."

"What's your favorite flavor?" I ask.

"Vanilla." She licks her lips.

"Really?" I chuckle, surprised by her choice, and squeeze her as she sits in my lap.

"Don't act so surprised. I like vanilla on occasion." She winks.

"I can handle vanilla, beautiful." I can't contain my grin. "Hey, Eddie," I call up to him.

"Yes, sir." Eddie turns his head.

"Two of the usual, but a vanilla shake for both of us." I order up the standard fare for when I visit here: a Shackburger, fries, and shake. "Hold on, I'll get you some money."

Kathryn slides off my lap so I can retrieve my wallet. I hand Eddie a hundred. "Thanks, Eddie.

"Yes, thank you, Eddie." Kathryn beams. I pat the seat next to me. "Get back over here."

"I guess you're used to bossing people around." She's being sarcastic, but she's right. I've fallen into this persona that demands rather than asks graciously.

"Probably. Something I need to work on."

"Yes."

"Noted." I file that promise away. "I'll work on my manners."

"You better." Her kidding becomes obvious as she tries to mask her smile with her seriousness. She peeks out the window toward the burger joint again. "It looks like there's quite a line inside for Eddie."

"There's always a line this time of night. Weekend or not." I pull her up onto my lap when I have a brilliant idea. "There are things we could do to pass the time." I wiggle my eyebrows as she smiles up at me. "Is that a yes?"

She answers by placing her lips on mine. Our tongues tangle in a sweet embrace as she straddles my lap. Her pussy presses flush against my already hard dick. "Is this what you had in mind?"

"Yes, but I'll add some of this, too." I cup her ass and pull her even tighter to me. I'm hoping to hit her in just the right spot.

"Oh God," she says, confirming my target has been met. Her head falls back as I continue thrusting forward.

"It's going to take Eddie awhile to get the food and the windows are tinted..." I squeeze her ass harder. "So undo the top of your dress for me, baby."

I lick my lips as she quickly glances outside the window and raises her hands. The ties of her dress drop to her lap and her full breasts are unveiled.

I cup her breasts in my palms. Her lips part as I kiss one of her nipples, suck it into my mouth, and flick my tongue over the sweet tip. I rub my thumb over the other nipple to increase her pleasure. Her hips begin to circle against my length. I join the dance as we move to a silent beat.

"Oh God. You're killing me," she says between breaths.

I kiss a trail up her flushed neck. Stopping at her ear, I whisper, "Feel good, beautiful?"

I resume my wandering along her jaw until I find her lips and we kiss. The passion increases along with my heartbeat.

"Yes. Don't stop," she murmurs against my lips.

"I'm going to make it worse and better all at once." She shivers at my words. "Hike up your dress."

Her fingers shake and fumble at the hem of her dress, but she raises it up her creamy thighs. I want to feel their softness, so I follow her hands with mine. One holds her sweet, lace-covered ass while the other finds the soaked satin between her thighs.

"You're so wet for me, baby." I pass my finger over her satin-covered clit and down to where she's wettest. As I drag my finger back up, I let it roam underneath the edge of the elastic and feel her flinch in my arms.

"Shh," I say as her breaths quicken. "Let me make you come. Enjoy the feeling."

She's so slick, but I want her wetter, and I want to be buried deep in her heat. I take what I want and plunge my fingers into her.

"Like that!" she cries and arches her back, bringing her nipples close to my mouth. Like a moth to a flame, I can't resist devouring her pink peaks. I lick and twirl my tongue in sync with my fingers circling in her pussy.

I fuck her with my fingers until her legs begin to shake. "I'm close," she says before letting out a cry.

"Ah…" Her body stiffens as her moans fill the silence of the car. I continue to stroke her gently through her release. Finally spent, she collapses against me in a silky red heap. I bury my face in her hair, smelling her Shalimar scent.

My impatient cock remains hard and desperate to be inside her. But when I lift my head, I catch a glimpse of Eddie walking out the door with takeout bags.

Shit! Eddie will see Kathryn topless when he gets back in the SUV. I have to cover her back up. Her breaths are beginning to even out as I weave my hands through her thick hair in search of the ties to her dress. I locate them, move her hair quickly to the side, and retie them faster than Houdini. I ease her dress down over her thighs just as I hear the sound of the driver's door opening. A flash of the interior lights sends Kathryn into hyperalert mode.

"Holy—" She hides her face against my shoulder before clamoring off my lap and falling into the seat next to me just as Eddie settles into his seat. She adjusts her dress around her legs, detangles her hair, and then gives me a serious once over. I return the look, and we both crack up.

"That was way too fucking close," I whisper as Eddie gets situated and closes his door.

"I feel like we're back in high school," she says after brushing her lips against my jaw.

"Your pleasure is mine." I stare at her mouth as she licks over her lips. My neglected dick twitches when I see them. "And believe me, I couldn't have done that to you in high school. I was fucking clueless then."

"Pardon me, sir." Eddie clears his throat.

"No problem, Eddie. Thanks for getting our burgers. Tell me you ordered one for yourself, too." He always ate with Tom and me. The three of us would turn on the some old school rap music and scarf down our takeout in the car. We pretty much resembled animals feeding in the wild.

"Yes, sir. Just like old times." Eddie smiles into the rearview mirror, holding up his shake. "Where do you want me to take you two? Back to The Pierre?"

"Give me a second, okay?" The question for the rest of the night is still up in the air.

"The night's still young..." I throw it out there, hoping she'll catch it and run with it.

"It's young and you're still hard as a rock," she says in a low and raspy whisper.

"True on both accounts. Any idea how to deal with the 'rock' part?" I smirk as she shakes her head, laughing.

"As a matter of fact, I have a brilliant idea. We're eating fast food, so let's go back to..." She squints her eyes. "What do you call my office again?"

"The harem tent."

"Oh, yes, the 'harem tent.' " She snorts. "Let's go back to my apartment tonight. We need some..." She stops and bends closer to my ear. "Gourmet fucking."

I can't hide my excitement when I say, "Eddie, drive us back to Kathryn's apartment but take the short way *through* Central Park." I place my lips against her ear so my next words are spoken in private. "He needs to hurry because now I'm hungry to get inside your sweet pussy. Fuck the food; I want to fuck you."

"Sounds good." I watch a slight shiver run over her body, and I imagine her nipples are now hard and pebbled for me.

"We need some music." I announce. "Hey, Eddie, play some Run-D.M.C. for old times' sake."

I reach through the divider to grab our burgers and shakes. "Vanilla for the most non-vanilla woman I know. Even your perfume is spicy."

"Always keep them guessing. A fabulous quote from my mother." She winks, and I smile as I imagine sassy Ava saying those words. I pass her a burger and fries from the grease-soaked bag.

Eddie drives through Central Park as we unwrap our burgers and prepare to sink our teeth into them.

"Looking forward to your harem tent if we don't end up in a fucking food coma first." She licks her lips and takes the first bite. And damn, all I can think is how I wish it was my cock in her hot mouth instead. Maybe later tonight I'll get lucky. A man can hope.

Chapter 17

After driving through Central Park, Eddie dropped Kathryn and me back at her apartment. We quickly settled into her overstuffed couch after eating our burgers and greasy fries. Kathryn had given up halfway through her meal and handed me the rest.

Maybe it was the lack of sleep over the last week combined with all the food, but my eyes grew heavy and I sank like a ship against her cushions. The promise of some fun in her harem tent might have been in jeopardy if she hadn't rescued me with coffee.

Two cups later, I am no longer drowsy.

"Thanks for the coffee. I'm more awake now." I quirk my brow and smile. "How about you?"

"I'm good." She places her cup on the table in front of us. A glow starts to form in her eyes when she says, "But I could be better."

"Anything I can do?" I lean closer as we face each other on the couch. "I'm more than willing to help."

"I figured you might be, but I want to be honest with you." She looks away for a second. "You remember the position we were in when I asked you to go back to memories from earlier in your life?"

"How could I forget that?" I give her a smirk and she matches it.

"True," she says with a laugh. "Well I've never done that position without my clothes on. My experience has been more on the clinical side, not actual participation, and I'd like to remedy that with you tonight."

She moves closer to me on the couch so our knees are now touching.

"So you're talking about the position where you straddled my lap, but with no clothes on, right?" Her response is an excited nod of her head. "Count me in on that—and any other position."

"Come with me, then." She rises from the couch and takes my hand. I follow her down the hall to her harem tent.

Darkness shrouds the room as she opens one of the double doors. She drops my hand and walks over to the light switch, leaving me feeling bereft of her warm touch. Once the lights shine, she dims them to a soft glow, exactly how they were during our first and only time in the room.

"Is this what all Tantra rooms look like?"

Kathryn busies herself with lighting various candles placed throughout the room.

"Most instructors like me decorate with some type of Far Eastern flare since the tantric concept came from India," she answers while adjusting the sound system. A melody of hypnotic beats plays through the speakers hidden throughout the room.

It transports me back to our first experience in this room. I walk over to the large cream-colored cushion in the middle of the floor and stare down at it thoughtfully. My cock comes alive at the memory of her hips pressing and grinding against mine. I never thought dry-humping could be so intense.

As powerful as our sex was that night, the emotional healing I experienced when I let my old memories and feelings flood my mind changed and liberated me. Since that night, I've spoken about my mother and my past freely with Kathryn on several occasions. I let myself go back to the days of my childhood after ten years of suppressing them, and I couldn't have done it without her showing me how.

"What are you thinking?" Kathryn stands next to me. I feel her gentle touch on my back. I shed my tuxedo jacket in the living room, so I can feel the heat of her fingers through my dress shirt.

"Back to our night here." I point down at the cushion before us and look down at her face. A slow smile builds on her lips. She remembers the night the same way, too.

"Let's relive it but make it even better. Skin against skin." She moves in front of me and unbuttons my shirt. She stands so close; I feel her breath against my exposed skin.

"Yes, skin against skin." I briefly shut my eyes as she moves her fingers over my shoulders and down my arms to remove my shirt. "Your touch feels like fire."

Kathryn kisses my bare chest and my nipples, tickling each one with her tongue. My cock twitches.

"I want you naked." I loosen the tie at her neck and pull down the short zipper at the waist of her dress. The red silk falls at her feet and only a pair of lace panties adorns her body.

"I hate these pants." She smirks as my belt and pants come undone under her hands. She pushes them down, along with my boxer briefs, and my erection points free and ready.

Kathryn goes to her knees and helps me step out of my pants. Once they're removed, my socks follow. I'm left standing before her with nothing covering me. I'm fully open and exposed as she eyes my cock.

Biting her lip, she lays her hands on my legs and trails them upward. Alternating one hand and then the other she encloses my erection and moves in a gentle exchange from the base to the aching tip. The hunger in her touch matches the hunger in her eyes.

"God," I moan while the feeling and sight of her holding me drives my senses wild.

She tongues the length of my cock, letting her long licks travel my erection, teasing me. Killing me slowly. She ends her journey at the crease on my head, tasting the liquid starting to seep out. Then she crosses over to my hipbones, lightly kissing along the way and making a trail up my torso as she rises to her feet.

I wrap my arms around her and draw her against me. We sway to the beat of the music as I inhale her scent. The fragrance of spice and sex mix together, searing into my brain. The hot combination triggers a sensuous high.

"Let's sit on the mat." She pulls me forward.

"You lead and I'll follow. You're the expert here, beautiful."

We sit cross-legged, facing each other. Our knees press together, and I notice she still has on her damned panties.

"You missed something." I shake my head while staring down at the offending piece of cloth. "Skin to skin, remember?"

"You're right," she says without hesitation while sitting up on her knees and easing her panties down her legs.

"Here, let me help." I curl my fingers inside the elastic waistband and yank them down. I should have been gentle because they rip in my hands. "Sorry, baby." I shrug while throwing them to the side.

"That's the second pair, you brute," she says, but the flame in her eyes betrays her feelings.

Instead of returning to the cushion on the floor, she climbs into my lap with her legs wrapped around my waist. My breath hitches as her wet pussy and my dick make contact, my hardness meeting her soft warmth. On instinct, I push forward as I grab her ass.

"Whoa." She holds me back by the shoulders. I loosen my hold while giving her a wide-eyed look. "Don't play innocent, mister. You know the rules. Slow with patience."

I smirk, caught in my hormone-driven actions. "Okay. I just can't help myself with your pussy so close to me. I have this strong urge bury myself inside you."

I ghost my lips over her neck and jaw line. Her breathing exhilarates as I kiss and suck on her tender skin. I end my path with a nibble on her earlobe. "I am ready whenever you are."

We're positioned nose-to-nose and eye-to-eye. I wait for instruction, but Kathryn stares at me without blinking. An intensity rolls off her, and I'm caught up in its waves.

"Remember the time with the coins and special massage when I brought you close to an orgasm then pulled you back?"

"Of course. How could I forget that torture? It was fucking sweet, but torture nonetheless."

"Tonight will be similar. We'll be reaching for plateaus before our release. As we get close to orgasm, we'll level off. Not stopping the pleasure completely, just savoring it. Then we will build from each new place. When we are at the final plateau, I'll tell you. There will be no holding back then. I'm aiming for the sweetest torture you've ever had."

"Me, too, baby." I bring my lips to hers in a kiss of thanks and expectation. "I'm the luckiest fucker to have you."

"I agree." She giggles as I kiss across her cheeks. "Okay, enough talking. And no moving below the hips as of right now." I frown and she smiles. "Don't worry, when the time comes, you'll know. Patience, you horny devil."

"I'll follow your lead." I hold up my hand like I'm swearing under oath.

"Rub your right hand over my chest, but don't touch my breasts." Kathryn takes my hand and guides my touch, rubbing circles around her chest and down her cleavage. It's similar to the motion she did when I first sat in this room with her. The night I faced my past and confronted the demons surrounding my mother's death.

She places a hand over mine as it lies over her heart. "Follow my lead."

Gently she glides her palm over my knuckles, teaching me how to touch her. Eventually she drops her hand to her lap, allowing me to explore on my own.

"Eyes," she says and I respond without wavering when I meet her gaze head on.

Her eyes appear a deep navy in the darkened room. Their beauty mesmerizes me, pulling me deeper into their spell. Her chin tilts down and she eyes me through her lashes.

"Breathe with me. I'll inhale and you exhale." Her shoulders rise, and I wait to inhale until she releases her breath.

We exhale then inhale. One breath followed by another.

Our eyes pierce and penetrate deep into each other's souls.

The tempo of the music matches the beat of our hearts.

The smell of the candles mixes with the scent of sex to intoxicate our brains like a drug. The subdued light from the flickering flames bathes us in sensual shadows.

Our senses are saturated and full of lust and something much more that I can't describe. Even the air tastes heavy.

Minutes go by as the sensations of the massage intensify. She eases herself against my erection. My breathing gets out of sync with hers when her pussy sits so close, and I can't take it yet. Scrunching my face and trying to refocus, I get back on task.

Once we are breathing together again, she squeezes her strong legs around my back. I reach around her, tentatively cup her ass, and press her even closer into my cock. I look to her in a silent plea for approval. She answers me with a curl of her lips.

Her hand at my heart migrates upward to my shoulders. The tips of her fingers play a soft melody on my skin, a relaxing tune. I'm tempted to close my eyes and drift away in her touch, but I know the rules and the importance of eye contact.

"Oh, Kathryn. Your touch," I mumble as my skin prickles in sensation, like fire racing over every inch of my skin. She kisses me, and I can't get enough of her taste. When our tongues start moving in a circle, her hips begin to rotate in tandem. She pulls her lips from mine and our eyes lock, but hers are even darker this time.

Step-by-step we climb higher up the tantric ladder. Our eyes stay connected, breathing together, our touches comforting. The wetness of her pussy presses against me as she slides over my cock with each move of her hips.

"I want to be inside you. Please?"

"Inside me is where you belong." My heart races when I hear her heated words.

She brings her hand between us and grasps hold of my cock. Her legs raise off mine just enough so my erection grazes the entrance of her sex.

With her eyes fixed on mine, she lowers herself onto me. The tip of my cock breaks through her folds, and her body stills as her eyes shine with desire.

It takes all my willpower to remain motionless and not shove my hips upward into her soft warmth. My muscles shake with need. Just one quick thrust and I'd be buried deep in her hot pussy.

She anchors her hands on my shoulder before she moves. Then finally, inch by glorious inch, she lowers herself, and my cock finds its home inside her.

"Oh!" she cries out while tightening around me. "God, so deep." She tosses her head back and circles her hips.

Her tits tempt me as she arches backward. I bring my lips to them and suck her nipple into my mouth. Her hips rotate around me faster and match the twirls of my tongue as it licks over hers.

"I have to slow this down." She's breathless and sits up so that we're once again eye-to-eye. She slows down her hips.

"Our first plateau," she whispers to me, her eyes hooded with want.

"I want more." I'm not above begging. She fulfills my needy request by raising and lowering herself on my cock. Her movements are deliberate and slow, making me ache inside for more. All I have left to do is thrust up and meet each push. I grab her ass harder, and try to hold back part of my desire to push ahead for more.

Minutes sail by as we continue to climb in our pleasure. Higher and higher we step until she slows us to an almost painful stop. We catch our breath and fix our gazes once again, neither looking away. A focused concentration gathers the sexual energy between us as the world around us has faded away.

I'm floating on a lover's high while Kathryn slides her hands over my body and her hips join my thrusts. She leaves me weak and defenseless as we push through plateau after plateau. I silently pray for mercy as my need to release inside her becomes more than I can bear.

"No pulling back this time." She attacks my lips, and I run my hands all over her body in a frantic act of desperation.

I hold onto her tight as I plunge ahead. My delayed release builds within me, and I don't want the powerful feeling to end. But I feel it tagging my back and running down my spine. Finally, it tackles me to the ground, and I explode inside her.

"Fuck!" I yell. Her pussy clutches around me as she miraculously joins me with her own climax.

Coming down from our mutual high, we collapse on our sides onto the cushiony mat. Our gazes remain stuck like glue. As our labored breaths begin to calm, a wide grin of shear bliss spreads across Kathryn's face. Pure contentment. I skim my fingers along her flushed cheek and move a stray hair away. Leaning in to kiss the tip of her nose, previously unspoken and guarded words leave me.

"Kathryn," I say seriously. The haze in her eyes evaporates as I capture her attention. "I love you." I pause as she searches my face. I hope she's not wondering if I'm feeding her a line. "Truthfully, I've only spoken those words to one other person in my entire life."

"Oh, Adam, I believe you. That makes your words even more special to me." She pushes her hands through my hair. I move my head to mimic the twist and pull of her fingers. "Part of me wants to say you're crazy for already feeling this way. We've known each other for such a short time. But I can't deny that I'm falling for you. Maybe we're both a little nuts."

"Perhaps." I laugh. "I've felt this way for some time. I think it really hit me when I thought you were going to die. The thought of something happening to you... of Simon..." I look into her eyes, pained at the thought. "I knew then there was something special about my feelings for you. They were deeper than I've ever experienced."

Kathryn brushes her fingers over my jaw and brings them back up to my hair. "I felt the same way when I heard Simon's gun go off and you fell to the ground. I screamed for you *and* for me. I thought I might have lost you. Just like when I'd witnessed Jean-Paul's death."

Her eyes blur with unshed tears.

"You witnessed his death?" I catch a tear as it runs down her cheek. "I had no idea."

"Yes, he was skiing ahead of me, but he turned, looking uphill to find me. He ran straight into a tree. Never saw it coming." She shivers in my arms. "All I could do was watch in horror."

"It's okay, baby." I squeeze her in my arms, comforting her as she quietly cries.

"You know my mother was right about you and me. You're a lot like Jean-Paul." She's smiling through her tears, and I smile back at her in relief.

"How so?"

"You and he are very much alike: rich playboy, never the same girl twice, closed off emotionally, etcetera. Then one day at a charity event, we met and crazy sparks flew." She laughs,

" 'Closed off emotionally'?" I ask with a laugh, knowing she's right. "But seriously? You met him at a charity event, too?"

"Yes, something similar to my mother's charity." Kathryn chuckles. "Do you think it's ironic?"

"Maybe it's fate."

"Maybe," she says, her somber mood disappearing.

"But you *did* meet the man of your dreams, right?"

She laughs. "There better not be a wife hidden away somewhere." She tries to punch my arm, but I intercept her wrist before she makes contact. Her body is underneath me before she knows it, and I've trapped the other wrist now, too. She squirms in a halfhearted attempt to free herself. But the smile on her face betrays her true feelings.

I bury my face in her neck. Her scent surrounds me. "Damn, you smell so good."

I kiss from her ear to her mouth. Our tongues play as she parts her legs beneath me. It's an invitation that can't be missed, and my already hard cock comes in contact with her wet need. I release her hands and rise up on my elbows.

"I want you again, beautiful." My voice is a raspy whisper. She answers me with a thrust up of her hips. I respond by lodging myself deep inside her in one very strong thrust of my hips.

"Adam." She sings my name over and over again.

"I'll never get enough of you, Kathryn. Never." Our movements become desperate and frantic, so different than our tantric sex. Maybe it's our newly professed love, but our desires burn through our bodies until we're left scorched and spent.

~

Startled awake, it takes me a moment to get my bearings and realize I'm in Kathryn's bed. The softness of her sheets and the heat of her body next to me are my reminders. But even lying in heaven, I can't stop my racing heart or the cold sweat from covering my body as the dream I had lingers around me in the dark.

Simon reappeared in my sleep again. The weird visions or hallucinations I've been having during the day have stopped, but the nocturnal visits have continued each night since the shooting.

My waking hours were crazy enough this week as I tried to calm my investors' fears, so I was relieved the daytime flashbacks stopped. The last one was at the fucking press conference on Monday. Just thinking I saw him standing there in the crowd... unnerves me. But

Simon still haunts my nights and robs me of sleep, one damn precious commodity.

Raking my fingers through my hair, I ease myself off the mattress and pad off to the bathroom. Standing in front of the sink with my palms spread out on the counter, I lean into the mirror to inspect myself. My face is pale— almost ashen—and the wide eyes peering back at me are unsettling.

I need to pull my shit together, and I sure as fuck need a good night's sleep. I can't exist on an hour here or an hour there. My days are filled with meetings and appointments, some lasting into the wee hours of the night. People rely on my business decisions, and staying on my game is critical.

Turning on the faucet, I cup my hands and gather some water to splash on my face. When the coolness hits my hot skin, I look up, expecting to see steam rising from the surface. I keep throwing water on my face until my fevered skin feels relieved.

It doesn't work, though, and I towel off the droplets.

Walking back into the room, I find my tux from last night. I'd brought our clothes back into the bedroom after our visit to the harem tent. I pull on my pants and put on my shirt, leaving it unbuttoned.

Rubbing my eyes, I head to the kitchen to make some coffee. As I'm walking through her living room, I notice my tuxedo jacket lying over the chair where I tossed it. My phone's tucked away in an interior pocket, and I grab it to check over my messages and emails. Even on a Saturday night my business emails pile up, so not checking for hours can add up to countless missed messages.

Before checking the emails, I scrounge through the kitchen cabinets, looking for Kathryn's stash of coffee. Once I find the pricey gourmet grounds, I brew a pot and swipe over my screen of my phone.

The first few emails are ones I was copied on and will be handled by Mrs. Carter on Monday. She filters out the fluff for me because I don't have time to search through each email for what's pertinent.

Scanning through my inbox, I stop breathing when I see an email from Thorpe. Before I open the email to see what he wants, I take a deep breath, prepping for the unknown.

I skim over his words, trying to gather Thorpe's tone and its basic content. He wants to confirm our meeting on Wednesday at two. He says I seemed a bit distracted last night, not that he could blame me. I imagine the shit-eating, condescending grin on his face as he wrote those words to me. Fucking bastard.

I fire off a reply. My fingers fly over the keyboard, spelling out just enough to convey that I'll be there as promised but keeping it brief. His words stir up the anger in me lying just below the surface. My only solace is knowing I'll see the look on his face when I reveal the facts of his illegal activity. I fucking can't wait!

Scrolling down further in my inbox, I see an email from Dr. Payne, the ER doctor who saw me after the shooting. I'm hoping it's the results from my STD tests. After opening up the email, I realize I guessed right. One word tells my story in text, CLEAN. Thank fuck. Considering my sexual history, I've dodged a big bullet... again. I grin, knowing I'm free to fuck Kathryn without a barrier. Skin-to-skin. My mind drifts for a few seconds as I dream about our next time together. I forward the email to Kathryn and include the words, "can't wait to be completely inside you" with it.

Next up are texts from both Tom and Patrick. They *need* to meet me for an early game of squash this morning and to discuss the week ahead. They've repeatedly sent me texts and are wondering why I haven't responded. I roll my eyes because they're up in arms after only a few hours.

I'm torn because I'd rather stay with Kathryn this morning, but the call of duty as Kings CEO wins and I send back a reply saying I'll meet with them in a little over an hour. The coffee I've made finishes brewing, and I open a couple of cabinets before finding the one holding the coffee cups.

I add some creamer to my coffee and the white swirls on the surface. While sipping the coffee, I inhale the aroma deep into my lungs. The fog in my brain fades after receiving its much-needed drug.

Glancing at the time on my phone, I believe there's enough time to whip up some breakfast in bed for my sleeping princess. I imagine her nude from the waist up as I set a tray plated with eggs and toast on her lap.

My mother was a big believer in a hot, protein-filled breakfast, and scrambled eggs are the only things I don't burn. Digging around in her refrigerator, I locate some eggs and butter. The frying pan hangs from a rack above the kitchen island; I take it down and heat it up on the stove.

I scramble the eggs in a bowl I've found and pop some bread in the toaster. After some stirring, I plate the steaming eggs and add the toast I buttered.

The tray seems bare, so I browse around the countertops for something special to add to the mix. My first serving of breakfast in bed to the woman I love needs a special touch.

An arrangement of unopened yellow tulips sits near her kitchen sink. I pluck one from the vase and head to the dry bar in the living room. I grab a small shot glass sitting beside the bottles of liquor. After walking back into the kitchen, I place the flower inside the glass after adding an inch of water. Perfect!

I add a cup of coffee to the tray, and my princess is ready to be served by her willing subject.

When I enter her bedroom, she stirs and pushes the hair from her eyes.

"Adam, what are you doing up so early?" She glances back at the clock on her nightstand before sitting up.

I grin, seeing her sleepy eyes and her hair tousled around her shoulders. I smile from ear-to-ear when the sheet falls into her lap, exposing her firm, full breasts. My fantasy come to life.

"Woke up and couldn't sleep. So I cooked you up a little something before I have to leave." She peeks up at the tray I'm holding. "It takes a lot for me to cook. Or I should say it takes a special someone for me to cook for them."

"Wow. I'm impressed and surprised." She moves back against the headboard and smoothes out the sheet on her lap.

"Don't be. Just eggs, toast, and coffee. Hard to fuck that up, even for me." I shrug. "I wanted to do something nice for you. It's going to be a busy week again for me. I may not see you until the birthday dinner for your mother on Wednesday night."

She pouts and I place the tray on her ready lap. I kiss her forehead before sitting down on the edge of the bed next to her. I smile as her eyes widen when looking over the food I've cooked for her.

"You've really surprised me." She reaches for my hand and weaves our fingers together. "Thanks," she says in a soft voice, squeezing my hand.

"My pleasure, beautiful." I push some of her wayward hair back from her face and trail my fingertips down her cheek, then her neck, and then along the side of her breast. Her nipples harden as I gently stroke them with my thumb.

"I want to remember you like this today." I slowly peruse her from the top of her sex-styled hair to the perfect curve of her round breasts. "An alluring sex goddess made just for me."

Chapter 18

Peters struts into my office at exactly one o'clock, our designated time. He's carrying a folder of evidence and wearing a broad grin. Both are proof of the damning material we have against Xavier Thorpe, my bastard of a father.

We have an hour to prep for the meeting with Thorpe. Hell, we've been prepping since Monday morning when Peters showed up with a stack of papers.

Endless pages of documents point a guilty finger at Thorpe. Investors handed large sums of money over to him, believing he was bringing business and commerce to an underdeveloped area in New Jersey. In reality, Thorpe used the money he schemed to prop up his failing hotel resorts along the East Coast. The amount taken from investors is obscene, probably in the range of five billion dollars.

He stole from legitimate businesses to keep flailing ones alive. It was the age-old scheme of robbing Peter to pay Paul. And nothing more than a smoke-and-mirrors charade that never pans out in the end because the unlucky *Peters* of the world always find out about the *Pauls*.

His prestige is the only reason Thorpe can keep his investors blinded. He is ruthless and cutthroat in his business endeavors and doesn't care who is affected by his hostile takeovers or layoffs. People are merely numbers to him. But all his dealings are above board, or perhaps like this one, they only appear to be.

I smile as I imagine the world learning about his deceit. His lawyers would scramble to bury the accusations. But at the same time, his stocks would plummet, and his gilded reputation would be forever tarnished. The press would have a field day. Even if he avoided jail time, the fall from his throne would be satisfaction enough for me.

"Good afternoon, Mr. Kingsley." Peters snaps me out of my reverie. He sets the folder in his hands down on my desk with a plop. "No need to guess why you have that smile."

"It's pretty fucking obvious, right?" I scoff and motion to a chair opposite my desk for Peters to join me. "I feel like we're ready. Don't you?"

"In every sense of the word." Peters points to the folder in front of me. "I have a copy of these papers with my assistant. She will fax them to the SEC and press outlets when I send her the word."

"I want you to take a vacation in a couple of weeks. The dust should be settled by then. You've earned some time off."

"Thanks, I'll take you up on that. Perhaps a trip to Fiji. I've always dreamed of going there." Peters looks out the window distantly. The man definitely needs to take a break, and truthfully, so do I.

"I'm thinking about hopping around the Greek Isles with Kathryn." I join Peters as we both look out the window. I imagine Kathryn dressed in a white sundress with her raven hair blowing in the island breeze, all the burdens of Thorpe left behind us.

Peters shakes his head and smiles. "Well, Mr. Kingsley, I'm happy for you. You think this woman is the one?"

"You've met her, right?" I can't help but smile, thinking of her.

"Yes, I have." Peters says, agreeing with my assessment.

"Hold on just a second." I raise a finger toward Peters and push a button for Mrs. Carter.

"Yes, Mr. Kingsley," Mrs. Carter responds instantly.

"I want you to research a vacation around the Greek Isles. Feel free to select the best options for us."

"I'll have the research for the vacation in order by tomorrow."

"Just email me the details. Thank you, Mrs. Carter."

"You're welcome."

I smile and end the call. I turn back to Peters and say, "So let's run through the meeting one more time."

I reach for the folder and begin thumbing through the papers. This is the first time I've had the evidence in my hands because Peters wants to be the source of Thorpe's wrongdoings, not me.

I've had Peters silently watching over Thorpe and his business activities for nine years, so I trust him on this issue. When investors find out about Thorpe's deceit, there won't be any evidence connecting me to his downfall. My connection to this mess and disclosing Thorpe's activities will remain hidden, I hope.

~

On the ride over to Thorpe's office, I check my phone for messages. Ollie and I have been exchanging emails this week since Kathryn told him we were half-brothers on Sunday night. Kathryn mentioned to Ollie that I was meeting Thorpe today. I open an email Ollie sent a few minutes ago.

> *Afternoon, Adam,*
> *I know you're planning on meeting our father today, and I wanted to warn you to be careful. The man's a crafty bastard.*

*Please be on your guard with him and touch
base with me after your meeting. It will put my
mind at ease.
Look forward to finally meeting you in person
tonight. We have thirty-two years of catching
up to do.
Your brother,
Ollie*

I put down my phone. I never imagined I would have a brother when I was young, and now I do. Ollie is right; we have so much to catch up on. If only I'd known sooner, maybe things would have been different

Eddie eases the SUV into a drop-off area outside the towering skyscraper belonging to Thorpe Partners. The monstrosity serves as homage to Thorpe's power and control in this city. A perch from which he reigns. The twenty pieces of paper I hold in my hands will make his empire evaporate. The building will remain—perhaps only to become a beacon of his corruption. People will pass by and point as they carry on whispered conversation about the once- great business giant who fell.

Eddie opens the door for Peters and me. With my head held high, I lead the way to the building's entrance. As I cross the patterned sidewalk, I notice faint Xs stamped in every few segments in the concrete.

"X marks the spot," I mumble under my breath and laugh at the display of Thorpe's obvious conceit.

"What was that, sir?" Peters asks as we near the building's glass doors. "Did you say something?"

"Nothing to worry about." I see my reflection in the glass doors, standing tall with my head held high, ready to face Thorpe.

I enter through the revolving doors with Peters trailing behind. My steps are quick and precise with my heels clicking against the shiny granite floor.

My first stop inside the lobby is the security desk. A couple of uniformed guards sit behind a tall counter. An electronic gate that requires a special access card blocks off the entrance beyond them.

"Good afternoon, gentlemen." The two guards give me the onceover. "My name is Adam Kingsley. My associate, John Peters, and I have an appointment with Xavier Thorpe at two."

"You're here to see Mr. Thorpe." Repeating my request, the guards eye each other in a silent conversation before turning back to me. "We will have to call his office and confirm."

"Understood." I lay my hand over my computer bag, hoping that its contents won't be searched. What I have hidden inside will likely change the name at the top of this building.

One of the guards dials a number and waits, still looking at me.

"Mr. Adam Kingsley is here to see Mr. Thorpe," says the gatekeeper. I swear he's getting off on this little power trip of being the king's guard. He waits and sits up straighter in his chair. He glances over me quickly and looks past me at Peters. I glance back at Peters. He's standing with his hands in his pockets.

"Thank you. I'll send him up." The guard hangs up his phone and turns his attention to me. "Mr. Thorpe's assistant said to send you upstairs."

"Thank you," I say with a hint of sarcasm. I've never had to go through such a hassle for a meeting before.

"I'll buzz you through the gate, and you can proceed to the bank of elevators on the right. Mr. Thorpe's office is located on the twenty-seventh floor." He hands me a keycard. "Insert this special card into the elevator's panel before selecting the floor. It's special access only."

I nod and walk through the gate with Peters as the guard buzzes us through. "Special access card. Smart. Something we should implement for my floor." I dangle the card before Peters as we wait for the elevator's doors to open.

"I agree. It's very much like the one you have at The Pierre. I'll get on it... after my vacation." The grin he flashes me reaches up to his eyes. "It's hard to believe that after years of doing surveillance, that part of my job will be over after today."

"Believe me, Thorpe would blow his fortune to prove his innocence." I can almost hear Thorpe's denial and protests now. "So be ready for some serious backlash over the next few days."

"True," Peters says, shaking his head and looking toward the floor. "He's not one to go down without a fight."

"Exactly. Guns will be blazing. Count on it." I reach for my phone and scan over my latest messages. Kathryn sent a text a few minutes ago.

Remember you promised to be careful today.
Call afterward. See you tonight.

She and Ollie are on the same page with their messages to me. I have no reception in the elevator, so I can't answer her text. I know she's going to be livid when she finds out I kept the real reason for my visit a secret. However, I'm certain she'll understand my motivation when reports come in outlining Thorpe's wrongdoings. This time I have documented and tangible proof that he can't refute. Unlike the assault Thorpe made on her where her words and accusations would have been pitted against his, I possess irrefutable facts.

Thorpe's attack on her and her family went unpunished, but today all his past sins will come back to bite him on the ass.

I tuck my phone back in my suit pocket and stare ahead at the doors of the elevator. I push my shoulders back and smooth my hand down the front of my necktie. I need to exude confidence for the meeting; my armor needs to be crack-free.

I've loathed Thorpe for years. He's felt the same about me, even before I took my first breath. I'm just one big fucking mistake to him, a reminder that he doesn't control everything in his well-crafted world.

I owe my mother everything for keeping me away from this man, but I blame Thorpe for my mother's constant state of melancholy. The results of today's meeting will be in her memory.

After she fled the city, pregnant and alone, she built her life around raising me. She never dated or had many friends. Men had flirted with her while I was growing up, but she wouldn't engage with them past a quick hello. I wish she'd married and moved on with her life. She never told me why she kept everyone at a distance, but she didn't' let me feel like I was a mistake or a burden. She loved with me with her whole being. When I went off to college, she'd call me daily, just to hear my voice. I felt guilty leaving her behind, but my mother forbade me from staying in Philly for college. She insisted that I attend MIT.

"Full scholarships don't happen to everyone," she'd said.

The elevator slows and the doors open to the top floor. I catalog all the lives Thorpe's fucked up—my mother, Ollie, Kathryn, Kathryn's father, and me, not to mention all the people out of work because of his selfish decisions. As I step off the elevator, I carry each name with me like a badge of honor as I prepare to shred his empire to pieces.

In silence, I turn to Peters and we pump our fists together. Our nerves are steeled and our plan flawless.

The affluent décor on the top floor is not understated, and no expense seems to have been spared. The walls are painted a shimmering gray and the furniture is modern and sleek, more fitting a luxury penthouse apartment in Soho than a business office. Even a small copier would seem out of place and gauche.

The space reeks of opulence and showmanship, a Manhattan setting fit for the city's emperor. A lone desk is positioned ahead of us, and an attractive young woman watches as Peters and I approach. The massive wall art behind her is made of large, shiny scraps of metal manipulated and polished into the letter X. I roll my eyes seeing the piece's grandeur and Thorpe's homage to himself.

"Adam Kingsley for Mr. Thorpe," I announce to the woman sitting behind the desk.

"Of course," she says with a stiff smile. She glances at Peters but her eyes don't rest on him for more than a second or two. "Please have a seat." She tilts her head in the direction of a few chairs.

"This is my associate, John Peters." I extend my arm toward Peters.

"Yes." She pauses and then says, "I'll announce you both." I shake my head at her odd response. I turn to Peters who just shrugs.

Minutes pass as we wait. The blonde never made a visible call to Thorpe alerting him of our presence. Perhaps she emailed him the message. Either way, we are left guessing and waiting.

Unannounced, the door to the left of the massive X swings open and out slithers the human snake himself.

"Gentlemen." Thorpe's voice booms through the space. He doesn't move from the threshold of his office. "Please, come in."

He retreats back into his office, leaving us with no choice but to obey his command and follow him through the door.

Clearing my throat, I stand and signal for Peters to join me. I'm one step ahead of him as we head toward Thorpe's office. Once inside, I look around and realize the entire floor of this building is Thorpe's office. *The entire fucking floor of the building*

"Well, fuck *me*," I mutter under my breath and scan the room from corner to corner. "I guess it's good to be king."

Peters hears me and snorts.

"Please, gentlemen, take a seat." Thorpe takes his seat behind a dark wood desk large enough to seat The Last Supper.

Another man sits to the side of the massive desk. The serious-looking character must be Thorpe's attorney. The legal pad and pen the man holds in his lap are a dead giveaway.

I stride up to the desk and shake the hand of the man I hate. "Good afternoon, Thorpe." Mister or sir cannot be forced from my lips. His last name will have to suffice. "This is John Peters. He's worked for me nearly ten years now. Almost back to the day I arrived in New York City."

"Mr. Peters," Thorpe says in a formal tone as he offers Peters a quick handshake.

Thorpe turns to his man. "This is my attorney, Davis Young."

We all shake hands and take a seat. Surprisingly, the hatred I normally feel when I'm in Thorpe's presence hasn't reared its head. Maybe it's the fact that I have a folder full of damning evidence sitting in my computer case like a ticking bomb.

"I have a busy schedule today, so let's get down to business about the New Jersey economic development."

I want to tell him about *my* scheduled evening plans with his other son, Ollie, but I refrain from getting too personal.

"Yes, I've been doing a little research," I say, reaching for my case and removing the papers secured in organized, bound folders. A congressional declaration couldn't look more official.

I hand the folder over to Thorpe and his attorney. Thorpe thumbs through the documents and tosses them on his desk. He snarls at me like a cornered dog.

"So, this is a poker game and you've laid down your best hand. You've made a big mistake, Adam. One that will cost you everything you've worked for." Thorpe pushes his chair away from the desk and stands. I jump back in my chair, startled. He walks around to me and sits on the corner of his desk. The position allows him to tower over me.

"The facts are undeniable." I nod at the discarded folder, and then I catch of glimpse of Thorpe's attorney, whose mouth is set in a definite smirk. He almost appears ready to laugh. This entire interaction feels off, like there's an inside joke that no one's shared with me.

But the facts of my case against Thorpe are clear. They're carefully detailed and redlined, while pointing to all the damning evident I have against him.

"Facts? Well I have some facts of my own." He reaches back and grabs a thin folder. "Here are some facts. I'll call them my ace in the hole." He thrusts the folder at me. I glance at Peters and he nods. I take the folder and open it up.

Pages of confidential information concerning Kings Capital's security software glare up at me.

Fuck! How the hell did Thorpe get his hands on these codes? These were the same ones Simon offered to sell to another company. In the wrong hands, they could be a deathblow to Kings.

"Shocked, I see." Thorpe chuckles. Speechless would be a better word, because my mouth won't move. "It's pretty simple. I have someone ready to put these documents into the wrong hands, so to speak. They'll have the security codes for every bank and website in the world who relies on Kings Capital for their firewall. The customer accounts and credit card information will be accessed within seconds. Your company will be ruined in a blink of an eye."

"How?" Finally I mutter something. The papers I'm holding shake in my hands. "Where did you get these codes?"

Thorpe glances at Peters with a sardonic smile. I turn toward my friend as a grin spreads across his face.

"Peters? You?" My voice quivers as a fiery rage starts to build in my temples. I clench my jaw as I speak through my teeth. "How did you get a hold of them?"

Peters looks at me with a mocking smirk. Dots get connected as my mind spins in fury. Simon had the codes and wanted to expose Kings.

"Don't blame Peters. He was only doing as he was told."

I hear Thorpe but continue to stare, seething, at Peters. I remember back to the moment I met Peters in a dark Brooklyn bar. He said he lived close by and stopped in for drinks about every night. He told me about how he was struggling financially, trying to make ends meet to support his wife. He was a private investigator and business was slow. At the time, I didn't have anything to offer him other than a friendly ear and a small job working for me. He proved to be an asset as time wore on. I trusted him. And not just me but Tom, Patrick, and even Simon.

"Nine years we've been working together. Was it all a lie? I thought you were my friend." I shake the damning folder in Peters' face. It takes all my strength not to slap him across the face with it. "You got these codes from Simon, didn't you?"

Peters scoffs at my pain-filled questions. His unaffected appearance supports his betrayal. "I did, on a silver-platter. And 'friends'? You're fucking kidding me, right? You've treated me like shit for years. Or maybe that's just how you treat all your friends. Look what happened to Simon."

Peters' words and cold demeanor cut into me. "The thing with Simon was different. What did I ever do to you? I paid you enough to live like a king."

"Thorpe paid me more." Peters says. "Money; it's the root of all evil, as the saying goes. I'm a selfish motherfucker, something you and I have had in common."

Anger rages through my veins, and I want to punch this bastard's head in.

"Besides, Adam," Thorpe says, and I turn to shoot daggers at him. "Do you think I didn't have an eye on everything you've done in your life?" Thorpe says. "Your mother didn't listen to me when I demanded she get an abortion. I even offered her money to pay for it. But she didn't take it. I hoped my *stain* would go away with you living in Philadelphia, but here you are, trying to bring me down. You're pathetic, and I'm glad no one knows you're my son."

"I don't want anyone to know you're my father either, you son of a bitch. You treated my mother like she was gum on the bottom of your shoe. You're the one who's pathetic." I spit out my words in anger, trying to defend my mother.

"I have watched your every move, your mother's, too. I never thought my mistake would rise in the business world alongside me. When Kings started out, I had to put Peters in to keep my interests protected."

He flicks his finger at the documents, the codes, I hold in my hands.

"This is my protection."

I can't process it all. Thorpe has been watching every move I've made all this time? I'm the biggest fucking fool. I hang my head as I try to gather myself; my entire world spins out of control.

"Peters, you can leave us now." Thorpe dismisses Peters with a wave of his hand, but I have something to say before he even thinks of leaving.

I throw down the papers on the desk and stand up. I rush to Peters and pull him to his feet by his lapels. In the background, Thorpe asks his attorney to call security, so I release Peters with a push and watch him land back in his chair. His red tie flies up and hits his chin. My anger hasn't subsided as I hold my fist close to his face. Kathryn's warning to be careful flashes through my mind, and it's enough to keep me from punching him.

"All about money, was it? The evidence you gave me about this Jersey deal is probably lies, too, right?" I point a shaking finger in Peters' face. The man's performance in my life is nothing short of Oscar-worthy. In the decade I've known him, I'd never have taken him for a liar.

"Yes, all those documents were fabricated," Peters says with no emotion. A wave of nausea races through me. Peters' betrayal is worse than what Thorpe can ever do to me.

"I trusted you. Gave you complete access—" Those last words are a noose hanging around my neck. Peters had special clearance to practically everything at Kings. I want to pull my hair out for being so naïve. "What else have you used against me, you liar?"

"I might have encouraged Marta in her obsession with you. I saw the opportunity arise when she started dating Simon and couldn't resist. You didn't even remember who she was. And by the way, she loves the penthouse you gave me," he says with a knowing smile.

"Why would you do this to me?" Peters' actions with Marta go way beyond spying for Thorpe. They're personal and vindictive.

"I was bored and tired of being treated like shit. It was a nice little diversion to keep me occupied." He tosses his head up with a chuckle.

"Because you were bored? You sadistic bastard!" I scream at a smiling Peters.

"Sit down, Adam." Thorpe's demand is like a slap in the face. How dare he think he can control me? I turn on my heel to face him and feel every muscle in my body strain as I lean forward. Through it all, the bastard is still sitting calmly on the edge of his desk. "We have matters to discuss." He points to the folder that dropped out of my hand as I went after Peters.

"Are you kidding? I'm not sitting down." I snap back. Peters rises from the chair and walks toward the office door. "Run, you fucking traitor!" I yell after him as he slams the door. I'll deal with him later.

"Here's my bargain for you," Thorpe says, and I jerk my head around to look at him. "You and I both know I can release these codes before you can give the word to change them. You don't really have much of a choice. Resign as CEO of Kings Capital and your precious company will be safe. Or watch everything you've worked for implode. ." An evil smirk slides over his face as he taps a single piece of paper on his desk.

I know what it is before I even look over its contents. My letter of resignation as CEO. My loss and his win.

"So what will it be?" Thorpe thrust a pen in my direction. "Release this signed letter to the press or I release the security codes?"

As I reach to grab the pen from Thorpe's slimy hand, I hear Simon's maniacal laugh echoing in my brain.

Chapter 19

What have I done?

I collapse against the wall of the elevator as it descends. My breaths fogs up the shiny metal where my face touches it. My entire career lies in ruin. Bending at the waist, I ride another wave of nausea as the reality of what just happened sets in.

Everything I've worked for, everything I've personally achieved, has been stripped from me with one stroke of a pen. I'm out and Thorpe wins. The only bright spot is that Kings Capital remains intact. Thousands of employees could've paid the price for my stupidity. Instead, I sacrificed myself. It was the penalty for being a fool.

I exit the elevators and lean one hand against the marbled wall of the lobby. Taking deep breaths, I try to remember which way to turn for the exit. I bring a hand to my heart—it's racing as if I've just run a marathon. I hear the clicking of shoes on the marble floor nearing me. I glance up to see one of the guards from earlier. He grabs my arm, and I pull it from his grasp.

"Sir, I'm here to escort you off the premises." In the time it took the elevator to reach the ground floor, Thorpe called security. Asshole. But did I expect anything less?

"No, I'm perfectly capable of walking out on my own." I snap back out of his reach. My reprimand echoes around the cavernous lobby. I want to keep my dignity. There's no way I'm letting some doofus guard strong-arm me to the pavement like trash.

Looking over the guard's shoulder, I see the exit. Beyond the revolving doors, Eddie waits. But my chest tightens and I can't seem to take a deep breath. I can do this. I push off the wall, brush past the guard, and concentrate on getting the hell out of here. I'm sure I'll feel better once I'm out of the devil's den.

Upon exiting, I tip my face to the sky, close my eyes, and try to take a deep breath. *Why can't I take a deep breath?* It begins to drizzle and within seconds, a steady rainfall covers the dirty streets of New York, clearing away the muck and grime. I stand there, getting soaked, but the rain doesn't have the same cleansing effect on me.

Lowering my head, I look toward the street. Eddie approaches me with an umbrella. His face is filled with worry. I step forward to meet him halfway, but stop dead in my tracks as I hear the haunting voice of Simon.

"Look at you now. The great and mighty Adam Kingsley left with nothing, just like me."

I spin around with a fist raised to face… what? Nothing but thin air? Of course, Simon isn't there. My mind is playing tricks on me, and I drop my fist. The quick turn on my heels, combined with the rain and my wobbly legs, makes me slide and tumble to the concrete. I have no time to break my fall, and I see my phone fly out of my hand the instant before my face hits the ground.

I will myself to not blackout, but my head feels as if it's split open from the fall.

"Now it's your turn," Simon seems to whisper in my ear. "You're lying on the dirty sidewalk, just like me. Let me hold your hand to hell."

What the fuck is going on? I shake my head in hopes of waking up from this nightmare. But pain begins to press against my ribs as I clutch my chest. I've never felt my heart pound so hard or so fast.

"Mr. Kingsley?" Eddie calls my name and kneels down on the sidewalk beside me. "Are you okay, sir?"

I can't catch my breath and a cold sweat runs over my body from head to toe. "I don't know what's going on." I pant between breaths.

"We need to get you to the hospital." Eddie holds my wrist and feels for my pulse. He stills his fingers when he locates my heartbeat. I glance up in my daze and see a grimace on his face. "You're as white as a ghost, your heart is racing, and you're short of breath."

I try to get to my knees, but they give out and buckle under me. Eddie grabs my phone, pockets it, and then helps me to my feet. He holds me up as I lean into him and slowly we make it back to the SUV.

Eddie helps me get in the car and closes the door. I recline the seat and wipe the sweat from my face. I'm cold and clammy, so perspiring doesn't make sense.

"Sir, I'm taking you to the same hospital you went to after the shooting," Eddie announces. I don't argue with him, because I think I may be having a heart attack.

"I need my phone." I say in an unsteady voice. "Gotta call Tom and Patrick."

Eddie glances at me before he pulls away from the curb. "What happened to you, sir? And where is Peters?"

How do I even begin to explain my complete fuck-up to Eddie?

"Peters has been lying to me for years." Eddie gives me a *you're shitting me* look. "He's always worked for Thorpe. A corporate spy."

"I can't believe it!" Eddie exclaims.

"Me, neither." I hold out my hand, and Eddie reaches into his pocket for my phone.

I call Tom's number first. "Hey, Adam. Why are you calling me on my cell?" We usually don't talk via cell during business hours.

"Tom, are you watching the business news?" My voice sounds weak and breathy.

"Adam, what's the matter? Are you working out?" Tom asks.

"No. Are you watching the news?" I repeat my question.

"Yes. Tell me what's going on?"

I'm shocked that Tom hasn't heard about my resignation yet. "I had a meeting that didn't go well. I'll call you back in a minute." I can't tell him I've resigned from Kings because I still can't believe it. I've spent years building my company. Years of blood, sweat, and tears. Everything I am is tied up in Kings, and now it's gone. I feel like a ship lost at sea, but I had no choice. The choice was between me and thousands of our employees as well as our clients.

The sweat pours off of me as my chest aches. I double over in my seat, unable to finish the call, and the phone drops from my hand. I hear Tom yelling in the background.

Eddie takes the phone from my hand and brings it to his ear. "Mr. Duffy." I watch Eddie nod as he listens to Tom. Even muffled against Eddie's ear, I can make out Tom's panicked voice.

The sounds around me fade away, and the daylight dims. I watch the buildings blur as we fly by them.

~

Once again I find myself in the same Manhattan emergency room being tended to by Dr. Payne. My heart has slowed down to a normal pace, and the overwhelming anxiety I felt has subsided thanks to a healthy dose of Xanax.

When Eddie practically carried me into the ER, I was taken back to an examination room before I had time to blink. Patients presenting with chest pains and shortness of breath are first priority.

The staff went to work one me as Dr. Payne gave them orders. First was an EKG that showed my heart beating fast as hell, but otherwise everything checked out all right. The blood tests followed, but the results still haven't come back yet.

The ER staff won't let Eddie in the room with me. Their strict privacy rule of "family members only" keeps him planted in the waiting room. I just want my damn phone so I can call Tom back let him know what happened. I'm sure Thorpe has already leaked my resignation to the news wires, and I imagine the buzz going around on every corner of Wall Street. Good news travels fast, but bad news travels faster.

I rake my fingers through my hair and cringe when I brush the small bump on my forehead.

"Fuck," I say under my breath just as the doctor walks into my room.

"Nice language, Mr. Kingsley."

"It's been that kind of day." I plop back down on the bed in a huff. "And I really need to get the hell out of here."

"Hold up there. We still need the results back from your blood work. Though I suspect they'll show nothing abnormal. You appear to be feeling better. No more shortness of breath or chest pains?"

"I'm doing fine now. That's the reason that I want to leave. I need to get ahold of my office." He eyes me as I fidget.

"Your office can wait." His stern look leaves me no room for argument. "Seems like the Xanax has done the trick. What has you so worked up? You uttered the word *Simon* under your breath a few times. That's the guy who shot you, right?"

"Long story, but here's the short version. Every now and then I have…" I'm not sure why I'm telling him this, because he'll probably label me as a nut job. "I don't know. Just weird flashbacks involving the guy."

"'Weird'?" He places his paperwork on the bed and crosses his arms over his chest. "Explain 'weird' to me."

"I've been having dreams of the shooting."

"Any troubles while you're awake?" He fishes out a business card and pen from the pocket of his white coat.

"Sometimes." I don't want to give away too many details here. I'm uncertain what the doctor will think. To be on the safe side, I refrained from telling him I've heard Simon speaking to me.

"I'm not an expert, but I see this a lot in the ER. Trauma can affect your brain. The shooting was traumatic and you're presenting with some symptoms of PTSD— post-traumatic stress disorder." He starts scribbling on the card. "I want you to give this psychiatrist a call. He's an expert in this area."

"Thanks." I pocket the card, and the doctor collects his paperwork off the bed.

"I'll be back with those results, but I'm fairly certain you had a massive panic attack today. Brought on by stress and those flashbacks." He nods and heads for the door.

Just as the doctor is leaving, the door swings open. Ollie Thorpe stands at the threshold.

"Ollie, what the hell?" I shake my head. How did he even know I was here? The doctor squeezes past Ollie and disappears down the hall.

"Nice introduction," Ollie says with tilt of his head.

"Sorry, you're just not who I expected to see opening that door." I get up from bed and walk over to him.

I extend my hand, but the greeting seems awkward and formal. He doesn't take my hand; instead, he wraps his arms around me.

My brother.

Hugging me.

An unfamiliar lump sticks in my throat, and I hold onto him tighter.

We break apart and I blink the moisture away.

"I have no clue where to start. First off, I guess I'll say hello." I smile at him and he smiles back.

"It's an awkward introduction for sure." He darts his eyes around the room. "But how are you? You look all right now."

"I'm all right." I take a deep breath. "It's just been one hell of a day—or last couple of weeks."

"How did you know I was here?"

"Eddie," he says. I scratch my head. Eddie has no clue about Ollie and me. "Kathryn called your cell phone. Eddie answered and we rushed over. I got in because I'm your next of kin. Half-brother and all." Ollie holds up my cell phone in his hands. I promptly grab it from him. "Looks like you missed it."

"And you're the only kin I have worth claiming in this town. It's been a fucked-up day all around." I swipe my finger over the touch screen, type in my security code, and scroll through the business news wire feed.

Nothing unusual pops up. Did my resignation letter not make the news?

"I don't get it," I say, confused.

"What's up?" He leans over to look at my phone's screen.

"There's nothing. My whole world should've blown up by now, thanks to Thorpe," I say, bewildered that my name isn't headlining any current business news.

"Eddie told Kathryn that you were frazzled after meeting him. What's going on?"

"A man who's worked for me for nine years, back to the beginning days of my business, was actually working for your— I mean *our* father all along."

"No fucking way!"

"Yes, I found out today the hard way, and Thorpe forced me to sign a resignation letter or let my company go down. This man had secure, highly controlled software codes he'd taken from my company; codes that would've opened up the firewalls for every client we have. Banks. Websites. Even the biggest online retailer."

"I can't believe this." Ollie shakes his head as his face twists in a frown.

"The catch was I had to resign or he'd leak the information and ruin Kings."

"That's corporate blackmail and totally illegal." Ollie paces the room, but stops and holds up his finger. "I'm going to call that bastard now. He'll take my call. Believe me. Besides, I haven't heard shit about your resignation."

"That's what isn't making sense."

Ollie pulls out his phone, hits the screen a few times, and then holds the device up to his ear. "Something smells like bullshit here."

"Yes, Natalie. It's Ollie. Tell Thorpe code red."

I scrunch my face at his words. What the hell does that means?

"Thorpe!" Ollie yells into the phone. I'm surprised he calls his own father by his last name, too. Just like I do. "What did you do to Adam?" Ollie press his phone's screen again.

"What does it matter to you?" Thorpe's voice rings out into the room. "And how the hell do you even know he was here?"

Holy shit, Ollie put Thorpe on speakerphone. "Wait, was it Kathryn Delcour and her big mouth?"

"Irrelevant. Back to the question. What did you do to Adam?"

I hear Thorpe chuckling in the background. My whole body tenses. My life has turned upside down, and he's fucking laughing at me!

"I just taught him a little lesson. Let him know who's really in control of his life. Have been since before he was born." My blood turns cold at his words.

"So forcing his resignation was nothing more than a power trip for you?" Ollie looks at me, astonished.

"Yes. Let's call it a mindfuck. He thought he could beat me at my own game, but he was wrong. It's funny, though. His actual resignation only occurred in his mind. What he signed is worthless. The next time your bastard brother wants to try to prove he's bigger than me, he'll think again. I can crush his world with very little effort." Another devious laugh comes through the speaker. My thoughts turn murderous as the conversation continues.

"I've heard enough. Go to hell, you sick and twisted bastard!" Ollie ends the call and turns to me, but I'm paralyzed as I process the last of the phone call.

"I didn't really resign... or did I?" I ask in hopes that Ollie will help interpret that conversation. How could he do something like that to me? It makes no sense at all.

"You're still head of Kings." Ollie sighs. "And our DNA donor is still a fucking asshole."

I collapse back onto the bed, my head in my hands. In the span of a couple of hours, I was going to pummel Thorpe, then I was forced to sign a resignation letter, and now I find out the letter was made-up. I close my eyes, weak from mental exhaustion. My heart begins to race again as cold sweat spreads across my body.

"I can't believe someone could be that evil," I mumble in shock.

"You're his biggest enemy. A mistake he couldn't cover up, so he uses all his power to try and control you."

"I don't understand that kind of hatred. What is 'code red,' by the way?"

"It's the only time my father will take a call from me. It means that something bad has happened to someone in our family. Rather apropos since you're my brother. No lies at all on my part."

"I guess not." I take a few deep breaths, trying to ward off another panic attack.

"I haven't spoken to him in three years. My mother had a health scare, and he had his assistant call to inform me that my mother might die. So I confronted him on his callousness. We agreed to use the code red to communicate moving forward. Otherwise I don't want to hear from him ever again." Ollie takes a seat in the chair across from the bed.

"I can't imagine what you went through living under his roof as a child." I wonder how Ollie turned out to be such a decent man.

"He was never around, something I'm grateful for."

There's a knock on the door, and the doctor comes back in the room. "You're good to go. The blood work came back normal. I want you to take it easy for a few days and reconnect with what's important in life. And call the doctor on the card I gave you." He glances between Ollie and me. "Are you two brothers?"

We look at each other and laugh. I say, "Yes, we are."

"Get him to take a long vacation, okay?" Dr. Payne asks Ollie with an arched brow.

"I'll do my best." Ollie responds with a grin.

"Take care." Dr. Payne's serious tone matches the look in his eyes.

The doctor seems like a smart man. Maybe I should take his advice and spend some time away from the office for a change. Just the thought of putting miles between me and Thorpe eases some of the tension in my body.

"I still can't believe you're my brother," he says, speaking fast after the doctor leaves us.

"No kidding." I give him a nod. "I have to be honest here. I wasn't sure you'd want to have anything to do with me."

"When Kathryn told me she was involved with you, I did freak out. You have a bit of a reputation." Ollie arches a brow and leans closer to me.

"I can't deny it, and I don't blame you for thinking that way." I raise my hands in concession. "I promise what I feel for Kathryn is genuine. That woman has totally knocked me off my feet."

"Kathryn's the most beautiful woman I know. Both inside and out. I'm rather protective of her, since we grew up together, side-by-side." It's good to know Ollie and I agree about Kathryn. "She really has strong feelings for you, so I promised to suspend my judgment for a bit. Then she springs the whole brother news on me. I was fucking floored."

"I figured you might be. I am the ugly secret. Thorpe has never said a word to anyone about me being his son."

"Doesn't surprise me. I'm just sorry I didn't know about you sooner," Ollie says. The wasted years spread as a frown on his face.

"I need to ask you a favor." I search Ollie's face as he waits for my request. "I know you don't have a reason to trust me, but I don't want to bring up what Thorpe did to me right now. I'd rather pick a better time to break it to Kathryn."

"Okay, just make sure you tell her today. She has a right to know." I nod. "She's crazy about you, and for that reason, I don't want to hear about you breaking her heart. *Capisce?"*

"*Capisce.*"

I call Tom before leaving my room and run through the events of the day: Peters' betrayal, Thorpe's threats and demands that I resign, but most importantly I tell Tom about the security codes Thorpe possesses. Tom freaks when he hears that confidential information was leaked to an outsider.

He brings Patrick and the head of our IT department into our call, and codes are changed immediately. A full-scale offensive is launched to secure everything that Peters *might* have gotten his hands on. They promise to work around the clock until everything is secured. I breathe a little easier knowing that nothing appears to have been compromised.

Tom and Patrick stay on the line after the head of IT disconnects. The guys convince me to let our attorneys look into civil or possible criminal activity on Peters' part. They also believe that Thorpe actions and blackmail should be turned over to the SEC. After all, we are a publicly traded company, and our stockholders could lose their shirts if the codes were truly released into the wrong hands.

I agree, but I don't have the fight in me today. Tom and Patrick have stood up for me and swear they have my back. I thank them and tell them to keep me posted. I also mention that I'm taking off until Monday, though I might meet them for a drink for Happy Hour on Friday.

Once I'm off the call with Tom and Patrick, Ollie and I head out to the waiting room. I see Kathryn standing next to the window. She's on her phone with her hand flying in the air as she talks. She turns and stops when our eyes meet. I swear everyone else in the room disappears around us.

She says a few words into the phone and then practically runs into my waiting arms. I wrap them around her and draw her to my chest. The familiar smell of her perfume works as a healing ointment for my frayed nerves, soothing me with her scent. After a few deep breaths, my shoulders drop and the knots in my stomach release. Kathryn has become my resting place.

"Are you okay?" She gazes up at me and feathers her fingers around the small bump on my forehead from when I hit the concrete. "What happened? Did Thorpe hit you?"

"No punches were thrown. I promise. Just a little fall outside of the building, and my heart was racing. But they doctor said I was fine to leave." I glance over at Ollie who gives me a warm smile. "But I could really use some rest."

"Let's get you home, then." She eases out of my arms and takes my hand.

Eddie stands a few feet away, and I motion toward the door. We've worked together for so long that words don't even need to be spoken between us. I watch him exit the doors and know he's about to bring the SUV around. But in the back of my mind, doubt creeps in. It's just a quick thought, but I wonder if Eddie's trustworthiness is for real? I want to push the idea away, but Peters' betrayal is still too fresh in my mind.

"So you finally met Ollie," Kathryn says while looping her arm through Ollie's.

"Yes, we more than met. I'd say we bonded. Don't you think, Ollie?" I still hold Kathryn's other hand in mine. She's sandwiched between us.

"Nothing like a son of a bitch father to bring two outcast sons together." Ollie and I exchange a smile, and I feel the bond between us deep down into my very soul.

The rain clouds from earlier have cleared, and the late afternoon sun peeks through the Manhattan skyline. Eddie brings the SUV around and gets out to open our doors.

"So, I'm going to walk back to my hotel," Ollie says as we all huddle together on the sidewalk.

"I was speaking to my mother when you came out to the waiting room. We're going to postpone her birthday dinner," Kathryn says while glancing between Ollie and me.

"Makes sense," Ollie says, confirming Kathryn decision. "I'm going to be in town until Saturday. So just let me know."

"I hate that we're not meeting on Ava's birthday, but I'm not sure I'd be good company tonight," I can barely drag my sorry ass to the car, let alone The Core Club for dinner.

I place my hand on Ollie's forearm before he leaves, but I wrap my arms around *him* this time and give him a quick hug. "I want to thank you for today, with Thorpe. You came to my rescue."

"I'm sorry for what you went through. He's a complete sociopath. My advice is to avoid him at *all* costs." Ollie presses his lips together. I have to agree with his assessment of Thorpe.

"Advice taken," I say. Ollie begins to walk backward away from us.

"See you crazy cats later. And Kathryn, see that my brother gets a bit of rest before dinner." Ollie winks before turning to continue down the sidewalk.

"Will do," Kathryn replies with a wave of her hand.

"It's just you and me now, beautiful." I lead her toward the SUV with my hand on the small of her back.

"Back to The Pierre," I tell Eddie before following behind Kathryn and climbing into the backseat.

"Sit here." I pat my thigh in a friendly invitation. As Kathryn moves to sit on my lap, I embrace her. "I have a bit of a headache." I complain.

"And I happen to have just the cure," she whispers into my ear as she massages the back of my neck.

~

Kathryn lies in my arms as we wake from a short nap.

"You promised to give me the details of what went on this afternoon with you and Thorpe after we rested." She looks at me with a stern eye, and I know I can't avoid telling her what happened today.

"I'm not sure where to begin. To say it was a complete fucking fiasco would be putting it mildly." I have her undivided attention now as she's raised up on her elbows.

"Oh, Adam. I had a bad feeling about this meeting from the second you mentioned it to me. What happened?" Her brow furrows in worry.

I take a deep breath before I begin. "First of all Peters has been working for Thorpe for years. The second I stepped foot in New York City, he had Peters get to know me. Gain my trust. And eventually sell me out."

"You mean Peters, your security guy?" She appears as surprised as I was when I was hit in the gut with the truth.

"Yes. Here I thought all these years that Peters was my most trusted source in this city. He's been monitoring Thorpe and his dealings for me for years. I bet not a fucking bit of it's even true." My temper starts to rise as I think about the years of betrayal. "After you told me about Thorpe's attack and how your father died, well, I asked Peters if we had anything illegal or damaging against Thorpe. I was ready to drop a bomb on the bastard's head."

"Adam, I thought we talked about this?" She seems hurt that I wanted to seek revenge for her.

"I know, I know. I wasn't going to do anything without having concrete proof. No hit men or anything like that.

Although, now I'm tempted." She shakes her head at me, and I smile so she knows I'm just teasing. "Seriously, Peters told me that Thorpe was doing some illegal transactions on a business deal. I believed what Peters said and decided to nail Thorpe's ass to the wall."

"But Peters was really working for Thorpe?" From the look in her eyes, I can see that things are starting to add up. "So the deal wasn't real. Peters just told you it was."

"Bingo. You're not only beautiful, you're brilliant." I push her hair behind her ear. Then teasingly I give her earlobe a little tug. Detail by detail, I run through the entire day's events. The resignation, the fall on the sidewalk when I came out of the building, and Ollie finding out that Thorpe had concocted the entire resignation as a ruse. The only thing I left out was the reason for my fall. The quick turnaround I did thinking Simon was speaking to me.

"I'm in shock." Her eyes are wide with disbelief. "How can a father do such a despicable thing to his son?"

"In his eyes, I'm no more his son than the homeless guy on the corner. I'm a stain—as he put it—that reminds him of a failure on his part."

"I'm so sorry, Adam." She rubs her fingers up and down my arm, her touch soft.

"Thanks, baby," I say, drawing her into my arms. We wrap our bodies around each other and stay locked in a lover's embrace. Each minute that goes by with her in my arms makes me forget some of the day's sting. But there's one more thing I need to share with her. My flashbacks with Simon.

"I've been having some strange things happen since the shooting." She rises up an elbow and frowns.

"What do you mean?"

"I've been having trouble sleeping at night." I take a deep breath before continuing. "Dreams of the shooting, starring Simon, keep disturbing me. Some of them have been graphic."

"I wondered why you weren't sleeping. Especially the night I found you drinking in my living room around 4 a.m. You should've told me." She doesn't say it to scold me, but simply that she wants me to share my life with her.

"I should've, but I kept thinking the dreams would go away and things would return to normal." I twirl a piece of her raven hair with my finger and look into her eyes. I need to see her. "I've even heard Simon's voice."

"During the day?" Her brow wrinkles as she waits for my answer.

"Yes," I confess after a brief pause. "It happened again today after I left Thorpe's. The doctor said I had a panic attack."

"Oh my God, Adam. I can't believe you're just telling me all of this now." Kathryn sits up on the bed, looking down at me. "Hearing voices is serious shit. I'm worried about you. All the stress and the shooting..."

"The doctor had a phrase for it—"

"Post-traumatic stress disorder?" She interrupts before I can say it.

"That's it."

She brings her hands to my chest. "I'm glad you told him about it... and me.

Chapter 20

"Adam, you're experiencing the classic symptoms of post-traumatic stress disorder, or PTSD. Flashbacks of the shooting, nightmares, and hallucinations in the form of hearing Simon's voice in your mind." The psychiatrist sums up all my issues in his assessment. It appears I have some troubles to say the least.

"I sound pretty messed up when you list everything together." I glance away from the doctor. I have no clue what the answer to my problems is, but I'm thankful he worked me into his full schedule two days after the ER incident.

"I'm most concerned about the daytime flashbacks and hearing Simon's voice. Those need to be addressed first. Have you ever had a flashback of *your* struggle with Simon? When he shot you—or grazed you, as you put it?" He taps something into his laptop as he awaits my answer. But I haven't thought back to the struggle Simon and I had with the gun or when the bullet hit me. None of it ever involved me.

"Not once. I have had nightmares of him shooting Kathryn. Killing her, actually. The times I hear him talking in my mind, he's mocking me. These episodes scare the shit out of me."

He nods as if he expected me to say this.

"Observing Simon's actions during the shooting likely caused the trauma more than what he did to *you* personally. When he held the gun to Kathryn's head, a person you feel strongly for, the feeling of hopelessness knowing you were the cause of his attack gave you the greatest anxiety. So I want to see you twice a week for the next month." The doctor meets my eyes with a serious stare as he waits for my response.

I've always thought shrinks and therapists were for weak people who relied on others to solve their problems. After sitting here for an hour, discussing what I've experienced since the shooting, I realize I was wrong. Completely wrong.

"Sure, I'll make it work," I say. The doctor's passive face changes to a smile.

"Good. Your first step to getting better is de-stressing your life and getting some sleep." The doctor returns to his laptop. "I'm going to prescribe a sleep aid for you. We'll start with that for now."

"Okay... but I'm not a fan of drugs." I have to be honest, but I also know I can't live with this anxiety and lack of sleep much longer. My body feels like it's being pulled down into an ocean's undertow.

"I'm not, either. But there's a time and place for them and this is the time. A few nights of uninterrupted sleep will make a world of difference." He taps his fingers on his keyboard, and I hear a printer churning somewhere behind him.

The doctor reaches back, grabs a piece of paper from the tray, and hands it to me. "Here is what I want you to get take. One per night, thirty minutes before bed. Now the de-stressing part. You may find this a harder pill to swallow."

He rests his hands on the desk, and gives me his full attention.

"I am recommending you take some time off—two to four weeks. A month would be best. You mentioned earlier that you haven't had a personal vacation in over a year. This needs to change. And by *vacation*, I mean a break from your cell phone, market analyzing, and emails. Totally decompressing. Your mental health demands it."

"A month? Two to four weeks?" What the hell? He's nuts. I shake my head as my mind runs through the fallout of taking this much time off. "I'm not sure it's possible right now."

"A month. Let someone else slay all the financial dragons for a while. You need the break before your stress breaks you."

I leave the doctor's office with a counseling appointment for next Tuesday, a cure for my lack of sleep, and my position as Kings' CEO to be put on hold, at least for the next month. Two are easily tackled, but one seems almost impossible.

As soon as I walk into the waiting area, Kathryn stands and comes to my side. A reassuring smile lights up her face.

"Hi," she says while reaching up on her tiptoes to kiss my cheek.

"Hello, beautiful." I reach out for her hand and lace our fingers together.

"How did it go?" she asks as we make our way to the elevator. "It looks like you survived."

"I told him *everything*," I say, summarizing the intense hour-long conversation. "He wants to talk about my mother's death next week." I swallow hard at the thought.

"I know it will be hard, but he has to know so he can help you." She gives my hand a gentle squeeze.

"True." Her words reflect the doctor's. "It wasn't easy, but I feel better after talking to him. I'm just glad to know he didn't think I was going insane. I was beginning to wonder after Wednesday."

"It's amazing how sharing your feelings can help." She has that knowing tone in her voice, and I turn to see her winking at me.

"Yes, I'm learning from the master." I bend at the waist and bow to her while she laughs at my display.

"You have come pretty far from that closed-off player I met at the gala." She inspects me from head to toe. "Yep, I think he's almost gone."

"I think you're right," I whisper and kiss the top of her head. "But the doctor believes I need a month away from Kings."

Kathryn eyes me, doubtful.

"I know, I know," I respond. "I'll see if I can make it happen."

"You do, and I'll take the month off with you," she says in a seductive voice.

"Well, that settles that," I say as we leave the elevator and walk into the lobby.

Exiting the building, we find Eddie still parked in front. We climb into the back seat and nestle together. She leans her head on my shoulder, and the scent of her perfume fills my lungs. A comforting feeling floods over me. I hold onto it, not wanting to let go.

~

I'm sitting in the Two E bar located off The Pierre's lobby next to the front desk. The discreet bar is tucked away inside the hotel, a hidden gem on the Upper East Side. The subdued lighting, quiet atmosphere, and conversational seating make it a perfect place to meet for drinks and a light diner. Tom and Patrick are scheduled to join me here any minute.

I haven't been back to Kings since I met with Thorpe two days ago. Though I've been on conference calls and answered a shit ton of emails, my physical presence has been missing from the actual building.

I asked the guys to stop by and unwind from the week. We also need to talk about what's happening with Thorpe and Peters and what fallout Wednesday might have had on our company.

Kathryn stayed upstairs in my penthouse because she wants Rosa to teach her how to make her famous meatloaf. The two get along like old friends, and I love how easily Kathryn has become a permanent fixture in my life.

I glance up from my scotch to see my partners stride into the bar. With suit coats thrown over their arms and ties loosened around their necks, the effects of the crazy workweek show.

"Hey, Adam." All eyes in the bar turn to Tom when his deep voice booms in the quiet bar.

"Hey, guys." I motion for them to join me at my table. A dutiful server follows behind, ready to fill their drink orders.

"Good to see you, Adam," Patrick says and drops his coat in an empty chair next to him.

"What would you gentlemen like to drink?" the server asks.

"What are you having, Adam?" Tom eyes my glass.

"The usual, scotch."

"Fine. I'll have the same," Tom says.

"Me, too," Patrick chimes in.

"What a few days you've had, buddy," Tom adds with a touch of sarcasm and a punch on the arm. "I've been trying to wrap my head around the fact that Peters worked for Thorpe the entire time he was supposedly your go-to guy. Nine damn years. I'm still floored, Adam."

"Tell me about it. It was the fucking shock of my life." I shake my head and take a healthy gulp of my drink. "Ken's working on the legalities of what Thorpe and Peters did with the Kings information. On Kings' behalf, he plans to file a complaint with the SEC on Monday morning. It's a long shot anything will touch Thorpe but it's worth a try."

"All the evidence we have against him is circumstantial and hearsay. He's likely hidden or destroyed all the documents he had by now. Plus, he didn't do anything with the codes before we changed them," Patrick says, summing up the situation.

We look at each other in relief. The consequences of a breach in the company's security firewalls would've been felt across the globe.

"Thorpe is known in this town as Mr. Teflon for a reason. Nothing sticks to him. Nothing. And he makes sure of that. But after what he did to his own flesh and blood, I don't think you have another choice. Someone needs to stand up to him. I'll stand behind you. You have my support." The usual stoic and cautious Patrick surprises me with the sincerity.

Before I can thank him, Tom says, "I'm in, too, Adam. It sickens me to think that Thorpe pulled such a slimy move on you. I can't imagine what you were thinking when you felt forced to resign. I say we do everything we can to expose this asshole."

"That's likely the only real result we'll have. Exposing him. You're right, Patrick. The SEC may not have enough evidence in the end, but Thorpe will have to defend himself as the investigation progresses. Who knows? Maybe other people will come forward. I'm sure there are countless businesspeople he's bullied in this city. Maybe our spark will get a fire started."

I say a silent prayer that somehow Thorpe will be held accountable for his wrongdoings this side of heaven—or hell, for that matter.

"You could be right. You may inspire others to stand up against him, too," Patrick says.

"Ken said the police haven't been able to locate Peters. When they searched his apartment, it was empty. Not even a sign that he lived there at all." Trying to stay calm, I take a deep breath as I relive the betrayal.

"Adam, you've been through a hurricane-size shitstorm. How are you doing, really?" Patrick asks with his brows wrinkled in concern.

"Honestly… I'm wiped out. I went to see a doctor today." I glance down at my drink as I decide to call my psychiatrist simply a *doctor*. I'm not ready to come clean with them about the PTSD. "I've been having trouble sleeping since the shooting. All stress related, the doctor said. He wants me to take some time off."

"Okay…" Patrick clutches his scotch as he waits for me to explain.

"He's advised me to take a month off. No emails, no phone calls. Nothing related to business. A complete break." I speak fast as I break the news.

Tom sits back in his chair and rakes his fingers through the mess of blond hair on his head. "Jeez, Adam. A month—"

Patrick reacts quickly and holds his hand up to interrupt Tom. "Take whatever time you need," he says. "We can handle Kings." He glares over at Tom, who's gone silent.

"Thanks, Patrick." I put my hand on his shoulder then turn to Tom. He's sitting up in his seat now and leaning my way.

"Patrick's right. Sorry, Adam. I just can't imagine you gone from Kings for so long." He gives me a warm smile, and it erases my concerns.

"I bet you all won't even miss me." I snort.

"If you stay away longer, we'll just change the company's name to Duffy Capital." Tom chuckles at his stupid joke, and Patrick and I roll our eyes at him. Always the wise guy.

~

The aroma of something cooking hits my nose the second my feet step over the threshold. I follow the delicious smell and the sounds of laughter toward the kitchen. I cross my fingers that chocolate chip cookies await me. I swear that's what I smell. My steps sound on the hardwoods as I approach the kitchen, giving me away.

"Adam!" squeals a happy and tipsy-sounding Kathryn. She's wearing a big grin, an oversize yellow apron, and a dime-size smudge of chocolate on her cheek. "You're back!"

She slides across the floor and hugs me around my waist. Trying to figure out what these two were doing up here, I look over at the counter and see a couple dozen cookies cooling. I glance at Rosa, who shrugs and looks over at a wine glass sitting beside a half-empty bottle of wine.

"Yes, beautiful, I'm back." I laugh at her playfulness. "And you've been drinking."

"Just a teensy bit." Kathryn pinches together her forefinger and thumb to show the universal sign for *teensy*. But one-half of a bottle isn't small when you barely weigh one hundred and ten pounds.

I kiss off the chocolate from her cheek. "That tastes good," I say and lick my lips. Rosa giggles and fans herself as I hold Kathryn close to me.

"Mr. Kingsley, you're going out to dinner, right?" Rosa asks while grabbing her purse from the counter.

"Yes, Eddie's downstairs waiting for us." I loosen Kathryn's apron ties, and she wiggles out of it. "No need for you to stay any longer, Rosa."

"Rosa and I skipped the meatloaf and went straight to dessert." Kathryn blows some hair away from her flushed face. It makes her look about seventeen.

"Good night, Mr. Kingsley and Ms. Kathryn," Rosa calls as she disappears around the corner into the hallway.

"Good night, Rosa."

I hear the clicking sound of the door as Rosa departs. Running my fingers through Kathryn's raven hair, I breathe in her appealing scent of wine mixed with chocolate.

"You know, I'm on vacation starting today."

"A whole month?" Kathryn asks with a voice full of hope.

"Yes, a whole damn month. I think we should get things started now." I smirk while picking her up by the waist and sitting her down on the kitchen counter.

"Humph." Kathryn lets out in reaction to my quick movements. "What do you have in mind?" She licks her red lips. Then I lean toward her and do the same.

"A lot of that." I kiss over her cheeks and end up behind her ear. "And tons of this."

I let my eager hand wander up her now-parted legs. I hook a finger underneath the lace of her panties and pull them to the side. Exploring her wet warmth, I find her clit. Once located, I press and move in quick vibrations. I'm relentless in my motions until she comes undone for me.

Catching her breath, she lays her head back against the kitchen cabinets. "What the hell was that?" she asks through a blissful smile.

"Just wanted to start off my vacation with a bang." I chuckle.

"Not that I'm complaining, but that was a one-sided bang, mister," she says with her hands on her hips.

"I think I'll survive. Now jump down from there. Eddie's waiting to take us to The Core Club for your mother's birthday dinner."

"God, I love you, Adam." *Finally*, she professes her love to me. All it took was some chocolate, wine, and a fast fingering. I can work with that.

"I love you too, beautiful," I say and kiss her chastely on the lips.

She follows my orders and hops down from the counter. I smack her sweet little ass as I trail behind her to the front door, hoping I make it through dinner.

~

"I still can't believe you two good-looking young men are brothers." Ava glances between Ollie and me. An approving smile spreads across her face.

"And we're the luckiest women in New York City," Kathryn announces. "To have these two handsome men in our lives, sitting here with us."

Ollie slowly shakes his head. "I think these two have had enough of the bubbly for the evening."

"Kathryn had a head start before we came." Her fingers trail a hot path up my leg under the table. I silently thank God for the dark corner and heavy tablecloth. She's kept me hard most of dinner.

"This is my last fifty-something birthday. Next year I'll be sixty, so let's keep that bubbly bubbling, please." Ava giggles like a schoolgirl who's just had her first sips of champagne. It makes me happy to see her enjoying herself.

"Well, you could have fooled me." I compliment her honestly. "I'd never believe you to be a day over forty." I imagine Kathryn aging the same graceful way as her mother.

"You always say the right words, Adam." She reaches out to my hand lying on the table and gives it a gentle pat. "When I met you a little over a year ago, I hoped I'd have a chance to introduce you to my Kathryn. She was still in Paris at the time, but I had this feeling. It's like I knew there was something special about you. You've always seemed so familiar to me."

"I trust your wise intuition," I add.

"Mother *does* know best." She winks. "This time that truly applies... You said you're taking off the entire month." She looks deep in thought as if she's scheming.

"Yes, the entire month. Going to try to make a clean break from the rat race." I hope I can really separate myself from Kings. Even as I sit here tonight, declaring my break, I'm thinking of investor calls that need to be made next week. I'm finding it difficult to relinquish control and relax.

"With a company your size, it can't be easy," Ollie concludes. "Ava has been trying to get me to come to the *light* and work for her at the Swanson Foundation. I'm not sure I can give up the rat race, though. I think I'll watch you and see how it goes."

"I want to step down as head of the foundation by my sixtieth birthday. I have a year to convince one or both of you gentleman to take my place." Ava purses her lips and taps her chin. Ollie and I exchange unspoken words and smile at Ava's determination.

But I wonder... If anyone can convince me to leave this concrete jungle, it would be Ava.

Chapter 21

Laurel Hill Cemetery, Philadelphia, PA.

The sun shines from an azure blue sky as I crouch down beside my mother's grave. I trace over the carved letters in her headstone and lay my hand on top of it. I slide my fingers back and forth over the polished surface. My mother is no longer here on this earth with me, but my light caresses on the smooth marble feel like a physical connection to her.

My visit to her grave today has one purpose: honoring her. Something I've failed to do over the last ten years.

I've rehearsed the apologies I need to say to her, but the words won't push past the constricting lump in my throat. Even my eyes fail me as they cloud with tears of pain and regret.

I bow my head into my chest and fall to me knees. The damp ground soaks through my pants and touches my skin. I collapse into myself and begin to shake as streams of tears run down my cheeks.

"Mom..." The strained plea leaves me and my confession begins. "I'm so sorry. I had no idea what you went through with Thorpe, but I understand that you left your dreams behind to protect me from that man."

"Thank you, Mom. You were a selfless woman, and I owe you everything."

Placing my hands on the top of her tombstone, I stand and brush off the fallen leaves stuck to the knees of my pants.

I kiss the tips of my fingers and touch them to the etched words: Flora Kingsley. Closing my eyes, I take a minute to say good-bye.

Reaching into my pocket, I pull out a tissue and wipe off my face. My vision clears as I walk back to my car. The passenger door is wide open, and Kathryn sits inside.

I kick some gravel as I near the car and alert Kathryn of my approach. She turns her head toward me and greets me with a comforting smile. My eyes begin to blur again because I wouldn't be here on this sacred ground if she hadn't fallen in love with me.

I make my way to the driver's side and climb in next to her. I reach across the console and take her hand. Raising it to my lips, I kiss over the soft skin of her knuckles.

"Are you all right, Adam?" She brushes her thumb over the back of my hand.

"Yes, I'm okay. I should've visited her grave years ago." I give her hand a gentle, reassuring squeeze. "Thank you for coming with me. I can't build a future with you unless I've dealt with my past." I turn the keys in the ignition, and with a lighter heart, I drive away.

Epilogue

You are cordially invited...

Adam wears a fitted black tuxedo, and I'm dressed in an ivory gown made for a princess. Tonight's catered affair is all for us.

The overpriced band plays our song as we dance alone on the floor. I lay my head against Adam's chest, and the sound of his heart's steady beat comforts me. I twirl my fingers in his hair, and he melts under my touch.

"What you do to me, beautiful," he murmurs as we move and sway across the dance floor. "I love and adore you."

"Please, say it again."

"Kathryn, my love. I adore you," he whispers sweetly in my ear while holding me tightly. I gaze up into his deep brown eyes and smile as I think back to what's happened in our lives over the last year.

"Sweet, sweet, Adam, I love you, too."

After Adam visited his mother's grave, he began to reflect on his life in New York City. The chase for power and money didn't hold the attraction it once did. He questioned if he wanted to stay in the rat race with all the other rats. The betrayals he faced from two of his most-trusted colleagues were hard for him to shake.

The biggest change came when Adam went to see to a psychiatrist as suggested by his ER doctor. My proud Adam admitted he needed help. Those sessions changed his life as he worked through issues he didn't even know were troubling him.

Every time he came home from his counseling session, his eyes shined a little bit brighter, his step was a little bit lighter, and his feet a little less in New York City. He was becoming a happier version of himself.

My mother realized the daily requirements of the Swanson Foundation were becoming to taxing for her, so she kept asking Adam to take over as its head. He had more money than he could possible spend in one life time and had considered stepping down as CEO of Kings Capital, so the resigning to head the foundation was a natural step. His transition to working full-time for the foundation took the better part of a year. He planned his break from Kings as I planned our wedding.

He had so many loose ends to tie up before he could walk away from the company that he created with his friends. Tom and Patrick supported his decision and made the mutual agreement to work as co-CEOs. It took two men to replace my Adam. He's that exceptional.

The SEC investigated the complaint Adam made against his father's wrongdoings. When the investigation was made public, other companies and individuals stepped forward to make similar claims of his father's bullying tactics. Even if his father doesn't face charges by the SEC, his reputation has been tarnished. Between Adam, Ollie, and me, not a tear was shed for Thorpe. "What are you thinking, beautiful? You seem lost in thought." He lifts my chin with his finger, and his eyes are filled with concern.

"I was thinking about the year we've had. When we met, who would have ever guessed that we would be leaving New York City to work for the Swanson Foundation in Ethiopia?"

"Are you kidding? When I met you, all I could think about was getting in your pants." He winks. I follow with a loving punch to his arm.

"You and your dirty mind." I roll my eyes at him, but honestly I do love our sweet and naughty banter. It's delicious foreplay. "I look back to where we both were. Me—a lonely widow and you—a lonely playboy. The year has been a perfect whirlwind."

"Yes, it has. But let's trade in the whirlwind for a nice island breeze." He smirks at me like the devil he pretends to be. I don't know how he thought keeping our honeymoon destination a secret was a good idea.

"We're honeymooning on an island?" I can almost feel the sand beneath my feet as I wait for his answer.

"Mrs. Carter's last job for me was locating a perfect island for the two of us, and I think you'll be very pleased. It's nestled off Brazil. The waters are the bluest blue and the beaches are white as snow. We'll have a cook and a housekeeper. But no one else will be there with us. Just you, me, and the sea."

"Thank you, Adam. It sounds perfect." I reach up on my tiptoes and give him a sweet little kiss of thanks. But he wants more from my lips and presses into me harder for a searing kiss.

We become lost in each other as our kiss deepens and our passions soar. The fact that we're in front of three hundred witnesses is forgotten until we hear them clapping, and our lover's trance is broken. Adam and I turn to the crowd and take a little bow.

Adam brings me back into his arms and spins me around as our song comes to an end. "Thank you for this dance, Mrs. Kingsley."

"My pleasure, Mr. Kingsley."

Thanks for joining us!

For the Reader

Thank you for taking a chance on an Indie, self-publishing author. I truly appreciate you choosing to buy and read my debut novel.

I'd love to hear from you too. Perhaps leave a review or a comment on my web site or Facebook page.
www.livmorris.com
http://www.facebook.com/LivMorrisAuthor

You can also connect with me on twitter. It's a favorite of mine.
http://twitter.com/LivMorrisAuthor

My five novellas in the Love in the City series are published in a boxed set.

All the best,
Liv

TEMPTATION

(Touch of Tantra #1.5)

by Liv Morris

Chapter 1

A sense of satisfaction hits me once I have all the necessary elements for my Tantra session in place. I survey the room and watch the candles' flickering flames bounce an amber glow over the silk tapestries. The soft music playing from hidden speakers sounds out a hypnotic beat. Like a rhythmic pulse—steady and paced. The setting and sensual ambiance are impeccable. I want nothing short of perfection for this session as it's my client's last scheduled visit with me. A grand finale of sorts. I'm looking forward to seeing him demonstrate his newly acquired techniques. Off with the old way, *getting off* with the new is my hope.

While I adjust a wedge pillow situated on the cushioned floor mat, the front desk buzzer sounds throughout my apartment, signaling my appointment's arrival. I leave my candlelit office, run to the in-house phone in my hallway, and pick up the receiver.

"Hello," I respond into the phone, winded.

"Mrs. Delcour, Mr. and Mrs. Browning are here in the lobby. They say you have an appointment with them."

"Thanks, Carl. I do. Please send them up."

"Yes, Mrs. Delcour." I appreciate Charlie's formal address, but referring to me as *Mrs.* makes me feel so matronly.

Being a widow at thirty-four makes me acutely aware I'm an unusual specimen. Old before my time, and very much on my own, I can't even remember the last time I went for a wax. That's something to add to my to-do list for later this afternoon at the spa.

Waxing hasn't been a big priority since I haven't had *real* sex in the last two years, although the thought of it comes to mind and more often than I'd like. The familiar craving of being with a man, having him fill and possess me, fills my thoughts and arouses an aching need in me I've locked away.

The problem is it takes two for the tango I have in mind, and I haven't found a single man in this entire city of millions who has raised my temperature or interest. All the men I've met have been mundane, at best, with absolutely no chemistry between us at all. I need a challenge. A sparring partner. A man with passion—or at least passion for me. A tangible heat would be nice, too.

A solid knock on the front door echoes through the marbled entryway, announcing the Browning's arrival.

One last glance at the hallway mirror, followed by a quick adjustment of my tight camisole, and I'm ready for the session to begin. This client is bringing his wife with him for the first time. He came to me as a referral. One of the first "it's all about me when it comes to the bedroom" men I've had the pleasure of teaching how to please a woman. Mr. Browning said the results in the bedroom were so great for him; he'd be my slave for a day in thanks. I begin to chuckle at that thought as I pull the door open.

"Hello, Ross." I greet the two happy and eager faces in front of me with a warm smile. "This must be Lily."

"Good morning, Kathryn." Ross gives me a light kiss on each cheek. His eyes dance as he pulls away from me. He's one excited man. "This is my lovely wife, Lily."

"Hello, Lily." Smiling at one another, we shake hands as I welcome her to my apartment and then motion them inside. "I've been looking forward to meeting you."

"Oh, it's so great to finally meet you, Kathryn. First off, I have to thank you. Good God. Where do I even start?" She giggles and collapses into Ross's side. He closes his arms around her. Their physical intimacy is apparent, and I can't help but smile, fully satisfied at what I see before me.

"No need to say another word. I can see you appreciate what Ross has learned." Lily looks up at me, nodding. I wink knowingly and offer my arm to Lily. It's time to get this show on the road.

We head down the hallway with Ross in tow. I peer over my shoulder and give him a big smile of approval. I have a wonderfully happy wife on my arm. A far cry from what he described the day I met him.

They are a young couple—early thirties and newly married. Recently, an old flame started making contact with Lily. It was a man she'd dated in her midtwenties. She claimed to have never been in love with him, but this old lover knew how to fuck her into oblivion, as Ross put it.

It made him take notice of their sex life. Ross knew Lily loved him, but he felt the need to up his game in the bedroom. I found that to be quite the understatement upon learning more. I remember him confessing on many occasions that Lily didn't climax during sex. He hadn't really thought much about why. Lucky for Ross, I'm not a dominatrix or he would've left my office with a sore and red ass.

Lily tugs my arm to get my attention. "I've been telling my girlfriends all about you, Kathryn. I can't believe what's happened in our bedroom."

Lily's voice fades away at the end. I glance her way and notice she's drifted off into her thoughts. If I wasn't holding on to her, I swear Lily would float off in some dreamlike state.

"I'm happy things are working out so well for you. Ross has obviously learned how to put this blissful smile on your face." I squeeze her hand and release our arms as we stand at the entrance to my guest bedroom.

Ross joins Lily at the door and pulls her into his side. She melts into his embrace and lays her hand across his chest. They could pass as lovesick teenagers. I have to shake my head and wonder if I could become a little sick from their sweetness before the session is finished. Yes, I might be a little jealous, I admit, but I am truly happy for them.

"I placed a couple of robes on the bed for you." Turning to face Ross, I continue. "Have you decided what you want to practice today?"

Ross exchanges a knowing smile with Lily. One she quickly returns along with a deep red blush. Their reactions to my question leave me slightly puzzled and curious what Tantra technique they've decided to practice for Ross's last session. I strongly suggested the Yab-yum to Ross last week, but something tells me he opted for something else.

"Well," Ross speaks with roguish smile. "I believe we have the Yab-yum down pat. However, I want to make sure I master the Yoni massage. I know it's very intimate and requires the woman to be naked, but Lily has agreed to it. What do you think, Kathryn?"

Damn. What a loaded question. I've studied and observed this massage of the female genitalia in teaching, even partially preformed it once for my Tantric certification. All my experience seems clinical now that I have real live people, my clients, standing in front of me. I knew someone would want to perform this massage during a session sooner or later. The joys of being a new teacher...awkward firsts.

"I'm fine with you performing a Yoni massage on Lily." I turn toward Lily. I need to see her approval, too. We just met, and this massage is one up close and intimate act. "Are you aware of what the Yoni massage entails?"

"I am," Lily answers quickly. Her eyes are bright and alight with enthusiasm. She appears to be game. Hell, I guess I am, too. "We've watched all the instructional DVDs you gave Ross. The only thing we have left to attempt is the Yoni massage."

"What makes you want to try it today in front of me?" I'm curious to know what has motivated Ross and Lily to choose this particular act with me as their audience. It's a rather bold move, in my opinion, since this is Lily's first time here with me. They will have to bury every sexual inhibition to have a fruitful session.

"I want to get it right." Ross's eyes are steadfast on mine and he's dead serious. There is no wavering in his expression. He wants to please his woman. And damn if she isn't some lucky lady to have her man want to please her like this. I stuff my jealousy away, knowing it's time to break the sex drought in my life. Pronto!

"All right, you two. Go ahead and change into the silk robes lying on the bed and meet me in my office." I gently tug on Ross's arm to stop him from following Lily into the bedroom. I need to clear up a few things before we go any further.

"I will quietly coach you through the massage. But I'm going to be watching Lily's reactions, and if at any time I'm not convinced she's comfortable with me observing, then I'll step out of the room and allow you two some privacy."

"Sounds fair enough." He looks away, in thought. "I did some research on this massage, and I read sometimes a woman will cry during this massage."

"Yes. It's not unusual for people to cry during any Tantra sessions. They tend to bring healing to people in the most unexpected ways."

"Do you think she might have trouble with this?" Ross's voice is now a mere whisper. I take that as reason to believe Lily isn't supposed to overhear our conversation, so I move closer.

"I don't think she'll have trouble with it. She might have some unexpected responses to what happens during the massage. Be prepared and know if she cries, her tears are tears of healing." I pat him on the upper arm in reassurance.

"Okay. I just want the best experience for her today, though." Sweet Ross. He wants her to feel nothing but bliss. However, he's lost focus of Tantra's true objective.

"Remember the basis of Tantra is intimacy and healing. Not an orgasm being the end game, although that's a wonderful side effect." I nod toward the bedroom where Lily disappeared. "Let an open heart lead you in the session today. I promise Lily will thank you in the end."

Chapter 2

I position myself next to the wedge pillow on the floor mat and wait for their arrival in my office. It's taking them some time to make their way to me and I'm beginning to wonder if they're having second thoughts. Perhaps all the bravado in the hallway was just that—*talk.*

My concerns are laid aside as they enter through the double doors to my office. Dressed in the black silk robes I left on the guest bed, their belts are secured loosely at their waists. Lily's robe hangs from her shoulders and is likely two sizes too big for her petite frame. I think she's even smaller than me.

Lily glances around the room, her eyes darting to the flickering candles, the tapestry covered walls, and finally resting on me kneeling in front of her. It's Lily's first time in my office, and I can tell she's impressed from the look on her face.

"Welcome, Lily." I smile at her while she returns my greeting with an inquisitive look. I don't think the room was what she expected. "Come over to the mat and sit down with me."

Ross takes hold of Lily's hand and they walk in unison across the scattered rugs to me. A sense of relief washes over me when I see Lily smiling my way. I believe she's absorbed her surroundings, and hopefully she's letting the sensuous atmosphere calm her nerves. Regardless, I know I must tread lightly in my approach with her if she's going to benefit fully from our time today.

Lily kneels next to me with our knees almost touching. I lightly caress her arm, trying to comfort and reassure her that I'm on her team of sexual discovery.

"Since you've seen a Yoni massage on DVD, you have a pretty good idea what you're going to be attempting." I catch Lily's attention and address her next. "Leave your robe on, Lily, and lie back with your upper body against the wedge pillow."

Lily maneuvers herself to the pillow and reclines against the soft cushion. Shifting from side to side, she settles herself in place and adjusts the front of her robe, making sure its length covers her sex. A sign for me to gingerly ease into nudity with her.

"I'm going to sit behind you on the pillow, Lily. I'd like to stay out of your peripheral vision and place the focus on you and Ross." Lily lets out a sigh of relief. Her earlier show of bravery has definitely worn off. I wonder how long I'll actually stay with them.

"Lily, you'll need to part your legs." She moves her legs apart as asked, keeping her hands relaxed at her sides. "Now, Ross, move between her extended legs with your knees touching the middle of her inner thighs."

"You're in the perfect position to start the massage." Ross rubs his hands over his robe-covered thighs. I sense his anxiousness to start, so I deliberately slow the pace. We will not be rushed today.

"I'll be gently coaching you two." I set my voice to where it's just above a whisper. "Before you begin touching, you're going to focus on breathing and eye contact."

Ross and Lily center on each other. "Focus on keeping this gaze the entire time."

The look Ross is giving Lily intensifies and turns into a smoldering gaze of need. A red-hot sexual energy begins to charge between them. I discreetly raise the volume of the music a notch or two with the remote I've kept close at my side. The gentle tempo of the song adds to the feeling of sex in the air.

"Take deep breaths in sync." My command is whispered but heard as they comply and take deep breaths together. "Deeper and slower now."

After a minute or two, I notice Lily's shoulders have drooped in a relaxed state and are no longer holding tension and excess energy. She appears calm, so I decide to move to the next step. Touching.

"Starting at Lily's forehead, begin." I give Ross the directive to commence the Yoni at Lily's Sixth Chakra, or the third eye. He delicately traces his fingers across Lily's face. Focusing on this area will help calm her mind and get her body ready to fully receive and focus on Ross's touch as he continues the massage.

Her body visibly responds to his touch as her nipples protrude against the silk of her robe. I can barely see Lily's lashes over the inclined pillow, but I notice them starting to flutter. "Eyes stay open and on one another." I reiterate the need for eye contact in a soft whisper.

Ross continues to caress Lily's body with his hands, lingering on her shoulders with the tips of his fingers gliding across the shiny black robe. I decide it's better for her to stay clothed at this point. No need to rush.

With gentle, up and down motions, Ross's hands sweep the length of Lily's arms. He stops at her upraised palms to delicately outline the creases lying within. A slight moan escapes Lily's lips.

I smile to myself, knowing how many nerve endings make up the erogenous zones that are littered across the skin. Many of them in the most unlikely places, too. Before Tantra, Lily most likely never thought she'd feel a clenching low in her belly from being touched on her palm's lifeline. But I saw her squeeze her thighs as Ross's fingers traced over her sensitive skin.

From where I'm kneeling, it appears Ross doesn't need much coaching from me on this massage any longer.

It's apparent he's read the material on the practice of the Yoni massage since he's now shifted his hands to her Fourth Chakra, the chest area right above the space between her breasts. His fingers remain on this exposed area, making small circles that extend almost to her collarbone.

Lily's skin is still covered by the robe's shiny silk as Ross skates over the fabric near her firm breasts on each pass of his circles. Impatient for his direct touch, Lily squirms in hopes of eliciting some contact with her nipples. Wisely, Ross catches on to Lily's desires and keeps his fingers away from them. The words *rush* and *hurried* are forbidden in Tantra, and Ross knows this from my earlier teachings.

Slowly, Ross drags his index finger from the exposed skin over Lily's heart to the knot in the belt of her robe. He repeats the seductive trail he made while easing his finger under the knot. Lily reacts to his teasing by widening the stance of her legs, welcoming him to move closer.

The responsive gesture shows Lily opening herself up and giving into the feelings being released inside of her. Each touch triggers more pleasure; eventually they will combine and build together to give her a tantric high, leaving her feeling nothing but sensation. Everything else around her will fade away in a blur. Ross's patient and soft lover's touch will overpower her other senses.

While keeping his focus on Lily, Ross lowers himself over her breast and eases closer to her aroused nipple. Through the silk, he draws it into his mouth, causing Lily to arch her back and moan. As quickly as he surrounded her, he removes his lips and pulls away. Eager for more, Lily spreads her legs further in an eager invitation of submissiveness. I can barely see the exposed top of her pubic bone as the robe's front edges separate. The interaction between them skyrockets. Lily confirms the sexual charge in the air by writhing as if she can hardly contain the pleasure exploding within her.

Ross looks up quickly, and his eyes dart from mine to the belt of Lily's robe. I believe he's trying to tell me what is possibly his next move, but I can sense a bit of hesitancy to pull open the belt and completely expose his wife in front of me. At this point, I think Lily's sufficiently lost in sensations and will likely yank the robe apart if he doesn't. I can tell she's ready for more as she moans softly.

I nod and it's the green light he seeks to proceed. Ross fingers the knot as he stares into Lily's eyes. She's practically panting now and shows no sign of stopping him. My presence is the last thing on her mind. She wants more of Ross's hands and fingers exploring her body and easing the ache within.

As I observe Lily and Ross, I realize for the first time that I actually wish I was the client in front of me. Maybe it's the intensity of the tantric massage, but I almost want to join in. It would be highly unethical and something I'd never do, but dammit, I'm so turned on watching Ross pleasure Lily

Perhaps it's time to cave in to my mother's demands to find the perfect man for me. How bad could a date or two be? I just need a little scratch to make this sexual itch go away. One night spent being touched by the rough hands of a real man. Add a willing tongue and a well-endowed...

Startled by my wayward thoughts, I stop my sex-starved mind from wandering down the street to the nearest bar in hopes of a hookup. Though my body isn't cooperating, I try to refocus on the scene in front of me.

I realize that as I daydreamed, Ross began removing the robe from Lily's petite body. Brushing the soft material from her shoulders and arms, she's now completely exposed. The velvety black silk lies in ripples underneath her, a shadowbox of contrast to her pale and luminous skin.

She's beautiful. Smaller but firm, her pert breasts thrust upward as she arches her back. Ross brings his hand back above her breast and trails his fingers downward to tease her nipples with a light touch. The movement has me biting my own lip to keep from moaning along with Lily. The sexual charge between them is making it difficult for me to stay professional.

Ross continues his caressing down to the juncture of her thighs and then separates his hands and lets each one travel down her legs. He keeps his fingers on the outside of her thighs, curving them under each knee—a forgotten pleasure. Lily shows how hard she's containing herself by gripping the edge of the wedge pillow.

Tantra is about prolonging and heightening the sexual experience, but I fear Lily will detonate the instant Ross touches anywhere near her clit. I hope he realizes this likelihood and delays his direct touch there. If he does, she'll likely experience the orgasm of her life. *Lucky woman.*

Ross slowly continues to ease his fingers down her legs. He circles her ankles delicately. With one hand he encloses her ankle, lifts it to his lips, and begins placing light kisses on the inside of her calves. Making his way up to her knee, he licks the underside at the speed of dripping honey. He somehow manages to keep his eyes trained on Lily even while they glaze over with desire.

Turning her leg away from him, Ross makes his way up her inner thigh. His nibble-like kisses are making Lily a twisting hot mess. Could she even orgasm without his direct touch? It's not uncommon in Tantra, but I hope she waits until either his fingers or mouth touch her clit. The feeling will be even greater for her.

As Ross nears the apex of her spread legs, he looks up at me and then focuses on the bottle of body oil next to my legs. I get his message loud and clear. The time has arrived for the central aspect of the Yoni massage.

I grab the bottle off the warming plate. *Nothing worse than body oil cooler than one's body temperature.* Ross takes the warm bottle from my hand and returns his focus back to Lily. Her body is still and tense, waiting and anticipating his next move.

Ross tips the bottle and starts to let a small stream of oil fall upon Lily's inner thighs, each toned leg getting a light coating of the warmed oil. Next he leans forward and kisses the area right above her clit, a true sign he worships her body.

After sitting back up, Ross begins to rub the oil against her skin, starting close to her knees and gingerly working his way up her inner things. The lines of oil are dripping as they run down the curve of her thigh, but Ross catches them, and Lily's skin begins to shimmer in the dancing candlelight.

Ross places his slick hands on the outer lips of her sex. He skates up and down, never touching her inner folds but making sure he caresses the intersection of her legs and body, an area tender and sensitive to the touch.

Lily tries to move her legs together, needing to relieve the sexual tension. Ross is on to her sneaky moves and pushes against her attempt. There is no escaping his slow and lingering assault. She has become his willing captive.

"Ross, Ross." Lily breathes his name—her first words since the massage began. The only other sounds are her soft moans and hums of pleasure.

Over and over, Ross rubs and massages the bare skin of her sex. His touch circles from the top of her mound down the sides of her outer core. He leaves her inner folds untouched, but each pass of his fingers gets closer to her clit.

Following the teaching of the Yoni massage, Ross deliberately prolongs Lily's need for release from the sexual build-up she's experiencing.

Lily starts to shake, and I wonder what's happening to her. Since she's facing away from me, I can't see her face. But it doesn't take long for me to realize she's actually crying. Tears of healing. A common occurrence with deep and intensive tantric sex. I can't suppress a sense of satisfaction knowing this special touch of Tantra has worked its way into her soul, exposing and healing scarred emotions she likely didn't know were there.

Ross appears concerned with the tears Lily is shedding. His eyebrows knit together in worry as he glances up at me, asking for unspoken advice on how to proceed from here. I mouth for him to keep going and circle my forefingers in the air in a sign to continue. He heeds my coaching, continuing to move his fingers over her sex. However, he brings his hand to her cheek and wipes away a few tears, acknowledging the agony her soul is experiencing.

Lily leans into Ross's hand and kisses his fingers. Nothing stops the tenderness between them as Lily's tears subside, and once again Ross focuses on caressing her intimately.

"Breathe together. Again," I whisper, my words blending around the beat of the music.

After several minutes with no sign of more tears, their coordinated breathing and centered eye contact draws them together once again. Any remnants of the tears Lily shed today are consumed with the passion Ross shows her as he administers his gentle touch over and over again. The oil glistens with her body heat and the friction of his motions.

He glides his fingers lower and turns the palm on his right hand up, and I know he's close to the last step in the Yoni massage. Ross uses his left fingers to open up her sex to him. Even from my vantage point, I can see she's wet and ready, dripping with need. As he begins to touch inside her, he smartly avoids her clit. She fidgets and bucks her hips, but Ross lays a hand on her thigh and helps to still her movements.

Lily begins to make whimpering sounds, and much to my happiness as their coach, Ross tries to soothe her with hushing sounds.

Moving forward to Lily, I speak softly into her ear. "Focus on his fingers, Lily. Absorb the sensations."

She follows my instructions and quiets her body. Ross moves his curved fingers in and out of her opening. The feeling is likely to be driving Lily to her breaking point as he touches and massages her G-spot. Ross moves his left hand upward, across her hip, inching over the soft curves of her stomach and finding her breast.

Ross squeezes Lily's aroused nipple. He tugs and elongates it as she arches her back. He's moving faster, but it's their first time at this massage, and I can tell the sensations for them are reaching a critical level.

Glancing down at her sex, Ross uses his thumb to massage her insides and presses it against her clit. With small circling movements, Lily ignites. Her legs shake far beyond the point of a slight tremble as her entire body tenses. Her cries of pleasure border on agony as she comes completely undone.

Nearing the top of her orgasmic mountain, Lily arches her back almost off the wedge pillow. I hold my breath and try to calm my own arousal while witnessing one of the most intense orgasms I've ever seen a woman have. The effects continue to roll through her body like waves, starting low at her hips and ending at her lips with a ferocious scream.

In a frantic hurry, Lily grabs for Ross as she descends from the high of her Tantra-induced orgasm. He collapses on her, kissing her face, neck, and down to her breasts before taking a nipple into his mouth.

He thrusts his hips forward as he moves between Lily's spread thighs. Lily brings her ankles together behind Ross's backside and joins the motion with every push. Ross awkwardly rises up on one hand, and I know what is likely to follow as he peels off his silk robe. Now that they're completely uncovered, I decide to exit stage left and flee out the door. My departure goes unnoticed by the two oblivious lovers ascending together toward the peak of tantric bliss.

Once I'm out of my office, I lean against a wall in the hallway. I've shuffled a few feet away from the door to try and respect their privacy even though I'm still able to hear the sounds of passion coming through the wall. There's no doubt I'm happy for them, but at the same time, I'm feeling a little frustrated about the lack of real sex in my life.

Here I am, a teacher of tantric sex who passionately teaches clients how to experience sex in the most blissful manner possible, and I've been stuck in a sexual desert for two years. Since the passing of my husband, Jean-Paul, I haven't been ready to fully give myself to another man. Sure, I've practiced Tantra for a couple of years and participated in countless sessions where things got close to the edge. But I've never been fully fucked by anyone in a session before.

Tantra opened a path of healing for me after Jean-Paul's passing. I was dead inside with a grief-filled heart. I want to share how Tantra can bring others closer to their lovers and possibly heal them in the process like it has for me.

It's odd, being unable to completely express myself sexually with a partner. I haven't found a man who turns my insides to molten lava, a burning desire where I am scorching with need and have to consume him or I'll die. I experienced this with Jean-Paul, and until I find another lover who inspires a similar type of passion, I'd rather just abstain. It's the difference between champagne and moonshine to me. I'll wait for the really good stuff.

Chapter 3

Running toward the curb outside my building, I flag down the first empty cab heading down Fifth Avenue. Once it stops, I jump in and give the driver my destination. I have an appointment to meet my mother at the Red Door Spa a few blocks down. Normally, I'd walk the short distance, since walking in the city is my main source of exercise. Not to mention that sometimes the traffic is so bad I can literally walk faster to a destination versus cabbing it.

However, I'm running late and it's past the midday rush, so traffic is light. Yes, there are several rush hours here. Nothing about traveling around this city is easy, unless you have a driver like my mother has. That's not my style, though. I'd feel too pretentious to have someone at my beck and call. I hated it as a child, especially during my teen years when I wanted to be my own person, able to come and go as I pleased. It didn't help that at the time, my parents' driver was a pervert, always staring at my chest and legs. The man was a certifiable creep.

My mother called this morning and asked to pick me up on her way to the spa. But I knew if my Tantra session ran late, she'd be upset and grill me with a ton of questions. Many of which would have answers that would make her extremely uncomfortable. She tolerates my career choice, but has decided to let the reality of my profession sit behind a shrouded veil.

I'm fairly certain today's session would freak her out. The rebellious bad girl in me can't help but smile wickedly at the thought. As progressive as my mother raised me, today's Yoni massage would probably make her blush.

Who knows, though? I like to think I am my mother's daughter.

~

Blasting through several yellow lights, my cabbie gets me to the spa in record time. I quickly tap the display screen in front of me and run my credit card through the reader. I added on a nice tip because he was quick and quiet, my favorite type of cab driver.

Approaching the mid-rise building, I notice the signature red doors I remember from my youth have been replaced by heavy, clear glass. A small sign posted by the entrance is the only identifying remnant of the infamous red doors.

After entering, I breeze past the lobby doorman and walk into the open elevator awaiting me. I press the button for my floor, run my fingers through my hair, and adjust my simple black dress and gray scarf as I'm whisked to the upper floors.

On the eighth floor, I stroll inside the confines of the luxurious spa. A quick glance at my reflection on the wall tells me why I'm here. My hair needs some TLC—I am several months overdue for a haircut. Actually I can't remember the last time it was trimmed and shaped, something I won't confess to my well-groomed mother.

I prefer a no-fuss routine when it comes to glamour. I tend to be a minimalist type of girl. With the exception of my red lipstick and mascara, I only wear makeup when I'm going out somewhere special. I'm amazed how lax my beauty routine became during the fifteen years I lived in Paris. One would think it's a city of flawlessly made-up faces, but in actuality the term *au naturel* applies to the styles there.

The beautiful young woman at the reception desk ends her call and looks up at me with a perfect, broad smile anyone would envy.

"Hello," she greets me warmly and glances over me with a discerning eye. "May I help you?"

I want to be snarky in response to her judging appraisal and say, *"What do you think?"* But I refrain and plaster on a fake smile, New York style. "Yes, I'm Kathryn Delcour. I have an appointment today. I'm meeting my mother, Ava Swanson. I believe she's already here."

She hustles from behind the tall counter that separates us; obviously the mention of my mother's name can move mountains—or at least put her small butt in motion. The Vanderbilt women are practically founding members of this spa. Other high-end establishments litter the Upper East Side and midtown, but no one does the complete head-to-toe beauty treatment like the Red Door. Hair, nails, and makeup, the Red Door is a one-stop salon for a special day or occasion.

"Yes, Mrs. Delcour. Your mother is here already, and I'm to escort you to the hair salon." I can't help but notice her staring at my unruly black locks falling over my shoulders.

"Thank you," I say as she leads me through the hallways covered with shiny white tiles. The décor is clean, minimal, and awash in soothing lighting. The walls are rounded curves which give the path to the salon a serpentine feel, like we're walking through a maze. It's a quiet and peaceful effect as we leave the harshness of the city behind.

We stop abruptly before an arched doorway, and the familiar sound of blow dryers and chatter comes from beyond the entrance. An older woman approaches us and smiles warmly at me. I return with a smile of my own.

"Hello, I'm Adrienne. Are you Mrs. Delcour?" She gracefully extends her hand to me but doesn't try for the traditional handshake. Instead she moves to my side and places her hand on my upper arm and pats me in a comforting gesture. I'm impressed she knows me by name; it's been well over fifteen years since I've been inside these walls, and I was a Swanson then.

"Yes, I'm Mrs. Delcour."

"How are you today? Good, I hope, and ready to be pampered." She doesn't show any sign of judgment at the current state of my hair, unlike the attendant who's disappeared and likely returned to her desk.

"My hair is crying for help." I follow with a little laugh and hold up the ends of my hair.

"You have beautiful raven hair, Mrs. Delcour. Enviable, really." I'm confident her compliment is sincere, and I happily follow her through the archway. I see my mother a few feet ahead of us, and it looks as if her stylist is close to having her hair perfectly coifed.

"Hello, Mother." I look at her reflection in the mirror in front of her as I speak my greetings.

"Kathryn, darling!" My mother holds her hand up to stop the stylist in his labors. She stands up from the brown leather chair and wraps her arms tight around me. She's always shown her love to me in an open and warm way without any societal pretense, unlike so many other mothers I knew growing up Manhattan. I never once doubted her unconditional love for me.

I hug her tightly and pull back a few inches, not quite leaving her loving arms. "You're looking beautiful as always, Mother. How are things going with the event? Everything in place?"

We're at the spa today in preparation for the annual Swanson Foundation fundraiser. It's the most important night for my mother's charitable work, where monies are raised from some of New York City's wealthiest residents. My mother began the foundation after my father's sudden death when I was nineteen. I know my father would be so proud of what she's done to help those in need in Africa. As a wealthy, attractive widow, she could've spent her days going to lunches, shopping, and planning her next getaway with girlfriends, but she chose to put her vast fortune to good use. Her money and energy have been focused on others, not herself. She is definitely my role model in life.

"We are as ready as we'll ever be. Natalie is great at helping put out any last-minute fires. Nothing has turned into an inferno yet." She winks at me.

My mother remains the heart and soul of the foundation with her optimistic personality while Natalie, her executive assistant, wears the mantle of a serious businesswoman. I'm not sure Natalie knows how to smile, although she could herd a few hundred cats, if needed.

"Good, Mother. I don't think there's a more capable assistant than Natalie. Now you can relax with me this afternoon."

"You're right about that. Natalie's priceless to me. I love being the face of the foundation, but the numbers and minutiae quite often bore me to tears. Because of her, I can spend time with my lovely daughter. It's been years since you've been in New York on Foundation night." My mother gives my arm a loving squeeze before she sits back down in her stylist's chair where his eager hands go back to teasing and setting her shiny gold locks.

"It's been years. Before I met Jean-Paul." I hardly ever mention his name around her, and I can tell she wants to comfort me. The look in her eyes radiates compassion back at me. I tilt my head and smile weakly, knowing it's time for me to move on with my life. Jean-Paul would want me to.

"Where are my manners?" My mother laughs as she twists in her chair and catches the eye of her stylist. "Marcus, this is my lovely Kathryn. We used to come here regularly when she was a teen. I believe her first trip with me was on her thirteenth birthday."

"*Enchanté*," Marcus says in a distant French accent before gently taking my right hand, raising it to his face, and then brushing his lips against my knuckles. The look he's giving me oozes sex. I imagine he's a favorite at the spa.

"Pleasure to meet you," I respond back with a chuckle in my voice. He stands beside me, rather puffed up and appearing quite proud of himself.

"Mrs. Swanson, where have you been hiding this beauty?" At his comment, I can't contain my eye roll while glancing in my mother's direction.

"She's been away in Paris for years, but I'm hoping she's back to stay now. She's started a new business here as well." My mother's pride is evident in her glowing smile. "It's a rather unique business, too.

I know this conversation isn't over when Marcus asks, "Oh, really? What type of business is it?"

The question needs to be answered, and I decide to give sweet, conceited Marcus something to chew on. "I teach a modern version of Tantra, the ancient practice of lovemaking. Perhaps you've heard of it?"

Marcus's mouth drops open, and I fear the comb and teasing brush in his hands may soon follow. He peruses my figure as I'm sure he's trying to figure me out or imagine me naked, teaching my craft. I glance over at my mother who's quietly enjoying my little show. Yes, I'm totally her daughter.

Before Marcus can respond or close his mouth, I feel a hand on my arm. I turn to see Adrienne at my side.

"Mrs. Delcour, your stylist is ready for you now." She politely gestures for me to follow her.

"See you in a few minutes, Mother." I bend down and kiss my mother on the cheek before leaving a stunned Marcus behind. I can't help but laugh as I follow Adrienne to my appointed chair. I truly enjoyed toying with Marcus and can only imagine what's going on in his mind or what he's asking my poor mother.

Chapter 4

An hour and a half later, my hair is trimmed, shaped, and blown out perfectly. I marvel at what a difference a little TLC has made as I see the long waves lying shiny above my breasts. Even though I've hit the town many times since my arrival back in the States, it's been awhile since I've let the sexy, dolled-up side of me out like this. I happen to like what it stirs up inside of me. An odd sexual energy flows through me, a feeling of expectation. I could just be high-strung from watching Lily and Ross's sexy Tantra session. I should've taken the time to calm the definite ache between my legs. The thought makes me shift in my chair

I meet my mother's stare, and I smile at her reflection in the mirror along the wall in front of us. We're sitting next to one another in counter-high chairs as we have our faces perfected by two very capable makeup artists.

"Look at you, Kathryn," my mother says sweetly to me while taking my hand in hers. "You're simply beautiful. So much of your father's coloring. Stunning."

"Thank you, Mother." I can't ignore the tears in my mother's eyes at the mention of my father. "You're beautiful, too. And Father would be so proud of you. The lives you've touched and the bridges you've mended in Africa. The work you've done is phenomenal. I couldn't be more proud."

"Thanks, darling. I've tried to live as Richard would've wanted me to. Wealth isn't something to hoard. We're very blessed, and it would be a sin not to help others. Someday, I hope you will carry on with the foundation. I'm not getting any younger." My mother doesn't look anywhere near her age of sixty, but what do I say to her desire to appoint me as her successor?

"You'll be at the helm for years to come, Mother. Besides, I haven't a clue about running a foundation." She releases my hand, and I hope I haven't offended her by my slight rebuff.

"I know, but think about it. I know you're invested in your business, but I'd love for you to be involved with the foundation in some way. Even coming in a day or two a week." The hopefulness I see in her is something I can't dismiss.

"We can talk more about it later, but a day a week seems doable. I'd love to learn more about what you're doing."

"Nothing would make me happier. Well, that's not entirely true. I'd love to see you find love again."

Her last words were spoken cautiously as if trying them on for size. Frankly, I'm not sure how well they fit me right now. I don't know if I'll ever find another love like Jean-Paul, and the saps I've met have been far from encouraging. I miss the feeling of being loved and loving someone with my whole heart in return.

"As you know very well, there'll be no replacing Jean-Paul." She nods and understands since she hasn't remarried after my father's passing. "But I am open to seeing what fate has in store for me. I haven't met anyone I've had an ounce of chemistry with."

"Ah, yes. Chemistry." Mother rolls the word over her tongue, slowly drawing out its sound. "The much-needed but often overlooked essential to long-lasting love."

"Exactly. After experiencing it, I'll never settle for anything else."

"And you shouldn't, dear." My mother knows a lot about chemistry. What she and my father shared was nothing less then an electrifying love. I remember my father staring at her longingly across the dinner table. The man was head over heels for her. He always had his hands on her in some manner, touching her shoulders, smoothing her hair, even a few pats on the ass. They loved each other with a deep passion.

"There's a man coming tonight I want you to meet." I begin to protest, but my mother cuts me off with a quick lift of her hand, a familiar gesture from times past when I tried to interrupt her and was overruled. "He's something else. Tall, dark, and handsome. Best looking man I've seen in years. I swear if I was younger..."

I watch in shock as my mother transforms into a giggling schoolgirl in front of me. Holy hell. Who is this guy?

"Okay, Mother. Now I'm super curious." I tip my head to the side, trying to process this person she's become in front of me. "I have a strange feeling you want to live vicariously through me."

"That's silly. I'm nearly double his age." She waves me off. "Just wait until later tonight. You'll see what I mean. He's giving a large donation to our foundation, and I'll be sure to introduce you."

"Who's this man and how old is he?" I'm failing terribly at appearing uninterested, but I wonder if I've ever heard of him. Although it's unlikely, considering I've been out of the New York social scene for years.

"His name is Adam Kingsley." The makeup artist applying my eyeliner stops cold and almost inaudibly gasps. I look up at her and find horror written all over her face.

"I believe he's your age, dear." My mother must not have heard a thing because she continued on with her description of Adam Kingsley.

"So I take it he's single, then?" Observing the alarmed woman in front of me, I notice her eyes have widened further, possibly thinking I'm interested in the man. One thing's for sure, I'm as curious as hell to meet him now... I think.

"Yes, he's very single and dates aimlessly, I believe. He's one of those men who needs the right woman to cross his path—very much the bad boy needing to be tamed. Much like your Jean-Paul." My mother adds the last comment with a wink. I'm not sure whether to be appalled or ask her more questions, but I do want to know more.

Before I can think of another question, my mother continues. "Trust me on this one, Kathryn."

I nod, not wanting to argue this point with her any longer. I'll meet this man if it's meant to be, but I have a feeling she'll make it happen one way or another.

"Mrs. Swanson, what do you think?" My mother's makeup artist pulls away and directs our attention to the mirror. There's no denying my mother looks every bit as lovely as she did twenty years ago.

"Wonderful job, Francis," Mother says, beaming while Francis smiles, satisfied with the result of her handiwork. It doesn't hurt that her canvas was beautiful from the start. "You have a magical way of making the years disappear. Thank you."

"Mother, you look great."

She scoots off her chair and straightens her casual black dress.

"Thanks, dear. I need to get moving, so I'm going to get my nails done now. I'll meet you back in the Relaxation Room." She kisses my cheek as I did hers when I left her alone with Marcus.

As soon as she disappears behind the frosted glass doors, my makeup artist spins around and faces me. I didn't miss the scowl that spread across her face at the mention of Adam Kingsley, and I'm rather certain she has more on her mind than the shade of my lipstick as she stands in front of me with her hands on her hips.

"It's none of my business, really. I do love your mother. She's probably the spa's favorite client, but this Adam Kingsley..." She begins to tsk-tsk me with her pointed index finger while shaking her head back and forth. It's easy to see's he's definitely *not* a favorite of hers.

"So you know him?" I give her an opportunity to spill what's on the tip of her tongue. I raise my brows to encourage her, hoping the floodgates will open up.

"I've never met him personally. I steer clear of men like him. He's a player of the worst kind." She bends toward me as I sit in my chair, and her voice becomes softer.

"I have this friend," she says out of the corner of her mouth as if she's giving me some super inside information. "She's a pretty well-known model in town. Gorgeous. Legs to die for. She had a little romp with this Kingsley guy. They met at some charity thing. She left with him, thinking they were bound for his apartment or a hotel room."

"Really?" I'm surprised this woman is ratting out her friend's secrets to me. I've always hated torrid gossip, but for some reason I'm thankful she's decided to share this with me. I feel as if she's trying to warn me after my mother's enthusiastic endorsement of him.

"Yes, but they didn't even make it to a hotel room. His driver drove the streets around her apartment for an *hour* while they had sex." She draws even closer to my ear. "That's not all. He dumped her right out in front of her apartment building—without even an awkward handshake good-bye."

"Wow. How did your friend take that?" This man sounds like a complete piece of work.

"She tried to brush it off as a lesson learned, but I think this man is very charismatic, and uses it to keep his dick happy." She shakes her head in disgust. "Good news, though...my friend's engaged now. To a nice, respectable man, too. For what it's worth, stay away from Adam Kingsley. I'm pretty sure your sweet mother has no clue what this man's really like."

I nod, agreeing with her assessment and warning. As she finishes my makeup with a nice red color on my lips, I can't deny I'm curious about this man, warts and all. It's likely the professional psychologist in me is raising her curious head.

Once the last bit of makeup has been applied to my face, I head back to the Relaxation Room and wait for my mother. I select a comfortable chair and find a complimentary mimosa has been set next to me. The sweet drink goes down smoothly and quickly to my rather empty stomach—empty because I had to rush out of my apartment without lunch to make it here on time.

By the time I've finished my drink, my mother still hasn't arrived. I rest my feet on the ottoman in front of my chair and gently lie back, careful not to mess up my freshly styled hair.

I close my eyes and recall my earlier Tantra session with Ross and Lily. Ross has begun to master the tantric sex trifecta I prescribe to: touch, simultaneous breathing, and constant eye contact.

I began my Tantra journey after Jean-Paul's death, and have refrained from fucking any man. There had been countless experiences of intimate touching, but no actual penetration. Right now I'm certain any sort of touching will not take away the sexual ache that's building up within me. It's making me so damn restless. Lately I've been getting lost in my own desires during sessions, which would be unethical and unprofessional if any of my clients were to find out. But unbidden I start to imagine practicing Tantra with a man I am truly attracted to, his hands caressing my body. Our breaths become synchronized while we stare into each other's eyes

I feel my skin warm under my clothes, and my nipples harden as if they long for the lover's touch I've created in my mind. The familiar ache between my legs makes me uncomfortable in my chair.

Damn if that mimosa didn't go straight to my head. I open my eyes and take a few calming breaths when my mother appears in the arched doorway, looking like a million dollars. She's ready for the event with her tea-length gown of navy blue fitting her exquisitely. I can only hope I age as gracefully as she has.

"Oh, Mother." I rise up out of my chair and walk across the small room to meet her, hoping the sexual fantasies I had just dreamt about don't show on my face. "You look wonderful and ready to go. I guess you have to head over there now."

"Thanks, darling," she says to me while reaching for my hands. "And yes, I have to get to Lincoln Center. Natalie just texted me that I'm needed."

"Yes. Time for you to kick butt and take a few names." She cringes because she's always hated the word butt.

"Kathryn. You and that mouth of yours." I want to tell her what I said was tame in comparison to my normal conversation, especially when it comes to my sex sessions. But I refrain and play the well-mannered daughter for her.

"Yes, Mother dear," I say mockingly, adding a smile to match. As I do, a woman from the spa crosses over the threshold of the arched doorway with a garment bag in her hands.

My mother turns to the woman as if she was expecting her and takes the bag. "Thank you for bringing this to me."

"My pleasure, Mrs. Swanson," the woman responds and quickly pivots to leave as she came.

"What do you have in there?" I nod toward the bag draped over her arm.

She locks her free arm with mine and walks us out of the Relaxation Room and back toward the women's lounge. "What do you plan on wearing tonight?"

"A little black dress I bought in Paris. It's perfect for an early spring night."

"I hope you don't mind, but I brought a new dress for you at Barney's yesterday. I was walking by a mannequin and saw it." She unzips the garment bag and pulls out a chartreuse-green dress. The shimmer from the rich silk makes me want to touch the fabric. It's so soft and luxurious. I also notice it's very low-cut, and my cleavage will be on full display.

"It's beautiful." I can't deny it. She picked out a stunner.

"You like it?" I nod in reply. Who wouldn't like it? "It looked like it was made for you. I couldn't pass it up. Black is the color for mourning. You need to be colorful tonight, Kathryn. I'd love for you to wear it."

I sigh, knowing she means well, but I hate to be pushed into anything. Deep down I know the dress would've drawn my eye, too. So I cave and take it from her, holding it up to my chest.

"Look at yourself in the mirror." She places her hands on my shoulders and gently spins me toward the vanity mirrors. "That color green, your light complexion, and the color of your hair. It's like the designer had you in mind when they created it."

"Thanks, Mother." I turn to face her and reflect her beaming smile. Who can turn down Ava Swanson when she's happy like this? I can't because her enthusiasm is contagious.

Chapter 5

The new green dress is wrapped tightly around my body, fitting like a glove. Gathering at my lower back, it highlights the curves Mother Nature gave me. Underneath, I'm wearing a black satin corset from a charming boutique I frequented in Paris.

The feeling of being confined by the tightly strung lingerie, with my breasts positioned high in my dress, is an erotic blend. My breathing is more labored than usual, and I can't place all the blame on the corset. The plain and simple fact is I need sex, because dammit, I'm strung up tight, literally and figuratively.

I can't remember the last time I thought about taking a few shots of tequila before I went out for the evening. But the idea tempts me now. Instead, I shake off the thought and prepare to leave for the night.

I place a sheer black wrap around my upper body in hopes of keeping the evening's chill away. After tossing one end of the wrap over my shoulder, I grab my clutch off the hallway table and walk out the door.

Tonight my mother's driver is taking me to the foundation event. He brought her to Lincoln Center a couple of hours ago, and now his entire evening is free as he waits for the event to conclude. I do love Armand, her driver. He's always on time, which means he's likely waiting for me outside the building since I'm running a few minutes late.

Once I've made my way to the lobby, I see the first other human being since I closed my door earlier. From the look on my doorman Carl's face, I believe this dress was a perfect choice because the usually talkative Carl is stunned to silence. His jaw also dropped open to his chest.

In a flirty fashion, I wave and blow a kiss as I pass by Carl. Between the hair and makeup perfection at the Red Door, my mother's gift of the dress, and the snug corset, I feel a sense of expectancy. Although I have no idea why or what I am really expecting to happen. It's likely the fact that I need to get out more and also this sexual drought I'm experiencing. I think finding the bar will be first on my list tonight.

~

The crowd in the reception room at the event is starting to grow. I see a few familiar faces as I sip my wine. I scan the room, looking for my mother and wondering if she needs any help, when to my right, someone calls my name.

"Kathryn Delcour." The rather loud and boisterous voice I recognize instantly belongs to Trudy Patrick. We were inseparable during our years at the Dalton School. She's been trying to set me up with every rich, single man over thirty-five she knows.

"Hi, Trudy." We exchange the obligatory side-to-side air kiss as we greet each other.

"Look at you." She pulls away and examines every inch of me as though she's trying to find my hidden barcode. "Your dress is classic with a touch of scandal to it. You are hot as sin, Kathryn."

"Back at you." She does look great, back in shape after having had a child only four months ago. "How's the baby?"

"Little Jack is the joy of my life." She smiles at me, and I can see the love in her eyes when she mentions him. "But I'm as tired as hell. You know I've decided to raise him without a nanny. If he doesn't starting sleeping better, I may have to hire one for the night shift. This getting up at three and four a.m. is killing me."

"If it's any consolation you don't look sleep deprived at all. I don't see a hint of bags or dark circles. You must be doing something right."

"I sure as hell hope so. I've decided raising a child is harder than working with the worst sons of bitches on Wall Street."

"But the jerks on Wall Street didn't smile up at you like you hung the moon and the stars." Trudy laughs and I join in, although a small part of me envies her. She has a perfect life—a charming husband and beautiful child— and here I stand, a widow at thirty-four.

"You're so right. I love when I walk into the nursery and scoop him up out of his crib. You'd think I hung the moon."

"Now that the weather is warmer, I'd love to meet you and Jack in Central Park for a walk. It's been a couple of months since I've seen him. I'm sure he's changed."

"Sounds like a plan. And *you* should be out in the park daily. Lots of hot man meat lurking on those jogging trails," she says while pointing at me in a scolding fashion.

"You're relentless." I lightly pat her arm, although I'd like to pinch her for being so pushy about hooking me up at every turn.

"I don't mean to push." She laughs and shakes her head. "Wait that's not true, I have been pushing you. I think you need a little shove to get into the dating scene here. New York City dating isn't for the faint of heart."

"I know you mean well. But between you and my mother, I've had my fill of 'let's help lonely Kathryn find a man.'" I add an exaggerated eye roll to drive home my point.

"Good old Ava. I bet she's been worse than me. Is there someone in particular she's trying to fix you up with?"

"She was telling me about a man who's supposed to be here tonight. Only problem is even my makeup artist thinks he's trouble."

"What's his name?" From her tone, I'm certain she'd be rubbing her hands together if she wasn't holding her nearly empty wineglass.

"Adam Kingsley," I answer and see a similar reaction from Trudy as I did with my over-sharing makeup artist. "I've seen that expression in response to his name before."

"You can't be serious. Your mother wants to fix you up with him?" Trudy glances around her, and I'm wondering if she needs to sit down. "He's the last person I'd ever think of fixing you up with."

"That bad?" She nods almost violently. "You've got to point him out to me. I need to be prepared."

"He gave a very generous donation at this dinner last year. Maybe his humanitarian side has blinded your mother, because the only thing I'd fix him up with would be his own hand."

"Holy shit, Trudy." I'm shocked at that statement and also the fact that somehow my mother was pushing this man my direction. "Do you see him here yet?"

"Not yet." Her words were like a sigh. "But you'll know when he's here. He'll be the most handsome man in the room. Hell, he's the hottest man I've ever seen. But don't let his looks fool you. I'd say the majority of the women in this room have succumbed to him at one time or another."

"No way." I give her a questioning stare, hoping she can read my look accurately.

"Good God! No, I haven't been one of his victims. I could give you a long list of his casualties in this room, though. It's really quite impressive."

"I'm glad you aren't one. But what is it they see in him if he's really so bad?"

"Just wait." Her assessment is scathing, but oddly I'm even more curious about this man than I was before. "When you see him, you'll get it. I think there are two good reasons besides his looks that make his sexual conquests as easy for him as breathing: his well-endowed wallet and cock."

I took a sip of wine at the most inopportune time because I nearly spit it out. I wasn't expecting those comments from Trudy. Well, maybe the wallet one. The size of his dick? No.

"You're serious?" I question her even though I can tell she's shooting me straight.

"Very." She takes my arm and we begin to walk. "There is a nice group of bachelors a few feet away I *do* want you to meet. I don't know the size of their cocks, but their wallets are in good shape."

"You're horrible, Trudy." I try to wiggle out of her hold, but she's not having it and brings my arm closer to her side.

She introduces me to the group of men. They seem like nice enough gentlemen. Smart, well accomplished, and remotely handsome. But after some back and forth conversation, I realize not a single one of them gives me any spark or yearning.

As an investment banker tells me about his latest merger in the works, Trudy moves closer to me and whispers in my ear.

"Don't look now, but there he is." I do exactly what she said *not* to do. I glance around the room. And I see him. He's easy to spot because I see a hot as fuck man at the bar. He's turned at an angle to me, so I can check out his features unnoticed.

"See what I mean," Trudy speaks into my hair. "I knew you'd know who he was without me actually pointing him out."

"You were right." I have to agree; he's even more handsome to me than my late husband. Something I thought I'd never think about another man. I browse over the crowd and see several women staring at him. A few are huddled together chatting and appearing to admire what they see. I turn away from him and his onlookers and try to refocus on the banker who's trying to hold a conversation with me.

That attempt only lasts a few seconds before Trudy is once again whispering in my ear. Only this time she's more excited.

"What the hell? He's looking at you, Kathryn. Staring, more like it."

I have no idea what comes over me, but I make a move I may regret later. I graciously peel myself away from Trudy and the suitors she's chosen for me and head to the bar Adam is standing at. After all, my wineglass is empty.

"Kathryn, where the hell are you going?" Trudy asks as I walk away. I wave her off with a little gesture over my shoulder.

As I walk close to where Adam's standing, I purposely avoid looking at his face. Instead, I decide to focus on his legs, so I'll know if he moves. When I'm a few feet away, he pushes himself off the bar and turns in my direction. I'll end up walking right to him unless I turn and hightail it back to Trudy.

Ignoring my pinging danger radar, I soldier on, feeling the heat of his eyes on me. I swear they're leaving hot streaks across my body. Even before I've made direct eye contact with him, I feel an energy already pulsing between us.

When he's no more than three feet away from me, I begin to raise my head. Inch by inch, I work my way up his long, hard body. There's nothing that could've prepared me for the sight of him peering down at me when my eyes finally met his. They are smoldering, hooded, and dark with desire.

Adam Kingsley is a sight to behold. Towering in height and muscular. Dressed to kill or make panties drop in his designer tux. I can't turn away. The pull is too strong.

I'm faced with a couple of decisions. Walk around him to the bar and completely ignore him or actually allow myself to meet him. In the back of my mind, there's one other option that pops up. Straddling him. My sex-starved body reacts to this idea as a definite humming flows through me, putting me on hyper alert. One that is focused between my legs.

Thankfully, I find an ounce or two of self-preservation as I stand before this man who emits sex from every inch of his tall frame. I decide there is only one way for me to leave with some dignity tonight if I meet him. Focus on resisting his charms instead of wondering what's under his tux.

I believe playing a little hardball with this man instead of fawning at his feet will keep me from succumbing to this instant connection I feel with him and also let me see what he's made of. Then, as if on cue, he moves toward me, and I immediately fire back a mocking smile because I'm not about to be one of his conquests. At least not tonight.

Hope you enjoyed the little snippet into Kathryn's mind. Liv!

Made in the USA
San Bernardino, CA
16 April 2014